Marianne, if you ___ *ing*
to pick up on it.

And why the he ___ *fect*
you like that? Pull ___ *-act*
like it.

She took a deep breath, then gave him her most professional, polite smile. "What can I do for you?"

He said nothing for a moment, just surveyed the room.

Okay then. Two could play that game. She crossed her arms and waited.

After a few moments, he hopped up onto one of her tables and swung his legs up, bending over as if stretching out his hamstrings. "Where are the assistants?"

"Sent them out for an early lunch. Figured it'd be a slow first day."

He glanced once more at the empty room. "Figured right."

"So." She slapped a hand down on the table next to him, her palm stinging and echoing against the thick plastic like a smack on flesh. "Are you in here for business or pleasure?"

He scowled. "Out of those two options, business, I guess."

"No time for pleasure?" Crap. Why had she asked that? He might take that for flirting. She wasn't flirting. Of course she wasn't flirting.

BELOW THE BELT

JEANETTE MURRAY

BERKLEY SENSATION, NEW YORK

THE BERKLEY PUBLISHING GROUP
Published by the Penguin Group
Penguin Group (USA) LLC
375 Hudson Street, New York, New York 10014

USA • Canada • UK • Ireland • Australia • New Zealand • India • South Africa • China

penguin.com

A Penguin Random House Company

BELOW THE BELT

A Berkley Sensation Book / published by arrangement with the author

Berkley Sensation Books are published by The Berkley Publishing Group.
BERKLEY SENSATION® is a registered trademark of Penguin Group (USA) LLC.
The "B" design is a trademark of Penguin Group (USA) LLC.

For information, address: The Berkley Publishing Group,
a division of Penguin Group (USA) LLC,
375 Hudson Street, New York, New York 10014.

ISBN: 978-0-425-27925-0

PUBLISHING HISTORY
Berkley Sensation mass-market edition / April 2015

PRINTED IN THE UNITED STATES OF AMERICA

10 9 8 7 6 5 4 3 2 1

Cover art: Boxer © Gabriel Georgescu / Shutterstock.
Cover design by Rita Frangie.
Interior text design by Kelly Lipovich.

To those wives who kept me sane during deployments,
field ops, TADs and long work hours . . .

You are my heroines. The Corps is a
stronger place because of you.

CHAPTER

█ I █

First Lieutenant Bradley Costa tossed his pack on the bed and sank to the mattress beside it. Fucking hell, what had he walked himself into?

The best—and most terrifying—opportunity of his life, that's what. He stood and shook his hands, a habit he'd yet to break, to release the nerves. He couldn't let it get to him, or else he'd be screwed before he hit the gym on the first day of training camp.

A knock at his open door jarred him from his self-induced pity party. He turned and saw a guy holding his own ruck, wearing a civilian "uniform" of khakis and a button-down polo shirt that was similar to what he'd worn on his own trip to Camp Lejeune.

"Hey, you Costa?"

"Yeah." Brad strode over to shake the outstretched hand. "You Higgs?"

"One and the same." The other man grinned, then squeezed a little in friendly warning before letting go. He was an inch or two shorter than Brad, with a more wiry build. But there was strength in the grip, and Brad didn't doubt the man could likely run circles around an opponent. Pushing past Brad, Higgs walked in and observed the tiny room, nodding in acceptance. "Seems we're lucky roomies while we're here."

"Seems like." Brad watched him warily. "I've claimed this one. Yours is that way." What the hell was this guy doing? The small single bedrooms of the Bachelor Officer Quarters were connected by a tiny sitting room and shared bathroom. Obviously, this was his room.

Making himself at home, Higgs tossed his pack next to Brad's on the bed and sat in the chair. "I like company."

Oh, good. He got the Chatty Cathy for a roommate. He could wait it out. He went to his own ruck and started unpacking.

"So you think you'll be here awhile, huh?"

God, he hoped so. He glanced up as he organized the top drawer with his workout gear. "Wouldn't have made the trip otherwise."

"I'm not big on unpacking, myself." Higgs stretched and laced his fingers over his stomach. "I figure I'll just leave things the way they are for now. See if I like the setup. If not, easier to ditch and go if my shit isn't spread out from here to kingdom come."

Brad snorted. "What, like you're just going to walk away from this if you don't like how it's playing out?"

"Why not? Life's too short to do shit you don't like."

Brad's hands tightened into fists around the top drawer. He'd tried for years, nearly a decade, to get the chance to come to training camp for the Marine Corps boxing team. Had been working for the goal—even just indirectly— since watching his father compete at age six. For the next twenty-three years, the goal had been at the top of his bucket list. And this moron was willing to just walk away from the opportunity?

Fucker.

And yet, if he did, it would be one less fucker Brad had to step over to make it onto the team. He shut the drawer and shrugged. "Probably right."

Higgs watched him for a minute, then snorted and stood. Most likely disappointed Brad didn't invite him to stay to paint their toenails and gossip about boys. As Higgs grabbed his bag, he said, "A bunch of the guys who arrived today are heading down to Back Gate."

Back Gate, as anyone who had been stationed at Lejeune knew, was a well-known bar frequented by Marines in their off time. Ironically enough, it was accessed the easiest from the main gate. "Okay then."

"You coming?"

Training day one started at oh-seven hundred tomorrow morning. And these jokers were heading out to get wasted the night before?

"Oh, yeah, I'll come. I'll even drive."

He wouldn't miss this train wreck for the world.

MARIANNE Cook slid into one of the remaining booths at the Back Gate, and wondered why, God, why, had she agreed to meet here for drinks with her mother again?

That's right, because her mother was boy-crazy. The woman—half her namesake—was nearly sixty, and still got giggly around hot men young enough to be her sons, if she'd had sons. So meeting in a bar where Marines hung out after hours was, quite frankly, Mary Cook's idea of a perfect night out.

Fortunately, her father was not only aware of Mary's boy-craziness but found it amusing. And since her mother would never even consider cheating on her father, Marianne found the entire thing amusing as well.

Until she was an unwilling accomplice.

The server stopped by, a little harried and definitely short on patience, and took Marianne's simple order of a bottle of light beer and an ice water and left. Knowing her mother, she'd be zooming in about twenty minutes late. The water would make the beer last longer. Only one, since she would be driving home.

A shout, a few jeers and a male insult erupted from the bar area. She glanced over for a moment. Nothing much to see. A group of Marines doing that weird man thing where harassment passes off as bonding time. Add in a few beers and it just cranks the volume up. Nothing she hadn't seen before. Though she'd missed the sight since she moved down to Wilmington for college, then stayed there for her first post-grad job.

And, she realized with a smug smile as the server wordlessly delivered her beer and water, nothing she wouldn't be seeing up close and personal, for a few months, at least. She was about to pick up the glass of water when her mother breezed in.

"Sorry, I'm late, I know." Mary slid in the booth in front of her. Before Marianne could lift the water, her mother snatched it from her hand and took a gulp. "Better."

"I'm glad," Marianne said dryly, taking the water from her mother and having a sip for herself. "What held you up this time?"

"Myself, of course. Then I was late leaving, and Western was a parking lot." Mary patted her hair, a mix of silver and blonde much like Marianne's just plain blonde. Where her mother kept her hair longer—eschewing the tradition of cutting it shorter as she got older—Marianne had chopped hers off to a short bob in college. They shared the same icy blue eyes, though. "Had to spruce up a bit, didn't I?"

"So you could turn all the men's heads." Marianne smiled and shook her head while her mother gave her order—a glass of wine—to the server when she buzzed by. "Daddy's a tolerant man."

"My favorite kind. As long as I come home to him at the end of the night, he's never considered it a big deal to flirt. There's never harm in flirting with a cute young man." Mary's light eyes laughed as she took another sip of water from her daughter's glass. "I thought I taught you that."

"Among other things." Marianne waited for the server to plop her mother's subpar wine down and scoot away before saying, "I got all settled into the apartment. Still have a few more boxes to get to, but I should be done with those tonight."

"I'm so glad you're back in town." Her mother took a sip and grimaced. "This is awful."

"You picked the location," she reminded her mother, taking a sip of the much safer selection of bottled beer. "And you remember I'm only here for a while, right? I'm not moving back to Jacksonville permanently. When the All Military games are done, my job's over."

"But you're here for now. And that makes both of us happy." Mary laid a hand on her daughter's arm, and Marianne couldn't help but smile back. She loved her parents; adored them. She knew she was fortunate to have been raised by people who taught her a love of independence tempered by a healthy dose of respect for those who reared you.

"I know. But if this job leads to bigger and better things . . ." She shrugged. No big deal.

Except it was. That was the entire reason she'd left her old job, taken the chance and moved back to Jacksonville. It was the opening to making her dreams come true.

"I think if you—oh!" Mary grabbed for her wineglass as something jarred their table. But her flushed, slightly annoyed look smoothed into sweet cream and dimples when she looked up and found a handsome young Marine standing before their table. And there was no doubt he was a Marine. They were impossible to miss. His dark, almost black hair was in a razor-sharp high and tight, his face was baby-smooth and he was wearing the unofficial off-duty uniform of a clean polo shirt and nice jeans.

"Sorry, ladies." He grinned lopsidedly, dark eyes lighting up, and Marianne instantly knew he was, if not drunk, well on his way to becoming so. "Didn't mean to bump the table."

"It's fine." Marianne smiled briefly, then turned to her mother, who was smiling not-so-briefly.

"Totally understandable. It's just so crowded in here, isn't it?" Mary played with the thin gold band necklace she wore every day—her own patented flirtatious gesture. Marianne rolled her eyes into her water glass.

"Maybe it was just the sight of two such beautiful sisters," the younger man said with a cheeky grin.

Marianne tried not to laugh, she really did. But a snort worked its way up. Seriously. The guy was twelve. Okay, fine, twenty-one, max. But boy, did he have some good, classic lines. Her mother glared.

"Ignore my *sister*," Mary said firmly.

"Oh, please," Marianne muttered.

"Can I buy you ladies another round to apologize?" He motioned a hand toward the sliver of bench left by Marianne, silently asking if he could also have a seat. She ignored the gesture and looked straight ahead, past her mother's shoulder.

Seriously. Hot Marines. Been there, done that. Okay, not *done that*, done that. That sounded wrong. But you couldn't grow up in Jacksonville and not have had a teenage fantasy or two about the constant influx of good-looking, uniform-wearing hotties driving through the front gate every morning. Naturally, if she'd actually dated any of them during her teenage years, her father would have killed her.

She was older now. More mature. Immune to the hype. Could easily see through that cocky *you-want-me* grin the infant wore.

And yet her mother ate it up with a spoon. "You don't have to do that." But she scooted over a few inches.

"I insist. I . . . need to . . ." A hand clamped down on his shoulder. His speech slowed down—way down—and watching the young man's face change was almost like watching a gear physically click into place when he turned to see who had stepped up behind him.

"Ladies." Another man—only this time, he was a *man*—stepped up beside the infant lady-killer. "I hope my friend here isn't bothering you." He slung an arm around the other Marine's shoulder in a grip that even Marianne could see was designed to restrain.

"We're fine," Marianne said easily. The infant was a little obnoxious, but she didn't want him in trouble. "Really, no harm done at all."

"This just makes things perfect, doesn't it?" Mary said cheerfully, missing the undertones. "A Marine for each of us."

"Marine? What gave it away?" The taller, older one smiled easily, but his grip on the young man never loosened. Like his younger friend, he wore the same distinctive military markers—medium brown hair in a high and tight, polo tucked into jeans without any designer rips or holes—but it wasn't so much a definition of who he was as it was just something he wore comfortably. He was probably in his late twenties, early thirties tops, she'd guess. Not old. But old enough to flip a switch from thinking *What a silly little infant* over to *Oh, boy, that's good to look at.*

And God. Hadn't she just told herself Marines did nothing for her? *Bad, Marianne. Bad.*

"The high and tights, of course. And the impressive . . . physiques. Impossible to miss!" Mary ran a hand through her hair, smoothing it behind one ear. "Will you join us?"

"I think we're quitting for the night. We've got an early day tomorrow. Don't we, Tressler?" He said it so mildly, Marianne wouldn't have picked up on the not-an-order order if she hadn't been watching their body language.

A little sullen now, like a child being told playtime is over, Tressler gave them a weak smile. "Thanks for the conversation, ladies. Sorry to interrupt your evening."

The other one waved and led his now-subdued friend off.

She couldn't help watching him as he approached the bar to pass off the man-child to another Marine while he settled his tab. Damn, now that was an ass made for jeans. The dark blue denim stretched comfortably over a butt she could easily guess would be tight enough to bounce a quarter off of.

"You're staring," her mother murmured.

Marianne snapped her gaze back. "Am not."

With a small smile, her mother traced the rim of her wineglass with a fingertip. "You know the reason I find it fun to flirt with men? Men I have no intentions of being with, and whom I know have no intentions of being with me? When I'm happily married to your father, and have been for almost thirty years?"

"I'm not sure I want to," she muttered, and killed the bottle with one last gulp.

"It's because it makes me feel feminine and pretty. A little alive. Your father pays compliments, but it's nice to be . . . seen by other people. It's fun, and harmless. And it makes me happy. What makes you happy?"

"Work." The answer was easy enough, on the tip of her tongue before she could even think. "I love my job."

"Of course you do. But I don't see you looking at athletic tape and Icy Hot the way you just looked at that young man's ass just now."

"Things you never want to hear your mother say," Marianne said to the ceiling.

Her mother raised a light brow. "Am I wrong?"

She was saved from having to answer when the server sat down another light beer and glass of wine. Marianne waved her hand to catch the woman's attention before she made herself scarce again. "We didn't order these."

"Sent over from the bar. Guy says he's sorry for the trouble and hopes you weren't offended by his friend's intrusion."

"Oh, that sweet boy." Mary gulped the last of her first wine and pushed the empty glass to the server before reaching for the fresh one. "He shouldn't have."

"No, he shouldn't have. We don't need drinks," Marianne said quickly, stalling her mother's arm. "Can you tell him we appreciate the gesture but—"

"Nope. He's already gone. And that was definitely no boy. They're paid for, so enjoy." The server winked and headed back to the bar.

So the other one—the one not using horrible pickup lines—had sent them. As an apology for his friend? Or more? She found herself searching the thinning crowd around the bar, just in case. But the server was right, both he and his younger companion—along with most of the crowd they'd come with—were gone.

"Looking for our mystery Marine, are we?"

She threw a crumpled up cocktail napkin at her mother. "Don't start. And I can't drink this. I'm driving home. My boxes aren't going to unpack themselves. I've got a to-do

list a mile long, and I want to have some pamphlets ready
to print for—"

"Oh, relax." Mary leaned back in the booth. "Sip slowly,
drink water, and slow down for five minutes. You're having
a drink with your mother; it can't be that sinful."

She debated for a good twenty seconds before grabbing
the bottle and having a fresh sip of cool, refreshing beer.
Fine. Five minutes, then back to real life.

*Mystery Marine, thanks for the drinks, but no
thank you.*

TRESSLER eyed Brad with childish mutiny from a corner of the wrestling mat. "You didn't have to fuck up my
night, man."

Not even minute one of training camp, and already Brad
was making lifelong friends. He closed his eyes and
stretched his back on the mat. *Tuck right knee to chest,
rotate back until crossing body, and feel the stretch. Stare
up at ceiling and not at idiot.*

They were in some semblance of a semicircle, waiting
for the coaches to begin day one. There were several sleepy
eyes in the crowd, and a few who looked like they'd been
pushed out of bed with a bulldozer. And of course Tressler,
who would have been worse off if Brad hadn't stepped in
and "encouraged" him to make an early night of it.

But did he get thanks for being the mature, levelheaded
one and keeping him from making an ass of himself? No.
Of course not. Maybe he should have let the kid keep talking to the mother-daughter combo. He would have gotten
a healthy slap eventually.

Brad had almost done just that. Walked on by, hit the
head, and gone home alone to get a solid night's rest. But
something in the way Tressler's younger blonde-haired

prey had looked—an interesting mixture of boredom and concern—had stopped him in his tracks. And though she probably hadn't meant it, the gratitude and relief when he'd taken Tressler in hand had shone in her eyes, making him feel eight feet tall.

"You're not my commanding officer here."

"Nope," he agreed easily. *And thank God for that.* He stared at the exposed beams that criss-crossed over the high ceiling of the arena. Dropping the leg, he let it fall a bit more, allowing the pull to stretch his muscles.

"I don't have to do what you say."

"Okay then." *Switch sides, stretch away, ignore moron.*

"I could have had her," Tressler continued, almost to himself.

Brad snorted. And he wasn't the only one.

"Knock it off, you two." Higgs, who looked a little rough himself, slapped a palm on the mat. The smack of flesh echoed off the high rafters of the gym. "I'm not listening to a bunch of whiny pussies for months."

Brad took the insult the way it was intended, with equal parts camaraderie and respect, and a little warning tossed in for good measure.

Sadly, Tressler didn't seem to have the maturity to do the same. "Who are you calling a pussy, pussy?"

"Jesus," Brad muttered, closing his eyes again when Higgs stood. "Knock it off, both of you."

"I agree."

The low growl took them all by surprise. Every Marine was on his feet, at attention where he stood, as the coach approached. He was a mountain of a man, solidly built but still huge. His dark skin only made the contrast of his white teeth, bared in a grimace, and his shocking white hair stand out that much more.

"Bunch of ladies, bickering and moaning. 'She stole my

boyfriend. She wore my favorite shirt. I saw her texting Tommy and I like Tommy so she can't do that,'" he mocked in a high-pitched faux teen girl voice.

A few chuckled before coughing.

"Yeah, it's humorous." He let his clipboard fall to the mat with a rattle. "Funny, when men can't be five seconds in each others' presence without acting like a bunch of middle school girls who got snubbed for the big dance."

Brad bit the side of his cheek to keep from smiling.

The man walked between the Marines, through them, weaving in and out on silent feet. Brad kept his eyes forward, the only warning of the coach's presence the change in atmosphere when he passed by. For a man who must have weighed two-fifty, he moved like a ghost. "I'm sent the few, the proud, the—what? What was that delicate term you used?" He paused by Tressler and Higgs, who both stared straight ahead. "'*Pussies*,' was it?"

Tressler said nothing. Kid had caught on, finally.

"Well, if that's true, then we've got our work ahead of us, don't we?" He made his way back to the front of the mat, where they could all see him. "At ease, boys. This isn't formation; this is practice. I don't expect you to salute and stand at attention around me. I'm your coach, not your commanding officer. And I'll tell you what—I want you to all check your rank at the door. I make the leaders in this gym, not some brass on your collar when you're back with your units."

He rubbed his hands together. They were the size of dinner plates. "I'm Coach Ace, and these are my assistants." He pointed a thumb over his left shoulder, toward a tall, lanky man with almost no hair and glasses. "Coach Cartwright." Thumb jerked to the right, to the short man with a shocking orange-red moustache that would make the Lorax proud. "Coach Willis."

He spread his arms out wide. "Coaches, this is what we have to work with. Let's see what we've been given. Men? Are you pussies, or are you Marines?"

As one, for the first time, the entire squad gave a loud "Oo-rah!"

CHAPTER

2

The smell of a fresh roll of athletic tape. The feel of sanitized plastic seats squeaking beneath her hands. The echo of ice poured by the pound into ten-gallon water coolers to be taken out for the athletes to rehydrate.

Marianne closed her eyes, breathed in deep and sighed with pure joy. This was her world. This was where she reigned with pleasure. Some athletic training rooms resembled nothing more than a dungeon, and even then, she was in her element.

But this one, she had to admit, was pretty decent. Probably because she was comparing it to her last job, where she had worked in a small high school that could barely field enough boys for a football team. But she'd loved it.

And she would love this, too. She just needed to get into the swing of things.

Levi, one of her college interns—she had *interns*!— walked in bear-hugging a big five-gallon cooler. His steps were more like a waddle thanks to the girth of the round plastic. "God, these guys killed this one fast. They're camels, I swear."

"As long as they're hydrated camels, I don't mind." Marianne helped him maneuver the cooler over to the massive industrial sink that stood in the corner of her training room. Before, at the high school, she'd have had to wash the cooler herself. But thanks to having not one, but two, interns earning credit for the semester shadowing her, the grunt work was out of her hands for the low, low price of writing weekly updates and a more lengthy end-of-semester evaluation.

It was a beautiful thing to move up in the world.

Levi popped the top of the cooler and dumped out the last dribbles of ice before running the hot water. He shook his head a little to get his shaggy brown hair out of his eyes, then rolled up the sleeves of his shirt. "I'll wash this one up and get the second cooler out there in a few minutes. Honestly, I don't know how . . ." His voice trailed off, and Marianne glanced over to see what had happened.

Nikki had happened. Otherwise known as assistant number two. It had taken Marianne about point-five seconds to realize Levi was in some serious puppy love with the cute golden-haired coed. His voice rose an octave every time she was in the room, and his eyes tracked hers like the family pet hoping for a stray word of praise.

Nikki set a towel in the laundry hamper—which the janitors would handle later, another perk of the new job—and grinned. "One of them already threw up. Less than three hours. That's gotta be a record somewhere."

Marianne started for the door. "Is he okay?"

"Oh, yeah, sure. He just puked in a trash can while running laps. Barely slowed down at all to do it. He's already back in formation and running with the rest of the crew."

"Probably just drank too much water too fast before running." She debated a moment, then decided to hold off on going out. No guy wanted the trainer running out there to baby him for something as simple as throwing up water. She wasn't their mommy and they weren't toddlers with scraped knees. Finding the balance of knowing when to step in and when to let them push on was part of her job. Baby the athletes and they didn't want to come to her at all. Ignore the potential problems and they could injure themselves permanently.

Nikki walked around to the sink where Levi was washing out the jug and reached around him for a sleeve of plastic cups. "I'm going to run these upstairs. Looks like they'll be using both the catwalk for cardio and the downstairs area for training, so I think we should have a second water station up there."

Marianne bit back a smile as Levi's eyes nearly rolled back in pleasure from Nikki's nearness. "Good idea."

Levi propped the clean jug on the drying rack and grabbed the cups before she could. Given Nikki's short stature, she would have had to ask for help anyway. "I'll go take them out. You can get the next water cooler ready." He darted out of the room before she could protest.

Watching these two dance around each other could be amusing for the next few weeks. As long as it didn't interfere with their work, she could appreciate others finding a little fun where they could get it.

Nikki fisted her hands at her hips. "I wanted to take it out." Her pout turned to a Cheshire cat–like smile. "Any excuse to check out the hot Marines, right?" She moved to the clean cooler and started scooping ice, raising her voice above the crashing sound of the metal breaking through the chunks. "How can you be stuck in here all morning and not have any urge to peek? Half of them aren't even wearing shirts anymore!"

"Old news." Marianne shrugged, but grinned back. "I

was raised here, remember? I think I got that out of my system in my teens."

"There is no way you can get 'hot guys' out of your system. I'd have to be half-dead before I couldn't recognize quality beef like that."

Marianne's mother would have agreed readily. Marianne just chuckled and went back to inventorying the bandages.

"Hey, Marianne?"

She turned to look at Levi, whose head was poking through the door. "Yeah?"

"The coach wants you to come out and meet the team. They're about to break for lunch, so he says now's a good chance to introduce you."

"Sure thing. Just a second." She finished up counting rolls so she didn't lose place, documented the number and set the clipboard aside and headed out of the room.

The air was the first thing to change. Moving from the cool, AC-infused air of her training room into the muggy, heavy, humid air of the gymnasium, she almost struggled to breathe for a moment. The lights were dim, coming from far overhead, and her eyes adjusted before she walked toward the group of Marines and the three coaches. The men were in formation, feet shoulder-width apart and hands at the smalls of their backs, eyes straight forward. Though she knew they could hear her tennis shoes squeaking across the floor, not one of them moved a muscle to see who was coming.

Too well-trained.

Putting on her professional, distant smile, she shook hands with the head coach, whom she'd met the day before. "Hey, Coach Ace. How's the first practice going?"

He smiled and shook. "Not too bad, Ms. Cook."

"Marianne."

He nodded in acknowledgement, then turned to the group assembled in front of him. She knew the drill, and faced the Marines. They'd all donned their shirts now—poor Nikki—but most were plastered to their fronts, leaving no imagination where their body shapes were concerned. These were fighting machines, well-honed. *Body fat begone.*

"Men, this is Marianne Cook, the athletic trainer assigned to our team. Her training room is behind you, to the left there through the double doors. I'll let her say a few words, then we'll break for a few hours to fuel up."

"Thanks, Coach." She waited a beat, then asked, "Can they relax?"

"Sure thing. Ease down, boys."

She watched their muscles relax, their bodies loosen up, their gazes swing around the gym and their shoulders roll to ease the aches. And as she took inventory of the Marines, she spotted the idiot from the night before. The one who had done a pathetic job hitting on her and her mother. The infant. What had his friend called him? Tress . . . something? His eyes caught hers, and he flushed and his mouth gaped a little.

Oh, yeah. She bit back a grin, doing her best to keep the professional mask on. Sometimes, pretending to be a ladies' man bit ya big time. *Nice lesson, huh, kid?*

"Hi guys. I'm Marianne; or you can just call me Cook. Either one. I respond to both." It'd be easier on everyone if they called her Cook. Seeing her as one of the guys would make the entire thing smoother. "I'm either going to be around here, observing and keeping an eye on you while you work, or in the training room. I've got two assistants as well, Levi and Nikki." She pointed toward the door, where her interns waved. Nikki's wave might have been a tad more enthusiastic than Levi's, but at least she wasn't drooling.

"I've also got some pamphlets here." She fanned the stack she'd brought out with her. She'd made them herself, and was pretty darn proud of them. "They talk about proper nutrition both before and after a training session to give your body proper fuel. I'll leave them outside my door so you can grab one on the way out."

She took a deep breath, about to give a quick, well-practiced speech on the importance of stretching and hydration—both of which could prevent a multitude of injuries themselves—when she saw another surprising face in the crowd.

The second man from last evening. The one who had stepped in when the infant had started bothering her and her mother. The reluctant savior. She knew he saw her; she was impossible to miss. His face was an impassive mask, eyes staring straight ahead, just a little to the left of her, like something on the blank wall behind her shoulder was more interesting. But his jaw clenched in a way that said he wasn't entirely unaware of her presence.

Well. Curious.

WELL. Shit.

Brad focused on the speed bag in front of him . . . mostly focused. The work was repetitive; he could work the bag by rote. But cruising on autopilot wouldn't get him his spot on the team. Already, he knew his skills weren't to the same par as others'. He wasn't as fast as Higgs, and—it galled him to admit—he wasn't as powerful as Tressler and his big mouth. A man named Sweeney took the prize for the most creative moves, with the sort of skill to see three moves ahead of his opponent and make the right choice. The man was like Bobby Fisher on a chess board, always calculating and ready.

But he had determination, guts and sheer refusal to quit.

And his conditioning was above the curve. While some dropped like flies in the heat, he'd stand out as going the distance. He couldn't beat them, but he could outlast them.

Please, God, let that count for something.

But right now he couldn't think about outdistancing his fellow teammates. No, of course not. His mind kept drifting back to the icy blonde with hot legs and a banging body. Oh, sure, she hid it under the obligatory baggy staff polo that might as well have been a potato sack and a pair of loose khaki shorts. But he'd seen her the night before in a formfitting tank top and hip-skimming jeans. The woman was stacked.

And all but walked around with a sandwich board proclaiming, *"Hands Off, Marines."* Shame, really.

He missed another combo, and Coach Willis' barking, rasping shout had him blinking and dodging the bag before it hit him square in the face.

"Costa! Christ on a cracker, what are you doing with that bag?"

Brad turned, then jolted back a step when he found the shorter man standing right behind him. He had to be barely over five feet tall. "Coach—"

"Swear to God, boys, swear to God." Willis shook his head, upper lip twitching. The motion sent his moustache into an awkward dance. Brad bit back a laugh. "If you can't keep your head in the game, maybe you shouldn't be playing it."

Shit, shit, shit. Daydreaming about the Nordic princess had scraped his concentration raw. "Sorry, Coach. Just lost it for a second. I'm good."

"You can go be '*good*,'" he said with a sneer and some air quotes for extra insult, "by running a few stairs and laps. Up, across, down, across. Ten rounds." When he waited, Willis rubbed a finger across his moustache. "Go. Now."

"Yes, Coach." He took off immediately, sprinting to the

first set of stairs. The gymnasium was set up with a set of stairs in each of the four corners, leading up to a catwalk above where spectators could watch games or events. The drill was simple enough. Run up a set of stairs, sprint across the length of the catwalk to the next stairs, run down, sprint across the gymnasium floor by the wall, back up again. Around and around he would go.

And where his dumbass mind would stop, Brad didn't know. Jesus. Daydreaming about a woman when he should have been giving every brain cell to the task at hand, no matter how mindless.

He blanked her out—blanked it all out—and put his energy into completing the sprint drill in the fastest time he could. His best hope now was to wow the coaches with his speed and commitment so they would forget about his momentary lapse.

He hit the ninth lap strong, pleased with his time, barely winded, when, on the seventh stair up, it happened in slow motion. His brain registered the sickening sound of pops from his right knee, followed by a grinding sensation from under the kneecap that instantly made him nauseous. Brad grabbed for the railing before he pitched face-first into the concrete step and busted something.

Easing his butt to the step below, he stretched his right leg out fully. It clicked. Fucking clicked. He bent it to ninety degrees. A dull sort of pain radiated out from his knee, sharpening like ripping teeth when he straightened it again.

The hiss of breath he sucked in echoed in the steel-and-concrete staircase. He was alone, so at least that cut out the embarrassment of looking like a weakling.

Come on, work, dammit.

He bent the knee, straightened it out, bent it again. Then he slowly stood and tested the supporting weight.

No collapsing, no absolute brain-numbing pain. Just a dull ache. So, maybe he twisted it. Easy enough to push through.

He walked up two steps and sucked in a breath again as the sharp pain hit. Okay. That wasn't going to cut it.

But what the hell else was he going to do? Move into the stairwell like a hobo? Screwing his eyes closed, he evaluated the two possibilities. Quit, or push on.

No contest.

He swallowed the nausea as he half walked, half jogged up the stairs to finish out the ninth lap. He'd lost almost all his edge in time, but as he jogged across the top of the catwalk, nobody seemed to notice he'd been missing from sight longer than normal. He kicked up the speed a little when he caught Higgs glancing upward, and gritted his teeth against the grinding feeling.

That couldn't be good. But damn if he'd let any of his teammates see his weakness. Not yet. They weren't a fully formed team, which made them opponents as much as a team. Boxing was tricky that way.

Sweat dripped from the back of his neck as he finished out his final lap, the pain causing every step to feel like twenty. So great, now he looked like an out-of-shape asshole. But probably better that than to get cut immediately with an injury.

Not that it was that bad. As he walked across the hardwood floor toward the large orange jug, he shook out the leg a little, making it seem like a normal stretch in case anyone walked back into the gym. There was no grinding pain now. Just a dull throb, like a toothache, and completely manageable. If this was how it would feel most of the time, it would be no issue.

Still, he'd use ice and heat after practice to be safe. He wasn't a complete moron.

"Costa!"

His hand crunched around the paper cup he'd glugged water from. "Coach Cartwright."

The wiry man who looked like a stiff breeze would

send him out to sea paced up. He had a wispy-thin voice to match. "Finished with your punishment?"

"Yes, Coach."

"Good. Go hit the weight room. Coach Ace is in there getting measurements and sizing up weight classes."

"Yes, Coach," he repeated, tossing the cup into the trash before jogging lightly across the gym toward the interior weight room.

As he pushed open the door, he found a long line of Marines ahead of him, with Coach Ace standing in the corner by a scale. He stepped up behind his roommate and another Marine, who were chatting.

Higgs turned and gave him a funny look. "Where've you been?"

"Conditioning," he said easily. No need to mention it was a punishment.

Higgs just shrugged, then tilted his head to the left. His blond hair was soaking with sweat, darkening it to a golden brown. "Have you met Graham Sweeney?"

Of course he hadn't. It wasn't social hour at the O Club, for criss sake. But he held out a hand to the man standing beside Higgs. "Hey, man."

Sweeney smiled easily. His darker, olive complexion and thick black hair made Brad think of Tuscan landscapes rather than a smelly, sweat-soaked gym room. "Hey. I was just telling Higgs here, I'm at my home base, so I've got a house out the back gate in Hubert. If you guys ever get sick of the BOQ or base food, come on by. We'll toss a few steaks on the grill and relax a little."

"Yeah, thanks, man. Sounds good." The offer was decent, but he wouldn't be taking him up on it anytime soon. He had enough to think about without adding budding bro-ships to it.

"We were just saying, too bad about Ramsey," Higgs said with a shake of his head. "Disgusting luck. I thought he looked good in warm-ups."

Brad thought hard and came up with a foggy impression of a built guy with gym-rat muscles and a semipermanent mean sneer. "What happened?" How much had he missed in ten dang minutes?

"Dislocated his shoulder using the bag." Sweeney grimaced. "Showing off, looked like to me. He's done. Went out fighting, though."

"It wasn't pretty," Higgs agreed. "I could hear him in the training room, even through the door. He was screaming at the hot trainer like she was ruining his life. Though I think it was the coach's final word, not hers, that put the fork in him."

Brad's skin prickled, and not just from the weak AC hitting his sweat-soaked body. Already, injuries were taking over. Part of him felt mental triumph at one less competitor on the field. But the other half of his brain reminded him he could easily be next.

The line shifted and he bounced on the balls of his feet as he stepped forward. Still fine. No sharp pain at all.

He'd play it by ear. Take it easy, stretch often and, if push came to shove, see a doctor out in town on his own dollar. One thing was for certain. There was no way in hell he was telling the sexy athletic trainer he was hurting. He'd rather take a bullet.

CHAPTER

3

Marianne watched the poor, trodden masses stand at attention while Coach Ace read them the riot act. It was a speech she'd heard a dozen times, from a dozen different coaches in a dozen different ways. The gist was always the same, though.

Sloppy, out of shape, pathetic performance, how did I get saddled with such a sorry bunch of losers? I shoulda gone to culinary school like my mama begged me to. Blah blah blah.

Standard first-day fare.

Normally, though, it was geared toward high schoolers, and was delivered with less . . . colorful language. She smiled as the Marines stood at attention, being reamed out by Coach Ace, then Coach Willis—Cartwright seemed to pass on this round of ass-chewing. They were stoic and focused. Quite a change from the typical eye-rolling, sarcasm-producing teens.

After a few minutes of the interesting pep talk, the Marines broke for dinner. According to her schedule, they had about ninety minutes to decompress, grab food, shower, run errands or do whatever else it was they needed to handle around base. There wasn't a ton to do on base, and they didn't have enough time to make it out to Jacksonville, sit through a restaurant meal and come back, though some of them might be stationed on Lejeune, and so could pop back home to see families or roommates. The rest were housed in the BOQ or barracks, having been shuttled in from whatever base they were stationed at.

She watched with an amused smile as most of the men walked straight past her. A few nodded politely or smiled, but most simply breezed by. None, she noted, stopped to take one of the nutrition pamphlets she'd put on a stool outside her door. She propped a shoulder on the wall by the door and bit back a grin.

Day one, everybody was a tough guy. No showing weakness. No whining to mama. Give them another week, and she would have a full house of Marines wanting ice packs, heat packs, cramps massaged out, lacerations taped up, ankles wrapped and who knew what else.

One Marine walked up to stand in front of her. "Ma'am—"

"Marianne. Or Cook, either one."

"Cook," he said, as she had suspected he would. He was likely in his early twenties, which made her several years older than him, and he had a cute spray of freckles across his nose that complimented the russet-gold hair. But oh, God, coming on base could really be a dual hit and stroke to the ego. Hot Marines watching her walk around like she was the sexiest thing they'd seen all day, and then calling her ma'am like she was their old-fart aunt.

"What's up?"

"Could I get an ice pack for the road?"

"Sure thing, come on in." She walked back to the icing station and grabbed a plastic bag, blowing in it to fill it with air and wrapping the edges around a bucket. Made for easier filling. "What's the ailment, Marine?"

That was the beauty of this job. She didn't have to memorize names or ranks. Shout, "Hey, Marine!" in a full room, and you'll get a full room answering you back.

He glanced around the room, as if he were waiting for someone to pop out and scream, "Surprise!" at him.

"We're alone," she assured him, biting on her lip to contain the smile.

He blew out a breath, then held up his left hand. Even from several feet away, she could see the last two knuckles were swollen. Likely dislocated.

"Ouch."

"Doesn't hurt," he insisted, a little too quickly in her opinion. "I just don't want it to swell more and cause problems later."

"Well, you're right on that part at least. What's your name?"

"Toby Chalfant."

"Well, Chalfant, you came to the right place." She tied the ends of the plastic baggie and brought it over to sit on the bench next to him. When she held out her hand, he hesitated. "I'll be gentle, I promise."

His lips twitched and he gingerly stretched his arm out to place his wrist in her grip. It hurt more than he wanted to admit—that much was obvious. When she wiggled his pinky and ring finger, his eyes squinted and his jaw clenched, though he didn't flinch or pull away.

"Ice, ice baby," she said and handed him the bag. "Would it do me any good to ask you to take the rest of the day off? Or to just use your other hand?"

He gave her a look that clearly asked, *Are you insane?* He was too well-trained—either by his mama or by a very proud gunny somewhere—to say it out loud.

"Thought so. Take it easy with that hand, try using the right more than the left. If you want to wrap it, just for the illusion of support and to keep the swelling down, come back ten minutes before the evening session and we'll do that. I can wrap both hands up to the wrists, if that would make you feel better about it. A lot of guys are wrapping just to protect against scrapes and mat burns. Nobody would think twice."

He gave her a grateful smile and stood, bag of already melting ice in his right hand. He headed out the door, nodding respectfully to the man who passed him in the doorway.

Another customer. She tossed the bucket she'd used into the wash bin and was ready to grab another when she noticed it was her handsome stranger from the night before. His shirt, a light gray, had a shadowy line running down the front from the neck to his waistband. His brown hair had deepened to nearly black with sweat. And his dark eyes were scanning the room in a slow, methodical way that made her think he was waiting to be ambushed.

And unlike sweet Toby Chalfant, the sexy stranger sent her heart into a different gear entirely.

Marianne, if you let your heart race like that, he's going to pick up on it.

And why the hell are you even letting this one man affect you like that? Pull it together! You are a professional—act like it.

She took a deep breath, then gave him her most professional, polite smile. "What can I do for you?"

He said nothing for a moment, just surveyed the room.

Okay then. Two could play that game. She crossed her arms and waited.

After a few moments, he hopped up onto one of her

tables and swung his legs up, bending over as if stretching out his hamstrings. "Where are the assistants?"

"Sent them out for an early dinner. Figured it'd be a slow first day."

He glanced once more at the empty room. "Figured right."

"So." She slapped a hand down on the table next to him, her palm stinging and echoing against the thick plastic like a smack on flesh. "Are you in here for business or pleasure?"

He scowled. "Out of those two options, business, I guess."

"No time for pleasure?" Crap. Why had she asked that? He might take that for flirting. She wasn't flirting. Of course she wasn't flirting.

If he thought it was a flirtatious remark, he didn't seem inclined to reply in the same vein. "I'm here for the job. Which, right now, is boxing and training."

"Of course. Name?"

"Does it matter?"

You know, he was a lot more personable the night before in the bar. "I'm working with the lot of you for the next several weeks. Yes, it matters. At least until you get cut."

She'd meant it in jest, more as a *general you*, not so much him in particular. But he scowled at her like he wanted to bite her head off, as if she'd meant it personally.

There was silence for another while. She bit back the next sarcastic remark and decided to wait him out. When he said nothing, she turned and headed to wash the bucket she'd used on the last Marine.

"Brad Costa."

Brad. She liked it. Short, strong, solid. Suited him—the stubborn male.

"I just need ice."

At that, she turned. "Why didn't you say so?"

He shook his head . . . whatever that meant.

She started scooping ice into a new bag and fresh bucket, tying off the ends with a simple flick of her fingers. "What's the ice for?"

"Does it matter?" It seemed to be a favorite question of his. He reached for the bag, but she held it out of the way.

"It does, in fact, matter. I'm supposed to keep an eye on you big strong boys, so if you have a boo-boo, I need to know."

"It's just preventative. Nothing hurts, and I want to keep it that way."

She raised a brow, indicating she wasn't buying the bullshit he was trying to sell. But since he wasn't offering any more insights, and she didn't want to have a three-hour standoff, she passed him the wet bag. He stepped down from the table—interesting that he didn't hop down like he'd hopped up—and headed for the door.

"You're welcome," she called at his back.

He halted, but didn't turn around. "Thank you."

She snickered as he walked through the double doors that led to the parking lot, then she made a split-second decision. Who said she couldn't thank him for the drinks the night before? Might be better to just acknowledge the first meeting, get that out of the way, and move on. Maybe he'd loosen up a little afterward.

Marianne sprinted after him, but as she hit the doors herself, she watched as he continued on to a car, limping more than a little. Everyone else was already out of sight, having raced off to make the most of their short break time. So he likely thought he was safe letting his guard down.

She watched the limp pattern as he shuffle-walked to his car, then eased into the driver seat carefully. Right leg, likely the knee. His ankle seemed to be rotating fine, but he was struggling to bend the knee to get in the car, which appeared to be a rental.

Might just be sore muscles. If that were the case, heat would be better than ice, which she would have told him if he hadn't been such a hard-ass about it. But he wasn't ready to discuss it.

So she'd observe and make notes. It was part of what she did, watching for potential problems and working to prevent injuries just as much as putting out the fires once one cropped up. A healthy team was the goal, and a healthy team was the sign of a damn good trainer.

Brad Costa, I will just have to break you down and get you to confess. You won't know what hit you.

IT was a train. A train had hit him. Right at the kneecap.

Jesus H. Brad continually bent and straightened his leg—though the "straighten" part was more theory than actual practice—while icing in twenty-minute increments. Day one, and he was already falling apart. These three-a-days were killers. He had to be back at practice in another thirty minutes, and he wasn't even sure if he should drive his damn car over.

Lying back on his bed, he whipped out his cell phone from his duffel and called his mom. He'd missed her call to him the day he'd checked in—thanks to being out at Back Gate—and knew she'd be worried.

When she answered, a little breathless, he checked his watch and knew he'd called during dinner time on accident. "Sorry, forgot you're an hour behind me now."

"Globe-trotting will do that to you." His mother's amused voice warmed him from the inside. "How's my favorite son?"

"Don't let Brent hear you say that."

"He's at college. What he doesn't know won't hurt him."

He laughed, because he knew she'd have said the same thing to his younger brother. They were all her favorites. "Tell me what's up with you guys?"

"What's not up with us? Sarah's got college applications coming out her ears, and your brother dodges my calls faster than you do." She sighed, the much belabored sigh of a mother hen who enjoyed her chicks and hated when they were far from the nest. "Bob started a new project in the garage. He swears it's a chair—"

"It *is* a chair!" he heard his stepfather call from somewhere else in the house. Probably the kitchen table.

"And it's a lovely one," his mother insisted.

Brad smiled. His stepfather was always trying a new woodworking project. The family had long ago resigned themselves to the fact that they would never be able to actually park their cars in the garage.

"I need to hear how you are. Making any friends? How's the food?"

"It's not summer camp." He groaned as he tried once more to straighten his knee. The pop and grind made him want to gag. That was just so wrong. "It's like boxing camp on steroids."

"Are you hurt?" With a mother's intuition, she poked at the raw spot with scary accuracy. "Are you in pain?"

"Pain is gain," he joked. She made a sound that said she wasn't amused. "I'm fine. I'm sticking with it."

"Making this team isn't the end of the world."

He sucked in a breath, then let it out slowly. *Here we go again.*

"Your father was proud of you, no matter what. Just trying, being invited to the tryouts . . ." His mother's voice choked, and he mentally cursed being so far away. "Making the team wouldn't matter. Your father would be pleased with you just giving it a shot."

He might be. But Brad knew he wouldn't feel right if

he didn't make it to the All Military games. Completing that final hurdle was something he'd felt pressed to do the moment he'd joined the Corps. Not by any outside source, but by something inside him.

"Giving it a shot's only the first step. I've got this, Mom."

A knock on the door had him tossing the nearly melted ice bag into the trash can by his bedside and shoving the heating pad—which he'd purchased at the MCX on the way home with all the stealth of a ninja—under his pillow. "Hold on," he called.

"Should I let you go?" his mother asked in his ear.

"Yeah, someone's at the door. Probably my roommate."

"Okay, baby. Go make friends!"

"Sure thing, Mom. Love ya." He fought a grin as they finished their good-byes. His mom liked to pretend he was at nothing more than overnight camp, making crafts, learning to paddle a canoe and singing camp songs around the fire at night.

Another knock reminded him why he'd ended the call. "Come in."

Higgs poked his head in. "You heading over soon?"

"Sure, yeah. Of course." Why, had he heard something?

Brad studied his roommate's face, but the man seemed completely oblivious.

"All right then. Want to just ride with me?"

Perfect. The solution to his driving dilemma. He'd been worried enough driving himself home after the morning practice, with the way his knee was aching. Now that it'd had over an hour to stiffen up, driving was a real concern. "Thanks. I'll just grab my gear and meet you out there."

Higgs nodded and shut the door behind him, leaving Brad back in blissful peace.

His head thunked against the wooden headboard. What kind of shit luck did he have? Maybe he really was too old for this sport.

Even as he thought it, he cursed under his breath. He wasn't even thirty yet. *Too old, my ass.* So everyone was younger. Big deal. He had more years of experience, and he'd had more years to build up a thick skin and a long endurance.

He'd just have to be careful from here on out. At least until the knee healed. Who knew, maybe by tomorrow he'd be up and running again full speed. The travel must have thrown his body out of whack. Or sleeping in a new bed. He'd catch up, he'd adjust and he'd be back on track by tomorrow.

Next week at the latest.

Now all he had to do was avoid the sexy athletic trainer with eyes who saw too much. If he wasn't careful, she'd sideline him as a preventative measure and his chance at the team would be done for. Nobody was going to wait around for him to heal. He wasn't the strongest or the fastest.

Higgs. They'd give Higgs a second chance if he injured something. He was faster than the wind out there, and everyone knew it. He'd run a circle around his opponent and deliver the knockout punch before they even blinked. What he lacked in professional, technical training, Brad could see he had in raw talent. His roommate defined the word *natural*.

So avoid Marianne Cook, keep his nose to the grindstone and don't act as old as Father Time while in practice.

His knee grinded like a rusty gear as he lowered his leg to the floor and stood.

Yeah, sure. He could do that.

HIGGS pulled up to the parking lot of the training center, but didn't turn off the car.

"Problem?" Brad hefted his gym bag from the floor of the car onto his lap, ready to make a break for it. His knee was already feeling better, and he needed to get it moving so it wouldn't lock up on him.

Higgs stared at the door for a few moments, then shook his head. "Nah. I'm good. Let's go in and kick some ass, old man."

Brad rolled his eyes, but bit back a grin. He wasn't here to make friends, but it was nice to at least like the guy he was sleeping next door to. "You can't be that much younger than me."

"Probably not. I'm twenty-eight."

"Twenty-nine." Brad hefted his bag over one shoulder—his right, so the strap crossed his chest and the bag hung by his left knee—and started for the door with him.

"And that's all that counts, Grandpa." Higgs grinned and slapped him on the shoulder.

"*Grandpa*," he uttered in disgust. "If anyone else starts calling me that . . ." he warned. He punched at the door so it flew open and into the humid air of the sealed-up gym. A few guys were already stretching out, early birds who were after more than just the worm.

"Hey," Higgs called out as he tossed his bag off to the side by the bleachers, out of the way.

Be nice; don't be a dick. "Hey," Brad said, throwing his bag beside Higgs' gear.

A small chuckle sounded behind him, but he ignored it while he changed shoes. When he bounced off the bottom bleacher to stretch on the mat—swallowing a wince on the landing—a few of the Marines smiled up at him.

Okay, clearly the joke was on him. With an indulgent sigh, he plopped down—careful of his knee without being obvious—and asked, "What?"

Two of the younger Marines smiled at each other before one said, "Nothing, Grandpa."

That little crack had them bursting into laughter like a second-grade class pulling a fast one on the substitute teacher. He glared at Higgs, who smiled angelically and held out his hands in a gesture that said, *I'm innocent, bro.*

Innocent, his ass. "Yeah, yeah," he grunted and stretched out his hamstrings. "You children can laugh all you want. Slow and steady Grandpa's here to win."

They laughed more at that, but he wasn't offended. Bullshit and jokes were a way of relaxing in the tense atmosphere their jobs created. If they were saddling him with a nickname, they thought he'd be here long enough to care what to call him.

He'd ignore the sting behind the name and call it a sign others were watching and thought he had what it took to stick for the long haul. He was ready to consider it a good thing. A positive sign.

Of course, he still punched Higgs in the arm on his way to jog a few laps around the outside of the gym for a warm-up and to test his knee.

Fair was fair, after all.

CHAPTER

4

Marianne watched with interest as Brad pummeled a bag. Most of the Marines she'd watched go through the circuit with the bag had started off focused, then slacked off as the coaches had moved on to study other students. Just going through the motions so they could move on to another, more exciting exercise.

But not Brad. He attacked the bag as if he expected it to feint left and throw him a sucker punch at any second. His dark eyes were laser-sharp and intense, taking in every small shift of the heavy bag as it swung on chains from the impact.

That sort of intensity was intriguing to her, as well as impressive. That he didn't slack off just because nobody was watching or because he could get bored spoke volumes about his training ethic, and his desire to be there.

And okay, yes, if she was being completely shallow—she was her mother's daughter; it was inevitable one shallow moment would slip in—watching him move and shift around the bag, his arms taut and precise, even while delivering powerful blows, was pretty much the sexiest thing she'd seen in too long to remember.

His biceps flexed with every jab, his calves tensed as he stayed light on the balls of his feet and the cords of his neck stood out in relief. In short . . . he was an amazingly delicious package.

He paused for a moment to bend down and grab his water bottle, and she admired the way his mesh shorts stretched over his butt. Yup. He had a body meant for ogling.

And then . . . yup again. He took the lust factor up to a ten by stripping off the soaking wet T-shirt and tossing it to the side with a loud, smacking *plop*.

His arms sported faint tan lines from short sleeves, but as far as imperfections go, it was all she could find. His skin was slicked with sweat, beads of it making the sparse hair on his chest glisten a little. Naturally, her eyes followed the line of hair down past his belly button and . . .

"Should we turn the air up higher?"

Marianne nearly bit her tongue holding in a yelp of surprise as Levi stepped up beside her.

"What?"

He gave her a clinical once-over. "You're flushed. Is it too hot in the training room?"

"On the contrary." She smiled a little and stepped back into her domain. "That gym is a sweatbox. Compared to that, it's like the inside of an ice bar in here."

That was a true statement. True enough, anyway. They kept it a cool sixty-eight in her room to help athletes coming in who might have overheated themselves. But the hot air from the gym wasn't the real reason she was flushed.

Just go stick your head in the ice machine, Cook. God.

She waited until Levi grabbed the towels he had come in for and darted back out before slowly edging her way to the doorway again—and immediately felt like a creepy stalker. She had every right to watch the guys train. That's why she was here; to watch, to educate, to help. She couldn't help if she was stuck in her room twiddling her thumbs and quizzing coeds on the skeletal system.

With a quick glance around, she stepped fully out of the door and into the gym. The air was thick with sweat; the salty scent nearly knocked her back a step. Thank God she'd chosen to wear shorts today instead of long khakis, like she'd considered. Her legs would be sweating in under a minute in these conditions.

A group of Marines sprinted past, one of them sending an abbreviated wave as they zoomed on by. She recognized him as Tressler, the one from the bar, and smiled a little. Even now, he couldn't keep himself from paying attention to a woman. At this rate, he was going to run into a wall if Nikki said three sentences to him.

A few Marines were with speed bags, but nodded respectfully as she walked by. A few more were running footwork drills, using short orange cones and a ladder formation marked out on the wooden floor with painter's tape. Coach Ace nodded as well while she walked past, then motioned for her to stop a moment.

"How are things, Coach?"

"Just what I was about to ask you." He leaned forward a bit, and she had the momentary mental image of a dark tree bending slightly in the wind. "See any problems yet?"

"Too early to tell. Everyone's a tough guy at this stage in the game."

He grunted, then walked up behind a lanky Marine at a speed bag and gave him a quick love tap to the back of the dome. "Keep your eyes on the bag, Marine."

"Yes, Coach," he answered quickly in clipped syllables, just as if he'd said, "Yes, sir," instead.

"I want tough guys, Ms. Cook."

"Marianne."

"Cook," he compromised. "What I don't want is idiots. I can't field a team from a bunch of half-busted men. And the Corps is going to get mighty pissed if I return their warriors broken and have the balls to ask for a dozen more."

She bit back a laugh. "Probably."

"Know anything about yoga?"

She blinked in surprise. "As a theory, or in actual practice?"

"Both, though the latter is what I'm interested in. I figure yoga might help these chuckleheads stretch out. They're all muscle, but most of them can't touch their own damn toes. I need all-around athletes, not meatheads built like freezers that can't move or evade a blow."

More and more she liked this man. "I'm not really a yoga girl. Pilates, though, that's what I'm into. But I don't believe I should be trusted to teach a class. I do know a friend who's certified in both. She also does some health coaching." She gave him a smile. "Want me to set up a yoga session? She could come here to the gym to do it. I think her schedule is flexible."

"I'd like that, yes. If you could be there, watching, that'd be great."

The thought of two dozen Marines twisted up like pretzels while chanting had her gasping for breath to keep the laughter down. "Yeah," she squeaked out. "I can do that."

"A trainer with a sense of humor." Coach Ace's lips twitched in what might have passed for a smile in some circles. "Wonders never cease."

"A coach with a brain," she said in the same pondering tone. "Wonders, indeed."

At that, he shocked her by barking out a laugh and slapping her on the back hard enough to send her forward a step before she could catch herself. "You're a good one,

Cook. Keep my boys healthy and we're gonna get along just fine."

"Likewise, Coach." She grinned and took two steps back, only to jump forward out of the way of a pack of runners. She caught sight of Brad at the head of the herd and smiled to herself.

Stop that. He's not on the menu. Nobody is. Work, work, work.

But since it was her job . . . She watched as he easily led the Marines with a fluid runner's stride. He wasn't burning a pace, but he also wasn't even breaking a sweat as they grazed around the outer corners of the workout facility. And then, when Coach Cartwright pointed toward a set of stairs, they disappeared from view. She waited a moment, knowing the drill.

And was surprised to see a different guy leading the pack when they burst through the doors on the catwalk above to sprint around the perimeter. Brad brought up the rear, and for the first time, he looked . . . not winded. But the effortlessness of his movement was gone. It was clear now every step was purposeful, as every stilted stride set him back from the pack.

He'd been running or moving for hours and made it all look like he'd just started, fresh as a daisy, and one set of stairs sent his body into recovery mode? She doubted that. His knee was in pain. Whether he'd come to the team with the injury or it had happened earlier the other day, she couldn't know. But the man was definitely in pain, and the stairs were the big killer.

She debated saying something to the coach, then held back. Not yet. He was going to be a tough nut to crack. If she was wrong—if something else was going on and she said something that got him kicked off the team—she'd be pissed at herself. And not only that, but nobody else would trust her going forward.

Fantastic. So her options were . . .

Yeah. Not fun.

BRAD stood warily, watching his balance as he walked without limping. It took something out of him to do it—mostly the breath he was holding in his burning lungs—but he managed. Already the pain was shifting down to more of a dull throb. The lower extremity version of a toothache.

Higgs was still shooting the shit with a few other guys, so he had some time to duck into the trainer's office and grab a bag of ice. Marianne had been wandering around, and he noticed her leaving the training room. If he was quick, he could duck in and back out again with a bag and no questions. Higgs would wonder what it was for, but he could shake it off as just swollen knuckles or some other shit. They were all going to be battling that one soon enough.

Higgs waved as he started toward the training room and called out, "I'll be a minute."

"It's fine," Brad said and ducked in. How the hell did his roommate make friends that easily? It was like the guy was a walking friend magnet. People just wanted to be around him.

He did a quick sweep, making sure neither of the two young interns was lurking in corners. But they hadn't been present all evening, so he figured he was safe. He let his bag drop to the floor with a thud and hurried to scoop some ice out.

"Can I help with that?"

His hand jerked, the handle flipping and tossing ice cubes over his shoulder to clatter on the floor. "Jesus H."

The female chuckle was low and throaty, and his mind went immediately to hearing that same sound in a dark room with a soft mattress under his back.

And now he needed to stick his nuts in the ice bag to cool them off. Great. He turned—with reluctance—and faced the trainer. She stood with her hands on her hips, smiling at him from a few feet away. She'd pulled back the top half of her hair tonight, letting the bottom part swing to just past her ears. It only emphasized her large blue eyes, which watched him with way too much intuition.

"Are you in a hurry?" Marianne stepped around the ice cubes and grabbed a rag. She knelt down and started mopping up the already melting mess.

Jesus H. "Sorry, here, let me do that." He bent down to take the rag from her, but she didn't let go. The odd little silent tug of war ended when he wrapped one hand around her thin wrist and made her look at him. "I spilled it—let me clean it."

She watched him for a moment, and damn if her eyes didn't seem to darken while she stared. Then she shrugged and let go, and he told himself he was just making shit up in his mind. He was tired. That's all. Just exhausted after a long day.

"I'll get a new baggie. Just one?" She stood, and God help him, it was all he could do to keep his eyes down on the wet floor and not focus on her ass, which was conveniently at eye level now.

"One's fine."

"Are you going to tell me what it's for?"

He let the silence drag out while he scooped the last of the ice into a bucket, then took it over to a sink and rinsed it and the rag out.

"Costa, if you're hurting, I can help. Or at least I can do my best."

"Not hurting. Just keeping ahead of it. Nobody likes swollen joints." He shook his hands out as he spoke, like he was flicking off water, and hoped she took that to mean he was referring to his hands . . . without lying directly.

One blonde eyebrow arched in a silent bullshit call, but he ignored that and held out a hand for the bag. "Thanks."

She kept it just out of reach. "Can we talk?"

"About what?"

She shrugged again, stepping around the nearest table to hop up and let her feet dangle. "Anything. You're one of the only guys out there that doesn't make me feel like a big sister."

He grinned at that, then made a face. "Was that a dig at me being old?"

Her eyes widened in innocence. "Of course not." She blinked coyly. "Grandpa."

"Dammit," he muttered, but without heat. He'd accepted it was just his lot on the team to be the oldest. Provided he made the team.

"Where are you from?" Her heels thudded gently against the wooden leg of the table.

"Illinois."

She waited a moment. "Me? I grew up in Jackonville. Moved away for college and my first training gig, then came back for this job specifically. Thanks for asking, chatterbox."

His lips twitched before he could catch them.

"Jeez, you really ask a lot of questions. I'm an only child, and that was my mom sitting with me the other night at the bar, though you likely already figured that out. Got any siblings over there in Illinois?"

He raised a brow.

"If you don't shut up, I'll never get a word in edgewise," she said with mock seriousness.

He turned to look at the wall for a moment before she caught the smile.

She grinned, totally onto him. "You can't resist forever. Eventually you'll crack under the pressure. I have ways of making you talk. Do you need a ride back to the BOQ?"

He nodded before he caught himself, then shook his head. It was like being slowly but methodically beaten by a teddy bear. Not painful, but difficult to keep track of all the whacks. "I have a ride back."

"Ah. Okay, well that's good."

Higgs took that moment to stick his head in. "Hey, Grandpa, ready to roll?"

"Yeah, sorry, I—"

"Oh. Did I interrupt?" Higgs walked fully into the room and looked back and forth between them. He didn't even bother hiding his curiosity—or the fact that he wanted to watch whatever he'd interrupted.

"No, I think we were done. I was just offering Costa here a ride back if he needed one, but looks like he's all squared away." Marianne hopped off the table, and Brad resisted the strong urge to wrap his hands around her waist and catch her fall. She was short enough to make the jump dangerous.

She landed softly with no effort.

Or not so dangerous, and he was just overreacting.

Higgs backed out slowly. "You know, I actually need to run a few errands, so if you could still give him a ride . . ."

"Higgs," Brad warned in a low voice.

Marianne shot him a smile as sunny as the hair tucked behind her ears. "Absolutely. No problem."

And just like that Higgs was running for his car. Damn traitor. *This.* This was why it never paid to make friends out of the competition. Guy probably thought he was doing him a favor or some crap, having incorrectly read the tension in the room.

Marianne motioned to a chair. "Have a seat. It'll just be a minute before I can lock up and go."

He settled on the squeaky vinyl chair and stretched out his right leg, resting the ice bag over the top of his kneecap.

No point in pretending it was his hand and waste the ice. Her eyes missed nothing, although she was busy shuffling papers around on her desk.

So, he gave it back to her and watched her in return. She wore less makeup than she had at the bar, though that wasn't a shocker. The polo was too big by at least a size, and she tucked it in and did that poof-out thing from the waistband of her cuffed khaki walking shorts. He'd bet money she intentionally made herself less sexually appealing at work. Habit? Or something she did only because of the current clientele? If she'd worked for a women's team, would she have stayed so toned down?

"Okay, ready to roll." She beamed over her shoulder, then nodded to his leg. "We can stay until your twenty is up."

"I'm good. It's not a big deal." He clenched his jaw to keep a grimace from his face while he stood. He couldn't limp this time. No wiggle room for the pain. "You really didn't have to do this."

"I like getting to know the athletes. Makes it easier when you guys are in here and I'm keeping tabs on everyone." She waited for him to walk out the door, then shut off the lights and locked up. "I'm parked near the front, so it's not too far."

"I'm fine."

"Okay." Her tone was cheerful, not a single hint of sarcasm. But maybe that was the beauty of it. It was so non-sarcastic, it made a full reversal and became the ultimate in comebacks.

Or the pain was eating holes in his brain like Swiss cheese and he was reading too much into it. She was a trainer. Not the KGB. She was there to tape ankles and hand out ibuprofen. Not to investigate his entire life.

She walked to a clean little Honda and opened her own door before he could do it for her. Fine. Fewer steps for him. He eased into the seat, and this time the grimace was as much from how scrunched he felt in the tiny car as from the pain of folding his right leg in.

"I know, I know," she said easily as he fought to slide the seat back a few inches. "It's small. But I'm small, so it's not wasteful."

"You've got a point." As he settled the ice back on his knee, he watched as she navigated the base roads easily and headed in the right direction without waiting for his guidance. "You know your way around."

"I'm not a military brat or anything. But you know, you live in Jacksonville long enough, you'll make friends with kids who live on base. Plus, I worked at the Dunkin' Donuts by the commissary for two very long months the summer after I graduated high school."

He smiled at that. "Nothing makes you work harder in school than a taste of minimum wage."

"Exactly why my dad pushed me into the job." She followed the speed limits exactly, made all turns at a snail's pace, and stopped for at least five full seconds at a four-way stop with nobody there. When he raised a brow, she wrinkled her nose. "The MPs scare me."

He couldn't hold back the laugh then. She amused the hell out of him, being intimidated by the military police.

"No, seriously, they do. Once, when my friend and I were driving home from work, they pulled us over. She just had a broken taillight, so they were reading her the riot act over that. But it made a big impression on my very sheltered seventeen-year-old self." She shuddered at the memory.

Damn, she was funny. "They can be pretty intense."

As she rolled to a stop in front of the BOQ, she waited while he grabbed his bag and the ice-bag-turned-water-balloon.

"Muscle or tendon?"

He stared at her for a minute in the dim light from the dashboard and street lamp. "It's nothing."

She bit her lip, and he could almost see her mind turning over another angle to approach it with. She wasn't going to let up. She was the teddy bear, and she could go on whacking him forever until he broke. There was no way he'd hold up under her scrutiny. So, he just said the first thing he could think of to hold the questions back.

"Have dinner with me tomorrow."

CHAPTER

5

Hair behind the ears or in front? Front. No, up. Clipped back. That's more casual. Makeup? No . . . okay, yes, because otherwise it would just look like she didn't care about her appearance at all. She wasn't vain, but a girl had her pride.

And this. *This* was exactly what Marianne had been attempting to avoid when she decided her career was more important than dating for the moment. This utter waste of time she was going through for this dinner. A dinner that was not even an actual date, but just a meeting between two people to hash out stuff and pass the time. Not a date.

Nope. Not at all.

Heels. Yes, definitely heels.

Pride, after all.

She sat on the edge of the bed and debated between two pair of heels, choosing the taller ones. Mostly because she was just short and taller heels made her more confident on a daily basis. And also, a small sliver of her admitted they made her ass look particularly fantastic with the dark jeans she was sporting. The tank top she'd picked out was an old favorite, with enough skin to look fashionable but not so much that if she bent over, she flashed her ta-tas for the entire restaurant. And the ombre pale-blush-to-hot-pink coloring was subdued and playful at the same time.

Holy shit, she was putting way more thought into this than she had dressing for any date in the last two years. And it was Not. A. Date.

A date might actually have a better shot at sneaking in behind that tough shell Brad Costa threw up at every turn. The man was a turtle. No matter which way you approached him, he would just duck into his hidey-hole and stay put. He was determined to keep himself aloof, for some bizarre reason. And not just from her. She'd seen it in action with the other guys, as well.

Just fine. Marianne was determined to crack the shell and find his soft center. Every man had one; some were just harder to find than others.

Brad's soft center was better at hiding than Carmen Sandiego.

Marianne was debating between two shades of—admittedly nearly identical—lip glosses when her cell rang. She groped for it, relishing the distraction from her wandering mind. "Hello?" she answered as she forced herself to just grab one and slather some on.

"Your father is holed up in his study for the evening. Come out and meet me for dinner."

"Hi, Mom." She blew a strand of hair away from her mouth. Why was it the instant anything glossy went on her lips, they became magnets for stray hair? Was this some sort of universal female rule, like you'll always have cramps during important life events, be on your period when you travel and be wearing granny panties when you get the chance for some impromptu sex? "I can't tonight. I have plans."

The instant the words left her lips, she forehead-slapped herself. If she'd had plans with friends, she would have said with whom. Which meant her mother would automatically assume it was a date.

"Ooooh, you do?" Mary purred. "Who is he?"

Yup. Marianne knew her mother all too well.

"Crap, Mom, I'm running late. I'll call you later, okay? Have a good night!" She hung up and threw the phone on the bed like it was a cobra waiting to strike. As if that would somehow prevent her mother from calling her back immediately.

As her mother's ringtone played, muffled by the bedspread, Marianne sighed. Not how she wanted to start the evening. But time to be a grown-up. She picked up the phone, careful not to accidentally hit a button and answer the call, turned the phone on silent, and sent her mother to voice mail purgatory.

She was a good daughter. She'd call her mother back.

Eventually. Like tomorrow. Night. Or the day after, at the latest.

Every good daughter has her limits.

On the drive to the restaurant, she reminded herself it wasn't a date. There was no reason to be nervous. And she'd only embarrass herself if she walked in there with anxiety. Go in like a professional. It's almost like a business meeting.

Yes. A business meeting. She was pitching her product—her services as a damn good trainer—to the client and hoping he would agree. An unusual venue for her profession, but anything to keep her mouth from tripping over words or—God forbid—blurting out something like, "You don't think this is a date, do you?"

The hostess at the restaurant pointed her in the right

direction, and she made her way there with confidence. Brad stood as she approached the booth, and she inwardly sighed with relief at seeing he'd dressed casually, like she had. His dark jeans and light green button-down shirt looked fantastic, but was definitely more comforting than if he'd dressed up.

"Hey, sorry I'm late. Last-minute call tied me up." She slid in across from him and waited while he settled down. "Have you ordered yet?"

He raised a brow. "No, I was waiting for you."

"Oh. Right." Dumbass. The server passed by and took her drink order of a glass of water and a bottle of Yuengling. At her order, he looked surprised.

"What?"

"Nothing. Just impressed."

"Because I'm a lady who knows her beer?"

"I'm always impressed with anyone who knows decent beer. Most of the guys I know don't even go for the good stuff."

"Well, I could order a girly cocktail and pay nineteen dollars for a quarter of a shot of vodka and three ounces of cranberry juice, but I'm just not in the mood."

He grinned, then turned his bottle so she could see the label on his own drink.

Yuengling.

The smile crept across her lips before she could stop it. "Nice taste."

"I think so." He watched her while he took a sip. The server brought by her drink and water then took their orders. He surprised her by ordering the salmon, grilled, fresh vegetables and a salad with oil and vinegar. Meanwhile, her steak, chicken tortilla soup and baked potato suddenly sounded like a gluttonous splurge.

"Training diet?" she asked.

He nodded. "I try not to go too crazy. I want a beer with

dinner? Dinner's gotta be decent. I'm not in the mood for alcohol or carbs? Maybe I go crazy and order dessert." He shrugged. "Moderation."

"Healthy," she added. "Realistic. I see athletes sometimes who go insane with their diet, thinking they're doing the right thing. And I can't fault them for wanting to be healthy." She debated a second, then grabbed one of the rolls from the untouched basket on the table. "But after a certain time, your body just needs a little something extra, you know?"

He was smiling at her a little, like he enjoyed her snatching a roll as if it were the last one instead of one of four. "Burnout's a real thing. I've known guys who wanted to make it into training camp as badly as I did and pushed it too hard."

"Is this the first year for you?"

"Yup. Life—and the Marine Corps—has a way of stepping in front of the best laid plans. Deployments, training missions or commanders who didn't want to sign off on the waiver to let me come. This is my first real chance."

He sounded so passionate, so determined. But not in a scary, slow-down-big-boy sort of way. "Why boxing?"

He smiled at the server who delivered his salad and her cup of soup, then glanced back to Marianne after picking up his fork. Their server hovered, as if waiting for Brad to notice her and suddenly swoop down and carry her to the back for a quickie. Brad didn't cooperate, and, with a sigh, the server disappeared.

"Why *not* boxing?"

She waited a moment, then set her spoon down in mock-disgust. "You've really got to stop monopolizing the conversation. I mean, really, Brad. It's just rude."

His lips curved, but he ducked his head toward his salad to hide it.

"Boxing is just my sport. I've been boxing since I was a kid. I would have joined the Marine boxing team years ago, if I could. And it seemed like every year that was denied to me, the desire grew. But, in retrospect, I probably would have taken it for granted if I'd made it in at nineteen like some of these kids have. So it's almost like the goal took on a life of its own in my head."

"I can relate to that one." She blew steam from her soup and tasted. "I've got my eye on a bigger goal, too. It's been hovering over me for a while. I think the longer a dream stays in your head, the bigger it grows, until sometimes it takes on mythological proportions."

He pulled an offended face. "Working with the few, the proud wasn't your ultimate dream in life?"

She couldn't help but laugh. The so-serious Brad, joking around. It was relieving to see his more human side. "Sorry to burst the ego bubble. It's great and all, don't get me wrong. And a step up from having to baby the high school basketball stars who were in my training room begging for Midol."

He froze with the fork halfway to his mouth. A piece of tomato plopped back onto his plate. "Why in the world . . . Were they on a dare?"

"No. It's mostly pain reliever, but it's got caffeine, which can cut headaches faster than straight ibuprofen." She shrugged. "Mostly I think they thought it was hilarious to ask. Some rite of passage. *Look at me, I'm so tough I can ask for Midol and not care.* I guess the trainer before me gave them out like candy. That had to stop fast."

"No kidding." He grimaced. "Do you like your job?"

"Not like; love." She ignored her soup completely and leaned forward, careful not to plop a boob in the bowl. "It's amazing what the right trainer can do for the right athlete. When they click, and they can work together on rehabilitation, or even prevention, or maintenance, it's fantastic. Seeing the athlete's performance skyrocket, and knowing you had a hand in that, is special. The human skeletal system is

an amazing and complex thing." She cut herself off. "Sorry.
I was about to dive off the edge of total nerdiness."

"No, I like it. I like seeing people enjoy what they do."

"Yeah. It feels good to have found that niche that was
meant for me." She waited while the server collected their
salad plate and soup bowl and replaced them with dinner
plates.

It was good, she mused, to have this easy flow with him.
Without mentioning his injury, she'd gotten why the team
was so important out of him, and he'd learned why she
honestly loved her job. Perhaps later on, if it was still appli-
cable, he'd come to her for help.

But more than that, she just enjoyed talking with him.
He was listening. And not the fake listening she knew
some men did where they nodded and made soft noises all
while mentally calculating how fast they could unbutton
the fly to her jeans or whether she would want them to
come inside after their date.

Frankly, the entire evening had been better than a lot
of dates she'd been on in the recent years.

But it is not a date, she reminded herself sternly.

Cutting into the steak, she sighed in pleasure—then
shot him a mischievous grin. "Your salmon looks . . . not
as good as my steak."

He scowled, but she could see the humor in his eyes.
"Your arteries disagree."

"I've trained them to appreciate when I feed them red
meat." She took a bite and moaned in pure pleasure, maybe
just a little louder than usual to bait him. But when her
eyes opened again, he wasn't laughing or shooting her a
playfully angry face. He was watching her mouth intensely,
like he was memorizing the shape of her lips.

"What?" She used her napkin to wipe her mouth and
chin.

He just shook his head and stabbed at a piece of broccoli . . . a little harder than necessary, in her opinion.

"The broccoli would like you to take it easy," she joked,
trying to regain the teasing lightness they'd had moments
before . . . before what? What had she done wrong?

He stared at his plate for a second, then up at her. "Sorry.
Tired. I just zoned for a few seconds."

That she could understand. "I hope you take your day off
to rest up. At the rate Coach Ace is going to push you, you'll
need all the reserves you can grab."

He nodded and went back to eating. But a moment later,
when a carrot landed smack in the middle of her split-open
baked potato, she grinned.

NEVER had Brad had to argue for so long in the parking
lot of a restaurant about following a woman back to her
house. Not because he wanted inside, but because, as he'd
told Marianne repeatedly, he wanted to make sure she got
back safely.

And of course, being who she was, she argued. Only
one beer and switched to lemonade, lived here almost her
whole life, could drive around town blindfolded, yada yada
yada.

Jesus H., the woman loved to argue. He'd just kept his
mouth shut and indicated she go ahead. She could fight it,
but he'd still make sure she got back safe. It wasn't a date;
he wasn't trying to get in her pants, good as they made her
ass look. But his stepfather would kill him dead if he knew
he'd gone out with a woman for any reason and not made
sure she'd gotten home safely.

He preferred to avoid his stepdad's wrath whenever
possible. That was self-preservation. The Marine Corps
liked their officers to carry a decent amount of self-
preservation instinct.

The entire drive back to her place, Brad debated whether to actually walk her to the door. Would she think he was a creeper who couldn't take a hint? Maybe just parking and making sure she got to the door would suffice. She'd just moved back; likely she moved back in with her parents, since the job was short-term. If it was anything like his parents' house, it would be well-lit and in a typical, nice neighborhood.

He was pleased with the thought that it would be safe enough to just drive past her driveway and do the honk-and-wave before making his exit when she surprised him and pulled into an apartment complex. The complex was decent, with good access to one of the side gates to base that would be less busy during the mornings. Smart.

But it also meant his theory of leaving her in her parents' well-lit driveway was kaput. He could still just pull the honk-and-wave. She wouldn't care. In fact, he'd bet Marianne would prefer it if he just drove off and left her to get inside herself. He should just count his lucky stars they'd made it through the entire meal without her harping on his leg or him slipping up and confessing about the pain.

The mere thought of annoying her had him smiling as he parked three spaces away and stepped out of his car.

He knew he was right when he found her standing on the sidewalk, hands on hips, eyes narrowed. The faint parking lot light made her pale shoulders glow.

"I can get into my apartment by myself, thank you."

The words were polite, but the way she forced them through her teeth told him she wanted to add a not-so-nice *Buzz off* at the end of that thank-you.

Why that made him grin, he had no clue. "I know you can get into your apartment. Humor me."

"Remember when you used to avoid me? That was fun." She rolled her eyes as he merely stood there, waiting, then shook her head and headed for the stairs.

"Nice complex," he said as they walked up. "Good view." The fact that her butt was directly in his line of vision didn't hurt.

"Easy access to base, and decent safety. I didn't need much more."

"I'm surprised you didn't move back in with your folks."

"I love my parents, but by doing that, I would have been committing myself to the loony bin. This one's got a six-month rental, which is perfect for me. And I'm surrounded by Marines. Best theft deterrent I know."

He glanced over the railing by the stairs to see a parking lot full of SUVs, motorcycles and pickup trucks, almost all with the Eagle, Globe and Anchor sticker on the back. No Marine's vehicle was complete without the EGA somewhere. "Probably true."

She walked to a door with a doormat out front. In bold black letters, the mat proclaimed, "Oh, no, not you again!"

She caught his chuckle and glanced down. "Yeah, housewarming gift from my dad. He's got a warped sense of humor. But it's also why he can put up with my mom like he does."

"She seemed like fun—the kind of mom you can have a good time with as an adult."

"She is. It was a little embarrassing as a kid. She's a strong personality," she added with a wry smile. "But now, I appreciate the ability to treat her like a friend as much as anything."

He watched her dig through the large purse she'd brought—or was that a duffel bag?—and come up with a key ring with about forty keys on it.

"Do you moonlight as a security guard or something?"

"What?" She glanced up as her fingers flipped through the stack of brass, silver and gold keys. "No, half of these are for stuff in the gym I need to get to. The main gym door, my training room, storage room, offices, more storage rooms. Then the apartment, the key to the twenty-four-hour gym, my storage locker here, my parents' place . . ."

He stepped closer, just for a moment, while she was distracted. He couldn't help himself. Away from the scents of the restaurant, he could appreciate her clean, cool fragrance. Like laundry and the ocean breeze mixed together.

She glanced up suddenly, startled at seeing him closer than she expected and dropped the keys to the concrete ground with a clang. Her fingers clench into fists, as if fighting the urge to shake.

Her eyes watched him, like a rabbit watched a chained dog in the backyard. How long was the dog's rope?

Even he wasn't sure, all of the sudden. Because in an instant, he wanted to kick down her door, throw them through the entryway and slam it shut with her back against it and him pressed into her like they could melt into one person. He leaned down just an inch, then she ducked.

Or rather, bent over to grab the keys, smoothly stepping two feet back when she popped back up. Her laugh was a little brittle, but she didn't look at him again as she continued to flip through the keys. "Stupid things. I do that once a day at least."

Wake up, Romeo. There's your sign.

"Here it is." She held it up, as if he needed verification, then inserted it into the lock and opened her door a crack. "Thanks for walking me up, and the company."

Rabbit running scared. He had the most absurd urge to let out a soft *Woof.* "Yeah, sure, no problem." His foot itched to block the door's closing, as if that would prolong the evening rather than have her calling the cops.

Time to go, Romeo.

"Have a good night." Hands in his pockets, he stepped back, gave her a nod and watched the door close.

MARIANNE'S fingers lost their grip on the clip hook key chain and forty billion keys and let them tumble to the entry laminate with a sharp thump and jangle.

Oh. My. God.

Had she honestly been that socially awkward just then? She turned, rested her shoulders against the door then thumped her head back against the closed door once, hard. Maybe some sense would rattle back in place.

"Marianne?"

She froze, staring into the dark living room.

"Hey, are you okay?"

Brad. He hadn't left yet. Why hadn't he left yet? She could ignore him. Pretend she hadn't heard him calling out.

Except he must have just heard her drop her keys and bang her head against the door. So that would only make her look like the coward she was and create even more problems later on. With dread, and more than a little confusion, she turned and opened the door sheepishly. Just enough to stick her head out. "Yeah?"

He watched her, and she got the vague sensation that he was mentally searching for signs of trauma.

"What did you need, Brad?"

He shrugged one shoulder. "Just heard a really heavy thump. I worried you'd fallen or something."

"I'll press my Life Alert button if I can't get back up." At her snappish tone, he raised a brow. She sighed. "Sorry. Yes, I'm fine. I just dropped my keys and . . . hit my head against the door."

Not really the full story, but it was technically all true.

He smiled a little. "Those keys seem pretty slippery."

"Sure are." When he didn't move, she looked around the breezeway. "Did you need something else?"

"No, I . . ." He huffed out a laugh. "No." Then his face changed as he watched her, and she knew instinctively what he was thinking. Just as he leaned in, he whispered, "Yes."

CHAPTER

6

There was that half second, that bright flash of aware-
ness just before he bent down when Brad knew he
could still pull away. It would have been awkward, and
he would have been embarrassed, but he would have done
it. Almost did.

Except for that moment when Marianne's eyes brightened,
her head tilted up and her lips parted in complete acceptance.
And then the moment to pull away was a distant memory.

The instant his lips touched hers, Marianne's arms
wound around his neck and pulled him closer. He groped
with one hand to find the doorway to keep both their bal-
ances, then used the other to palm her lower back and pull
her body into his.

She tasted like summer. Like cool lemonade, with a
hint of the key lime tartness from their shared dessert. He
licked inside her mouth to see how long the taste would
last. Her tongue met his, circled around, danced in an

instinctive move that made him moan and press against her until her back slid into the doorjamb.

She gasped into his mouth, but didn't break the contact. His hand bunched in her shirt until he could feel the smooth skin of her back with his thumb. He stroked there in the same circles his tongue made, and she melted even more into his body. That tender patch of skin, so simple and yet so sensual, nearly had him rocketing off without her, like a horny teen who had held off for too long.

A door opened and closed somewhere else on the floor of her building, and it was the signal he needed to break the spell. He gripped her shoulders with both hands—damn that sweet, bare skin again—and pulled away, waiting until her eyes popped open before letting go.

"Steady?" he asked cautiously.

She blinked, then looked down at one of his hands. The tanned skin of his fingers, hand and wrist made hers seem even more pearly white. Luminescent.

"Yeah, Romeo. I'm not going to swoon, if that was your hope." She grinned, then shrugged one shoulder until he let go of that one. But he couldn't quite break the contact altogether. She raised a brow, then shrugged the other.

He held on.

She blew out a breath, stirring the blonde hairs that clung to the corner of her mouth, but not moving them. She growled and swiped at them with an impatient push of her hand, but they stubbornly clung to her lips.

Not that he could blame them.

Before she hauled off and punched herself in the face, he brushed the hairs back behind her ear, tracing the outer shell before caressing the lobe and dropping his hand away.

"Lip gloss," she muttered.

What that had to do with hair, he had no clue. But he wasn't going to ask. Women were a rare, special breed. It was best to not get too many details, or it might scare you off permanently.

"You okay?"

"I'm fine," she said quickly. Then she glanced around, like she was waiting for someone to pop out and scare them. "I'm fine."

"You said that already."

She nodded quickly, and it was like she couldn't stop once she'd started. Her head just kept bobbing. He cupped the back of her neck and pressed a kiss to her forehead.

That stopped her.

Clearly, she wasn't *fine*. But he wasn't about to push. He had no clue what the hell had just happened, or why *he'd* been the one to initiate it. But he knew he needed one gigantic step back to assess the situation.

More than that, he just needed to get the hell out of there before he did something embarrassing . . . like kiss her again and not stop.

Shoving his hands in his pockets—*good-bye, temptation*—he took one more step toward the stairs. "Thanks for dinner."

"I didn't pay," she reminded him, one corner of her mouth quirking with a smile. That her humor was returning was a good sign. It meant maybe they could just . . . ignore whatever the hell had happened. And she wouldn't be turning his ass in for harassment or whatever.

"Right. So I'll see you tomorrow then." When she opened her door all the way and took a step in, he waved and beat a hasty retreat.

Cowardly, maybe. Or just smart.

Sure. We could go with smart.

SHE'D kissed him. Oh, God almighty, she'd just kissed one of her athletes.

For the second time that night, Marianne let her head beat against her front door. No need to worry about him coming back this time. Brad had hustled it out of the building like his boxers were on fire.

Did he wear boxers? Or was he a briefs man? Maybe a boxer briefs kind of guy . . .

No, Marianne. Bad Marianne.

She was about to embark on a serious campaign to move up in the ranks of the training world. How the hell would she explain to future bosses that she had a habit of lusting after her clientele? No NBA star wanted a trainer staring at him with puppy dog eyes, and no coach or team owner wanted their investments being cared for by a woman with a record of dating the players. They wanted a serious businesswoman with talent, end of story.

Walking into her kitchen, she forced herself to pull in a few deep breaths, then let them go again. Just like Kara had taught her.

Yoga was so not her thing, but the deep breathing had been a godsend on more than one sleepless night.

With a calmer head, she took one more breath. This was not a problem. Opening a cabinet, she got down a glass for some water. Not a problem at all. They were both adults, and they could both laugh about it tomorrow morning. Chalk it up to a couple of good Yuenglings, a great meal and decent company.

No, not decent. Excellent company. Sexy company.

Bad Marianne.

She would act like it was nothing, and so then it would become nothing. Wasn't that what Kara was always preaching? Visualize the goal, sense the goal, *blah blah blah*, reach the goal?

Come to think of it, maybe that *blah blah blah* part was more important than she had thought.

Draining the water, she put the glass in the dishwasher

and went to get her cell phone out of her bag. Three missed calls from her mother. Fantastic.

Ignore.

She'd call Mary back later, when she wasn't still buzzing from the adrenaline rush of that kiss. Her mother could sniff out pheromones through the phone lines. When it came to men, dating or anything remotely embarrassing, Mary Cook was on the hunt.

Instead, she thumbed through her contacts and found what she needed. She breathed a sigh of relief when a voice answered.

"Kara, hi. Is it too late to call? I have a few questions about that whole *visualize the goal* thing you tried to teach me that one time."

BRAD'S back had barely done more than bounce on the mattress when his door opened.

He draped his forearm over his eyes and groaned. "It was closed, numb nuts."

"But not locked. Smells like someone wants company."

Brad threw his pillow without looking. He heard it hit a wall. Pointless.

"Where'd you go?" When Brad didn't answer, Higgs wandered around the room. Brad tracked his roommate's path by the sound of his voice. "I know you were out for a while. And given you dressed up—"

"Jeans. I'm wearing jeans. In what world does that constitute dressing up?"

"—you probably weren't going out for a drink at a titty bar."

Gross. The last time he went into a titty bar, he was nineteen, eager to prove he was a mature adult to the other Marines in his platoon, and vomited up the beer they'd given him—illegally—behind the Dumpster in the alley out back.

Ah, youth.

He decided the best way to make his chatty roommate go away was to stop answering. Sometimes, mosquitos got high on the attention of being swatted at.

"And the group didn't go out tonight anywhere. I know, since I would have been invited before you," Higgs continued. It was true, but that didn't account for the tightening in Brad's belly at the honesty. "So I'm left to conclude you had a date."

That one word had all his hackles rising. No, not a date. Not dating the trainer. "Wasn't a date."

"Ah, he speaks." As if that were an invitation, Higgs sat at the edge of his bed, within kicking distance. Brave SOB. "And as you didn't feel the need to denounce the other options—"

"You did for me," he pointed out.

"—I am left to conclude—"

"Again."

"—that it *was* a date, and that you are embarrassed by her. Which makes this all the more interesting." Flopping back, he laced his hands behind his head. His elbow bumped Brad's. "So tell me more."

"Hold on, I forgot to put on my nightgown and grab my curlers. Do you want to do my hair, or should I do yours first?" Brad asked with as much of a sneer as he could work up.

"You got curlers? Go for it. No judgment." Higgs shrugged. "She a stripper? Married? Ugly as sin?"

"What? No!" Brad sat up and shoved at his roommate. The man didn't budge.

"So there *is* a woman. Damn, you're bad at this." Rolling to his feet, Higgs chuckled as Brad threw his second pillow—this time with perfect aim—at his back. "Just saying, if you've got a girl, and you want to keep her quiet for whatever reason, it might be a good idea to be more discreet. Take her down to Topsail Beach or something. But don't leave the BOQ dressed like you're gonna meet her father. Guys talk." With a wink, he closed the door behind him.

He didn't *have* a girl. First off, the whole *have* part was insulting. And secondly, Marianne Cook was most certainly not a girl. Those had been the curves of a petite bombshell of a woman under his hands. That kiss had been with an active participant. The thoughts that had rolled around in his mind all the way back to the BOQ had been of two consenting adults.

And now his dick was semi-hard, with no hope of sharing the fun of remedying that problem. Fantastic.

The worst part was, he'd enjoyed the evening. He was struggling to remember the last time he'd had such a good time with a woman, even his sister. Marianne was funny, smart and could clearly hold her own around a bunch of hard-ass Marines. That was appealing in more ways than one. Even if there'd been no spark, he'd have been happy to call her a friend and hang out. He had no doubt she'd be the kind of girl to flirt platonically with you one minute, then drink your ass under the table the next.

But that spark. That damn spark . . .

His lips were still tingling from the contact. He might have initiated the kiss, but she'd hopped on that ride without a second glance behind her. The things they'd do to each other if they got naked on a bed. Or a couch. Or against a wall . . .

He groaned and rolled over on his stomach. His erection pressed painfully into the mattress, an apt punishment for letting his mind wander down the can't-go-there path.

She was intelligent, and she was cool. She'd probably laugh it off with him, if he managed to play it right. Marianne wasn't the kind of woman to go running to a superior for a single kiss that they'd both participated in. She'd probably go right back to annoying the hell out of him about his knee, come to think of it.

Captain Rock, meet Major Hard Place.

MARIANNE jingled her keys—all forty of them—in the palm of her hand as she walked into the gym. She tossed them up and nearly bobbled them on the catch. And her mind turned, unbidden, to the last time she'd dropped them, and what had followed.

Bad Marianne.

She took a deep breath and opened the auxiliary doors to the main gym, where the mats and conditioning equipment were—and immediately felt like the air had been sucked from her lungs.

Despite the fact that it was only seven in the morning, the heat was edging up on unbearable in the gym. With only a few windows, and high ceilings, the dark room seemed like it should be a cool haven from the summer sun. But instead, the arena turned into an oversized sweatbox in ten seconds flat. Hydration and stretching would be key, along with regular breaks. She'd have to speak to Coach Ace about that.

Several Marines were already there, stretching or chatting on the main mat. Coach Willis—who sort of reminded her of Danny DeVito with some wicked facial hair—was there, but the other two coaches weren't around. And, because she couldn't help but search him out, she noticed Brad was MIA. With a sigh, and with the realization she wouldn't be able to grab him quickly before practice for a chat to clear up the night before, she unlocked her training room.

The instant she opened the door, before the lights even went on, she knew something was wrong. Flicking on the light, she sucked in a breath and immediately gagged at the smell.

Gauze wraps and athletic tape covered the room, as if

the place had been TP'd by a high schooler. They hung from the ceiling, from light fixtures, wound around fan blades and chair legs. The place was a spiderweb of sticky substances. She couldn't even walk into her training room. She'd have to hack at the stuff with scissors like a machete through jungle brush.

Heating pads and pillows lay in a heap on the floor, soaked in what she could only assume from the smell was the alcohol she diluted and used as a cleaning agent. Someone had written more than one foul word over the walls in what looked like the same permanent marker she used to mark files. And two of her exam tables had been tipped onto their sides.

And . . . *Oh my God*. Was that a puddle of *pee* on the floor? What. The. Hell.

Marianne's eyes started to water from the alcohol. She closed her eyes, pulled her work polo over her face to blot at her leaking eyes and to cover her nose and stepped back out of the room, only to bump into a body.

"Sorry," she managed to mutter quickly. "Sorry." But there was no way she was pulling her face out from the shirt until she'd wiped all the tears away and had taken several more giant steps away from the stench.

"Hey," a deep voice said. Not one she recognized by sound. "Who's in there?"

"Cook," she said, then pulled away from the steadying hands and took one more step back before pulling the shirt down around her nose. With still-watery eyes, she saw one of the older Marines—his name began with an H, but she couldn't place it just yet—watching her with concern.

"Everything okay?" He started to say something else, then his nose wrinkled. "What's that smell?"

She said nothing, just pointed toward her room. Who could talk with that stench burning the hairs in her nostrils? She had to find a janitor, and Coach Ace, and call her supervisor. They'd have to triage what supplies could be salvaged, see if the ice machine was still functional, set up somewhere else for the time being in case—

"What the fuck?" She heard Brad's voice before she saw him around the other Marine's arm. His voice was a low growl, followed by a tight, "Where's Marianne?"

"I'm right here," she answered, waving a hand over the other man's shoulder. Cautiously, she lowered her shirt all the way and took a delicate sniff. No lingering burning smell. She was probably safe. "Thank you very much . . ."

"Higgs," he offered with a charming smile. "It's Higgs, ma'am."

"Cook," she returned, then smiled back.

Brad was by her in an instant. After a cursory glance at Higgs, his eyes leveled at her. "What the hell happened? Are you okay?" He took a step toward her, as if he was going to hug her, then pulled up at the last second.

Higgs, looking between them, deserted the field. "I'm going to look for Coach Ace."

"Oh, I'll do that," she started, but he was already out of hearing range. The man moved like the wind. "Damn it, I'm responsible for the mess, not him. He needs to start stretching."

"Pull off the trainer hat for a second and look at me." His voice was so calm, so intense, Marianne followed the instruction without thinking twice. His eyes bore into hers. "Are you okay?"

"It didn't happen while I was here. I just found it five minutes ago." She rubbed the heels of her hands over her cheeks to wipe off the last of the tears. "Wow, that stuff's lethal in that large a dose."

She saw his eyes dart around, then he reached out and brushed a hand down her arm, shoulder to elbow. Just one light brush, nothing dangerous. But the support, the contact, the obvious *I'm here* sent an extra ounce of steel to her spine. And she felt ready to attack the situation head-on.

Nodding once, she gave him a slight smile. "Guess I've got my work cut out for me today." She pulled her cell from her pocket, ready to make the first of numerous calls, when she heard a shriek. She slid the phone back in her pocket with a sigh. "And looks like Nikki's early."

"You'd think she saw a snake," Brad muttered, and she gave a watery chuckle. Okay, so she wasn't quite as composed as she wanted to be. But she'd get there.

"Yeah, well, you should hear her when she does the laundry. Watching her pick up sweaty towels with two fingers while gagging is pretty entertaining." She pointed to the mat and gave him her best stern face. "Now go stretch, Marine. I don't want to see you in my . . . um, see you wherever I'm camped out later because you've got muscle cramps."

He raised a brow, but didn't fight her on it. He tossed his bag to the side, into the same pile as the rest of the duffels, and jogged over to the mat, where his potential teammates were stretching and jumping rope.

With another heavy sigh, she walked back to the open door of the training room. Nikki was still there, still as a statue, one hand draped in a practiced pose over her chest.

"What happened? Who would do this?"

At that moment, Levi ambled up, earbuds in, head nodding along with the music. He pulled up to a halt when he saw them at the doorway, then glanced in. With a low whistle, he pushed a hunk of hair out of one eye and leaned over Nikki's shoulder to survey the damage further.

"Damn, what happened?"

"I don't know," Marianne said quietly. She grabbed both their arms and pulled them away from the stench. "But let's get to work."

CHAPTER
7

"Day three, and who's ready to go home?" Coach Ace barked as Brad and his potential teammates held their plank positions over the mat. A drop of sweat rolled down Brad's forehead, caught momentarily in the lines etched between his brows.

Please don't run into my eye. Please, for the love of all that's holy . . .

He nearly breathed a sigh of relief—if he hadn't been focused on steady breathing already—when it rolled down his nose instead and splashed harmlessly to the mat beneath his face.

"Nobody wants to go home?" Coach Ace walked through the rows, pausing to step over one man's legs, weaving back around to nudge another's ass down with the toe of his shoe back to proper plank position. "Sure is hot in here, boys. I'd like to go home myself, I think."

The Marine next to Brad moaned, and Brad risked a

quick glance over. The kid's face was red as a third degree sunburn, and his arms were shaking like a sapling in a hailstorm.

Hell, Brad's arms were quivering themselves, but he wasn't three seconds away from knocking a tooth out like his neighbor.

"Breathe," he whispered harshly.

The kid blinked furiously as sweat ran down his temples and shot Brad a nervous look.

"Breathe," he said more forcefully. "Now. In. Out."

The kid did as Brad commanded, and some of the redness faded out, revealing the freckled skin of his cheeks. So at least he wouldn't pass out.

"Flex your arms," he demanded, and the kid did immediately. His entire body focused to a sharpened point, and while he still vibrated with concentration, Brad noted with some satisfaction he'd stopped shaking hard enough to shift the mat. Which was good, because Brad was done helping. He had to focus on his own performance. Head down, eyes forward, push through the pain that was radiating from his knee up to his hip.

Coach Ace's black gym shoes came to a halt just inside his line of vision. Brad didn't move a muscle. Another drop of sweat rolled off his forehead and landed on the toe of the coach's shoes. Neither man moved.

"You looking to take my job, Marine?" came the man's growly, low voice.

"No, sir," he said through gritted teeth.

A whimper came from behind him. They were all dying.

"You think you can coach these youngins better than I can?"

"No, sir."

There was a long pause, then a quiet "Release."

As one, they collapsed to the mat like two dozen puppets

who'd all had their strings cut simultaneously. Most of them sprawled like broken dolls. A few tried to regain their dignity by crawling up to sit half-flopped-over. None of them were looking all that hot at the moment.

Brad leaned over and wiped his face clean with the bottom of his shorts.

"You're dismissed for the night," Coach Ace said. "If we called your name earlier, you need to see Coach Cartwright for your additional strengthening exercises. He's got your sheets. You'll have nobody to blame but yourselves if you get cut."

They crawled, rolled and dragged themselves over to the area where they'd dumped their bags. Most were shaking their limbs out, trying to regain feeling. A few looked as though, if they tried to stand, they'd vomit.

Brad stood slowly, rolling up like a ninety-two-year-old man coming out of his favorite recliner. Creaky bones and all. Twenty-nine, and already too old for this shit. But he'd held his own.

"Hey." The red-faced freckled wonder bounced over to him. Brad mentally cursed the recoverability of the young. "Thanks for earlier."

Brad grunted and rolled his left shoulder, shaking out his right leg at the same time. He hissed in a pained breath when his knee throbbed and made the same grinding feeling it had been doing all through evening practice. He covered the hiss with a cough, reaching for his water. Right. Like dry mouth was the problem.

"You really pulled my ass out of the fire," the kid went on, hovering while Brad debated the merits of putting his shirt back on or digging through his bag for a clean one. The old one was gross, but putting on a new one meant doing laundry that much faster.

Damn you, decisions . . .

"I'm Chalfant. Toby Chalfant. I'm with 2nd Recon." The

kid held out his hand for a shake. Brad stared at it a moment, then took it. Easiest way to get the kid—Chalfant—to back off was to follow along.

If Chalfant noticed Brad's less-than-warm greeting, he didn't act like it. "Anyway, so I was wondering if you do any coaching on the side or anything."

"Coaching," he muttered, going with the old shirt. Nasty, but he wasn't out to impress the ladies. He was keeping himself as sane as possible with as little laundry as possible. "I'm here for a tryout, kid. Same as you."

The "kid" was at least three inches taller than him, and spindly. But Brad had noticed him, and not just for his height. He had spirit, and a willingness to learn. Unfortunately, learning at this stage in the game wasn't the point. You were here to show what you already knew. Brad doubted the young, cheerful Chalfant would make the team, unless injuries kicked more than the usual amount out.

Which reminded him of his own issue, and how he was going to sneak a bag of ice from the storage room Marianne Cook had reconned for her training room.

"Well, you know, if you ever wanna grab lunch or anything, my friend's got an apartment here. I'm staying with him most of the time, since it's more private than the barracks. We could hang out and watch some practice videos, maybe you could give me a few ideas . . ."

The hope and eagerness in the younger man's eyes was about to kill him. Unable to bring himself to kick a Marine for being young and naive, he lifted one shoulder. "Sure, maybe sometime."

"Costa!"

The barked word had Brad's back straightening. Coach Ace had a voice that could make a SEAL piss his pants. As if sensing now was definitely not the time to hang around, Chalfant gave him a grimace of sympathy and waved before jogging off to get his bag.

Without any hitches in his step, without any pops or cracks from any joints.

Effing junior Marines.

Sweat-heavy shirt on and his duffel bag hitched over one shoulder, Brad turned and walked back to the coach. Every step was a deliberate choice to not limp or wince, to stay strong and not show any weakness.

"Costa," Coach Ace repeated when Brad halted in front of him. "I've made a decision about how things are going to run from here on out. You're the oldest one here."

Jesus H., was there a newsletter circling or something?

"I'm going to be asking you to take on some of the younger men. They're your responsibility to keep motivated and out of trouble."

Brad blinked, then rubbed at one temple. "I don't understand exactly what you mean, Coach."

"Consider it a tryout for captain. I watched you turn Chalfant's focus from the pain to the gain in ten seconds flat. Sometimes, the motivation has to come from within the nucleus of a team, not the staff supporting it. I want to see how you handle that responsibility. So . . . get to know your mini-platoon." He handed Brad a sheet of notebook paper with four names on it. "This is your new job."

"My job is to box, sir." Brad stared, unseeing, at the paper. He was struggling as it was to keep up and not get cut or kill himself. Now he had this added on?

"Now your job is to box, and to keep your mini-platoon in line. Consider it a bonus, without the pay increase." Coach Ace slapped a hand on his shoulder and walked on, calling out Higgs' name.

Something told Brad that Higgs—who was barely a year younger than him—was getting his own mini-platoon. When he saw Coach Ace hand Higgs a sheet of paper, the theory was confirmed.

He read the names on his own sheet, half-amused,

half-groaning to see Chalfant's name at the top. The other two were quiet guys he didn't foresee any major problems with. But the last one . . .

Tressler.

Damn it all to hell and back. That moron was his responsibility now? What kind of sick joke was the universe playing on him?

Now he was a Marine, a boxer and a babysitter.

MARIANNE grabbed the wrap and sat back down on her low stool to examine the ankle hanging over the bench. "I'm going with a tendon strain, not a sprain. Give it two days of rest—"

The Marine, Bailey, coughed out what sounded like, "Bullshit." She ignored that.

"—or, barring that, do your best to stay off it whenever you're not in practice. Elevate, ice and heat, ibuprofen and no jumping or running outside of practice."

"But Coach Cartwright just gave me a list of conditioning to do outside of practice," he said quickly, leaning forward to hover over her while she wrapped the ankle.

Her hands didn't pause in their work. Over, under, around. Check for circulation. It was soothing work, something she enjoyed and had no problems with. Wrapping ankles wasn't beneath her, like some trainers complained it was. "You'll just have to find other ways to condition yourself. Like getting extra rest. You know, being properly rested before a practice can almost double your performance."

He looked skeptical.

"No, really." She glanced around, then remembered she wasn't in her regular training room. "I've normally got my pamphlets. There's a great one I did on how many hours of sleep a night each individual needs. It's got some scientific research about—"

"Forget it," he muttered and sat back. The movement was so jarring, the table scooted three inches and she had to roll forward on her stool once more.

"That sounded pretty disrespectful, Marine," came a lazy voice from behind her.

As if he'd been hit by lightning, Bailey sat up straight, nearly kicking Marianne in the nose on reflex. "I apologize, ma'am. I'll do my best. I can grab some of those pamphlets on my way out."

"Cook," she reminded him, for the third time since he'd huffed into her makeshift training room. "Just Cook. And you're fine. Being injured is never fun, but you—"

"I'm not injured, ma—Cook. I'm not injured," he added again to Brad, who'd walked in and hopped up easily on the second table. He let his duffel fall to the floor and lay down, lacing his fingers over his stomach as if he had nothing else to do and all the time in the world to kill.

She knew better. He wanted ice for his knee, and didn't want anyone else to know.

"Whatever you say, Marine." His voice stating he was purely unconcerned, Brad closed his eyes and tuned them out.

Or, if he hadn't tuned them out, then did an impressive job faking it.

She finished the wrap and gave Bailey's calf a light slap. "You're done. See me again before evening practice and we'll check the wrap and go from there. And Bailey," she added when he slid his shoe back on. When he glanced at her, it was panic she saw in his eyes. "Don't hide it. I'll find out eventually if you're hurting, and how bad. But it's only going to get worse if you keep the truth from me."

He nodded, gave her what she assumed he considered a courteous nod and left the room. With a sigh, she began cleaning the remnants of the tape she'd used and wiping down the bench with cleanser.

"What's wrong with him?" Brad asked in a low voice. He didn't move a muscle or open his eyes. If one didn't know better, they might assume he was at full rest. But Marianne knew, better than most, that looks were deceiving. He was fully capable of being on alert in under a second.

"I don't fix and tell. So," she said, changing the subject, "how was practice?"

He grunted, then raised his arms until his hands were cushioning the back of his head. His shirt was drenched in sweat, and it stuck to each plane and dip of his chest and abdomen.

Talk about a work view. God, the man was gorgeous, with his clothes both on *and* off. She'd spent more time than she'd like to admit watching the way his body moved in nothing but shorts while he worked the mat with a sparring partner earlier. When she should have been inventorying rolls of gauze to see how many supplies they'd lost to vandalism, she hadn't been able to stop staring. His back had been a slick, tanned work of art. Knowing the way the muscles moved and stretched under that skin, how hard they'd be to the touch, had almost been as sexy as actually touching him.

"I think that spot's clean."

Brad's dry words snapped her back to reality. She glanced down and realized she'd been wiping the same spot on the empty table for the past . . . oh my God. Three minutes. She'd lost three minutes staring at Brad's stomach. Flushing, she turned and tossed the rag in a bin, putting the spray bottle away and organizing her already well-ordered, meager supplies.

"Did you need ice?"

He chuckled from behind her, as if knowing exactly why she couldn't turn around and look fully at him.

"We have gallon bags for ice right now, since whatever asshole tore apart my training room decided to use a roll of the regular ice bags as saran wrap for light fixtures."

When he made an inarticulate sound, she turned to look at him. He sat up now, legs still extended on the table, watching her.

"Do you know what happened?"

She lifted her hands, then let them drop. "Best the MPs could come up with was kids. Most likely choice is teenagers who live on base and were bored last night. The doorjamb was broken, so that's how the MPs assume they got in. From there, they just created havoc. Nothing of value was stolen; it was just a big-ass mess. Typical teenage rebellion stuff."

Brad's brows drew down, as if not satisfied with the answer. Frankly, neither was she. But what the hell was she supposed to do about it? Run around playing Inspector Gadget? She didn't have time for that junk. Her supervisor had come to survey the damage, promised the janitorial staff would be over quickly—which they had been, and they were currently working to put right the training room—and that the obscenities would be painted over after everyone left so the walls would be dry by morning. Tomorrow, she'd begin the painstaking process of starting fresh in her room and praying that new supplies arrived ASAP.

"Obviously, you've got a lot going on, so I'll grab my ice and go." He eased down—again, not nearly as nimbly as he'd hopped up—and moved with cautious steps to the small ice machine.

She could have done it for him, but it was a test, in her mind. She wanted to see if he'd let his guard down around her, let her know what was bothering him physically.

He clearly wasn't ready to talk yet.

"I've got to make some calls tonight. I've been put in charge of a few Marines." He sounded so disgusted by it, she had to smile. "Something about keeping track of them, or keeping them on task, or something. If they need a babysitter, they shouldn't be here." He let the lid of the ice machine slam down harder than necessary, but she didn't scold him.

Zipping the bag closed, he stared at it. "I'm not here to mother people. I just want to box, and do my best."

"I don't think anyone wants you to be their mother," she said softly. "I think they see a leader in you. Above and beyond the obvious rank situation. You've got something in you that guys look up to."

He raised a brow at that. "What, being old?"

"There is that," she conceded, and grinned when he laughed. "No, there's more. I watch you . . . all of you," she added quickly when he flashed her a grin. "The younger guys watch you. And sometimes, they want to show off for you. When one of them whizzes past, you just keep going at the pace you've set, and it doesn't bother you."

"Oh, it bothers me," he said darkly. Settling down in a chair, he rested the ice bag on top of his knee. She ached to sit in front of him, to use her hands to massage at the different points, to prod and find the problem so she could *fix* it. It was her calling, and it was painful to sit back and not be allowed to do her job.

"Just think about it." She waved at his knee. "Want to talk?"

"About this? No. About other things?" He sucked in a breath, then shook his head. "Not really, but it needs to be done."

Oh, great. Here came the "it's not you, it's me" speech. Honor and duty and whatever. "There's not much to talk about, is there?"

He watched her a moment, shifted the bag a little to the outside of his knee then looked down. "Probably not."

"I should apologize, actually."

He looked like he wanted to argue, but she held up a hand. Manners had him holding back, though he looked like he would rather not. "I do need to apologize and just get this out of the way." With a deep breath, she put on her most remorseful face. "I know it's hard to resist this." She indicated her entire body. "It's rough, being so hot. The number of men I've had to swing at with bats to get them to back up . . ." With a dramatic sigh, she rolled her eyes. "But you know, eventually everyone has to take the hint. You'll just have to do your best not to lust after my luscious curves."

The corner of his mouth kicked up. "It's a tall order."

"Being a Marine? Kid stuff." She *pffted* that. "Keeping your hands off Marianne Cook? Good luck." She laughed when he did. "It's fine, Brad. Seriously."

He looked relieved. And she hoped, with the humor she'd practiced with Kara, the situation wouldn't be awkward for either of them now.

"Which Marines?"

When he blinked, shifted the ice bag to the inside of his knee and shook his head, she knew he hadn't followed.

"The ones you're in charge of. Your babysitting job," she added with a silly face.

He reached into his bag and, from one of the outer pockets, pulled out a folded sheet of paper. She took it and sat in a chair next to him.

"Chalfant is a good guy, and he's one that idolizes you."

"He's known me three days," Brad growled. "He doesn't know me enough to idolize me."

"He senses something in you to aspire to." She let the paper fall to her lap and faced him. "Why is that such a big deal? Why are you fighting being a role model? You lead people all the time when you're at your regular job. So why not here?"

"I'm here to box."

"You're here to be a part of a team."

"Boxing isn't a team sport."

"The Marines are not a solo act."

He narrowed his eyes at that, but said nothing. She considered that a point in her favor.

"These two I don't know very well," she went on, running

her finger over the middle names. And this last one . . ." She started to laugh, then her belly cramped and she doubled over with laughter. He grabbed for the paper, but she rolled her chair out of the way. "No . . . oh," she gasped out. "You're babysitting Tressler. Oh, this is great."

"That little half-wit has nothing but trouble written all over him." Brad lunged to get the paper, but she danced out of the way. The ice bag fell to the floor with a plop as he caged her between a table and the wall of the storage room she'd commandeered for her temporary training room. "List back, please."

She pursed her lips together and held it behind her back. With a shake of her head, she made a "nope" sound.

He snaked one arm around her back and gripped her wrist, but didn't pull her arm out. Instead, he flexed, bringing her body flush against his. Through the thin mesh of his athletic shorts, she could feel his erection growing. Her own nipples tightened in response to being pressed against his wet shirt and hard chest.

Oh, sweet mercy. She was going to do it again. She was actually going to kiss him again; this time in her training room.

There were at least seventeen things wrong with the last part of that statement.

She couldn't remember a single one of them.

His eyes changed; his pupils dilated slightly, darkening them. And he made a sound in his throat she interpreted as frustration and lust, a fifty-fifty combo.

A cough at the door sent them both into panic mode. He stepped back quickly, catching himself on the table when his right leg wobbled. She breathed, then crossed her arms over her chest as if she were cold to cover the fact that her nipples were so hard they hurt.

She saw Gregory Higgs standing at the door, a cocky smile on his face, one shoulder propped against the doorjamb.

Oh my God. How long had he been there?

"You ready to go, roomie?" he asked with a drawl she hadn't heard before. When Brad flipped him off, his smile only grew. "Sorry, didn't mean to interrupt a training session. I can come back if you've—"

"Bite me," Brad muttered, then picked up his bag and hefted it over his shoulder before pushing past Higgs on his way out the door. No good-bye, no "Sorry about that" or "See ya later, Marianne" or "Sorry we got interrupted, I'll come back and finish this later."

Bad Marianne.

With her face feeling like it was on fire, she surveyed Higgs. "Did you need something, Marine?"

He watched her for a moment, then shook his head slowly. "Nah. It's cool." He waited until she was looking straight at him before he said again, "It's cool."

Hoping that was his way of saying he would mind his own business, she nodded in gratitude. "Thank you."

With a wave, he pushed off and disappeared.

Marianne sank onto a chair and fanned at her face, then picked up the discarded ice bag Brad had dropped and rested it against her throat for a moment.

That had resolved exactly nothing.

But it had been a whole lot of fun.

Bad Marianne.

CHAPTER

8

B rad pulled the door shut on Higgs' car and waited for the blow.

But his roommate put the car in drive and pulled out of the parking lot without a word.

After two minutes of silence, they pulled up to a red light. Lunch traffic around Mainside was always ugly, and he knew they'd wait through at least two red lights before they were moving again.

Higgs seemed content to fiddle with the radio.

Brad cracked first. "Nothing was going on."

Higgs looked at him, then back at the light. "Okay." He inched forward as the light turned green and cars attempted to move. They made it halfway to the intersection before it went red again.

"I mean it. Nothing happened."

"Okay."

"Damn it," he said with a groan. His head hit the back

of the seat and he fisted his hands. "This, on top of all the other shit we have going on."

"*This* what? Nothing happened," Higgs said easily, then chuckled when Brad shot him an evil glare. "Come on, man. So you've got a boner for the cute trainer. She seems okay. If nothing actually happened, then just stop going in there when she's alone and you'll be fine. She's usually got those two college kids around anyway. And if you hadn't noticed, people are starting to break down and go in there to get taped up. She's not going to have a lot of downtime to play sexy games like Chase Around the Table with you, anyway."

Brad groaned again and wiped a hand down his face.

"Besides, you've got someone else, so stick with her." When he glanced at Brad, he raised a brow. "The other one, the woman you went on a date with. Take her out again. Get your mind off Cook." Brad made a strangled sound and Higgs snorted. "What, did the other chick dump you already?"

"No," he said, trying hard not to clench his jaw.

"So then . . . oh." Higgs whistled through his teeth. "Oooooh."

No, the man wasn't slow.

"Just shut up about it. Nothing happened." *Nothing much.* "I don't want her to get fired for some bullshit excuse."

"Nobody's getting fired. Unwad the boxer briefs, Costa." Taking a turn easily, Higgs sighed. "I'm not saying anything, except to be careful. You're a big boy, and I'm your roommate, not your mommy."

"Damn right."

"But she's nice. Don't be a dick about it."

Famous last words, Brad thought as they rolled into the BOQ parking lot. He'd already invited her out to dinner once under false pretenses. She thought he'd asked to be a decent person and make nice. He'd asked to keep her from bugging him about his knee.

He still worried she might say something, might insist on checking him out and then might insist on telling the coach. He couldn't let that happen.

But what the hell did he do with Marianne Cook?

"GO back to the part where he pushed you against the wall and ravished you in a storage locker." Kara Smith waved the hand not holding her wineglass in circles. "And then rewind and tell me again. Rewind and tell me again. Rewind and—"

"I get the point, but there's nothing to rewind." Laughing, Marianne topped off her own glass and eased back into the comfortable sofa. Unlike her own sparsely furnished apartment, Kara's modest three-bedroom house was homey and comfortable. It felt lived in, without the stuffy feeling some places got when they'd been overdecorated with a bunch of impersonal stuff the owner bought because it looked good. Kara only brought things into her home if they meant something to her or were functional. The furniture was easy to sit on and the tables were full of knickknacks and clutter, as well as adorable finds from local stores.

The house was much like the woman herself. Kara was beautiful, but comfortable with it. Her auburn hair, which Marianne happened to know could fall in rich waves nearly down to her butt, was pulled up in a messy bun. She usually wore her clothes with meticulous attention to detail, but was now wearing sweats with dried paint on the cuffs. And her face was free of makeup.

"Something happened," Kara argued, then picked up a cookie. "These are sinful, by the way. Only let me have three. Three and a half. Which, rounded up, is four."

"You can have as many as you want. And no, nothing happened. We were interrupted before . . ." She sighed when Kara shot her a knowing look. "Okay, yes, we were interrupted before something actually could have happened. Probably *would* have," she conceded, to her friend's smug delight. "Oh my God." Sinking farther into the cushions, she covered her eyes with the non–wineglass holding hand. "What the hell is wrong with me? I was going to make out with someone in my de facto training room. I'm a sadist. I'm a sex fiend. I'm—"

"A healthy red-blooded woman who shouldn't ignore her own body's cravings. You know our cravings tell a story."

Sensing a lecture about her chakras or her chi or something, Marianne steered the conversation another way. "You still doing yoga privates outside studio time?"

"When I can get them." For the first time that night, the strain of what Marianne knew was a heavy financial burden etched lines into her friend's brow. "I'm lucky the studio owner doesn't mind me giving privates on the side. I guess he could technically call it competing business, but he's good about it. Knows I need the money." Brightening a little, she sat up straighter and set her wineglass aside. "Why, are you interested in some privates? You don't have to pay me, you know. We can work it into our hangout times."

"Uh, no. Not for me." She sighed, knowing she really should be better about her own stretching regimen. "Actually, the head coach—remember me telling you about him?"

"Big man, deep voice, good coach, nice guy?" Kara nodded.

"That's the one. Coach Ace asked if I could bring some yoga into the team's routine. He's really committed to keeping them healthy, and he thinks doing some team yoga would be a good way to do that."

Her friend beamed. "What a fabulous idea! I'd love to come in and do a workshop. I'll email you my studio schedule and you just tell me what time's best for the team.

If I'm not in the studio, then I'm available to teach a private."

"When do you work on the blog?"

She waved that off and took another cookie—number five, by Marianne's calculation, so she hid a grin. "Late at night, early in the morning, between classes at the studio in the office. It's one of those added bonus things. I don't schedule specific time for it. It gets done during all those pesky moments of downtime."

Pesky little moments most people looked forward to. Kara, on the other hand, seemed to find them the bane of her existence. If she wasn't doing nine things at once, she considered herself bored.

"You might have to start scheduling in time soon," Marianne pointed out. Kara's blog chronicling her struggles with her son's allergies and providing resources and information for those who were battling similar issues had been picking up steam recently, with a few articles featured on major websites. "And it's great passive income."

"Nothing passive about it. It's work." Kara smiled softly. "But it's nice work. I like it."

Just then, a blur ran through the room and landed on the couch. Marianne managed—barely—to catch her wineglass before she bobbled it.

"Hey, Mom. I'm starving."

"Starving, huh?" Kara stroked one hand over her ten-year-old son's hair. "But I just fed you last week."

"I've got a hollow leg," he said with a grin that told Marianne this was an old routine for them. "Can I grab a snack?"

"Take some cookies," Marianne offered. When Kara looked up, she grimaced. "Sorry, was I supposed to ask you first if it was okay? They don't have peanuts or peanut butter." She fumbled for her phone in her purse at her feet. "I can bring up the recipe so you can see the ingredients if you want. I got it from Pinterest."

Kara looked hesitant, but Zach shook his head, answering first. "Thanks, but I can't. I've got snacks in the kitchen. Can I have one, Mom?" he asked again.

Eyes blinking rapidly, Kara nodded and shooed him out of the living room. "He's always better at it than I am." Her voice was soft as she watched her son disappear into the kitchen. "I always hesitate, just a blink, before I say yes or no to something. I keep asking myself, *Should I take the risk this time? Will he resent me for saying no again?* But he never does. He's just so . . . easy." She said the last with a sort of humble bafflement.

"Probably because his mom's a kick-ass mother."

At that, her friend gave a watery laugh. "I've missed you." She let her head drop to Marianne's shoulder for just a moment. "I know you're not here forever, but I'm so glad you're back."

"Me, too." She picked up the plate. "Eat another cookie."

BRAD jabbed, jabbed again, threw a left hook that took his opponent by surprise and watched as Armstrong went to his knees on the mat. Even with the protection of the headgear, Brad knew the hit was a hard one.

"You dropped your damn guard again, Armstrong." He pulled his gloves off and tossed them to the side, then spit his mouth guard out in disgust. Squatting, he waited until Armstrong's head raised. Pupils were responsive, not fixed or dilated. "You're fine. On your feet, Marine."

Coach Willis wandered over and leaned over the single rope used to outline the practice ring. "Trouble?"

"There won't be," Brad assured him as Armstrong shuffled to his feet. "We've got it covered."

The short coach nodded, but instead of walking off, planted himself in one of the metal folding chairs nearby and crossed his ankles. He was settling in to watch, clearly.

With a sigh, Brad made sure Armstrong was steady before showing him exactly when he'd dropped his right arm enough to give Brad the opening. Armstrong nodded in agreement, then asked to go again.

Brad threw the same combination, but hooked with the right this time to catch him off guard. But he blocked as he should and kicked out a punch of his own while Brad's balance was still moving forward, catching him in the shoulder. Brad rubbed at the area and grinned when Armstrong hooted in triumph.

"All right, shithead, you tagged me. Tressler, get in here."

With a puff of breath and a smirk, Tressler slid his mouth guard in. "I'll go easy on you, Armstrong."

Brad rolled his eyes and hopped over the rope to watch. Willis rolled to his feet and stood beside him. After a moment, he grunted.

"You gonna correct that form?"

Brad looked down at him. "You're here. Are you going to correct that form?"

"They're yours."

Brad didn't quite understand how the whole mini-platoon thing was supposed to work. Was this a test of some kind? To see if he was willing to go the extra mile for the team? Or to see if he would put his own training first and foremost, making himself the best boxer he could be?

Who the hell knew anymore?

Biting back a groan, he called a time and walked back into the ring to correct Armstrong's form.

Again.

This was the practice that wouldn't end. Already they'd worked well into what would usually be their lunch break. There wasn't a Marine left who wasn't wilting like day-old spinach. Normally Brad thrived on outlasting everyone else, but even he was feeling the strain on his stamina.

All he wanted was a bag of ice for his knee, a half-decent meal from the salad bar at the commissary and his quiet room. But no. He wasn't getting any of that.

And he definitely wasn't going to have company in his room, either. With a glance back at the training room, where he knew Marianne was restocking shelves with new supplies, he battled back the urge to ask her over for a one-on-one consultation.

Terrible idea.

He was just full of them.

MARIANNE finished stacking the last box of cooling pads on the metal shelf and nudged it into place with her knee. Man, it was boiling balls hot. They'd had to turn the AC in her room off to stop the spread of the scent of alcohol. But now that the smell had dissipated a little, the AC was working overtime to catch up. It hadn't quite gotten there yet.

"That should be good. I can handle the rest from here. Take your break."

Nikki looked more than ready to haul ass out of the hot room. Marianne had an idea she'd be heading to the main gym where the Marines who lived and worked on base typically worked out. She said the scenery was "inspiring" for her job. Marianne snorted delicately at that.

Levi hesitated, even when the object of his youthful desires had bolted for the door. "Are you sure? There's more to do."

"Yeah, but we don't all have to be here. One of us does, while they're working out. But since it looks like they're not stopping anytime soon, no need to punish you guys. Get out, remind yourselves what fresh air smells like."

He smiled a little at that, then reached for his backpack under the desk. "I'm not sure you should be alone, after what happened in here the other day."

It was sweet, his worry over her. She gave him an unconcerned smile. "That was at night, and nothing's happened since. Plus, I've got about twenty-five Marines that are three feet away. I'm pretty sure if anything happened, they'd be in here in two seconds flat to protect the womenfolk . . . which would be me."

At that, he lifted one shoulder. "Okay then." With a hand raised in a wave, he headed out. Likely, she thought, to chase after Nikki and ask her to eat with him.

Young lust. Such a sticky, tricky web it wove.

There were more boxes to unpack, more wraps and tape to settle. Files she needed to properly put back where they belonged. But something made her edge out of her office to watch—what she hoped was—the end of practice. It was already two in the afternoon, and they'd barely stopped for more than a few water breaks. With the rate and intensity the guys were practicing at, their bodies were burning fuel at an alarming rate. Blood sugar was going to become an issue very quickly if Coach Ace wasn't careful.

She'd talk with him afterward about it.

The gym had been divided into multiple crude minirings. Rope looped over tall traffic cones outlined the different areas where boxers were sparring. If she had to guess, she'd say they were going at fifty percent power. Enough to work on deflection, evasion and some tactical maneuvers, but not enough to knock one another unconscious.

Save that for the Air Force, boys.

She watched as Brad walked into his ring to grip the upper arms of one boxer. He maneuvered him around, all but throwing him like a rag doll. Bending, sliding, swooping him around as if in some bizarre dance move. She knew he was demonstrating the different angles to use when blocking, but it looked hilarious from where she was standing. He was hands-on with the younger guys. More hands-on than he probably wanted to be, or would admit to. But she saw it in the way the younger guys treated him, watched him, spoke to him.

They had mentally placed him at the top of the pile, as someone to aim for. Not based on his skill or speed, but based on his endurance, his knowledge and his work ethic.

He wouldn't see it like that, though. He'd see it as them just watching the competition for weaknesses. So analytical, so pessimistic.

She grinned. He was so damn hot.

Even Tressler, cocky little shit that he was, quietly emulated Brad. As Brad showed Chalfant a combination, Tressler stood behind, mimicking the moves without being obvious. Committing the combination to muscle memory.

Coach Ace walked to the middle of the floor and cupped his hands. "Marines! Assemble!"

There was an initial scramble to head to the center mat. She saw Brad hop the rope, then immediately hitch a step in reaction.

He needed to be checked out. It could be something so minor it would need nothing but some stretching and extra heat and ice. Or it could be much worse. He could be putting his career as a Marine on the line, and for what? The chance to fight in a ring?

Pro athletes were being paid for their performances. In a way, though she disagreed with it, she understood the desire to push through the pain. But to risk his career—his real career—for the happiness of being on the boxing team? It didn't compute.

Soon enough, she would have to make him trust her and fess up.

COACH Ace waited until they were quietly lined up in formation before he began. "I know I pushed you well through lunch. Nobody complained, nobody fought back and nobody asked for a break. Thank you for pushing through."

Brad mentally breathed a sigh of relief.

"The reason I asked you to push through is because there is no practice tonight."

That brought out a murmur among the guys. *Probably already making plans to hit up a bar or find a willing woman,* Brad thought with an inner eye roll.

His eye caught on Marianne standing just outside her door, wearing her polo shirt and capri-length khakis, with her arms crossed over her breasts.

Suddenly, the idea of a willing woman wasn't far from his own mind.

"Instead of meeting at the gym, I want you to spend some time with your assigned platoons. Leaders, you're in charge of making that happen. Your choice how, your choice where." At the surprised silence, the coach's dark face creased into a smile. "Gentlemen, boxing is a sport of one against one inside the ropes. But never let yourself forget that this is a team. First, foremost, always."

Brad heard Higgs mutter a low "Oo-rah" from behind.

The second they were dismissed, Chalfant raced over to him.

Jesus H.

"What are we going to do tonight?" The younger man caught up with Brad as he turned to grab his bag. "We could see a movie. Or maybe watch one at the apartment. Oh! Dinner." His eyes grew wide with anticipation. "We could go to this place my roommate told me about. It's in Wilmington, but we've got the time, so—"

Brad tossed his cell phone at him to make him stop talking. "Put your number in there, then give it to the others. I'll let you know when I figure shit out."

"Oh." Looking a little like a kicked puppy, Chalfant

looked down at the phone in his hand. "So . . . okay. I'll just . . ." He rotated the phone a bit, then wandered off, thumbs moving over the screen to put his number in.

"That went well."

Brad turned to see another Marine standing there. Sweeney, he remembered. The one who owned a house out the back gate.

"What went well?" He leaned against the pushed-in bleachers, waiting for Sweeney to continue.

"I do believe that's the kid's hopes and dreams you're crushing under the heel of your shoe." With a small shake of his head, the other man leaned companionably next to him. "They're babies."

"They're not even ten years younger than us."

"In some ways. Half these guys haven't even seen a deployment yet. You know how that shit ages you." He let his head fall back against the hard plastic. "Grandpa."

"If I'm the Grandpa of this outfit, you must be my two-minutes-younger twin brother. Plus," he added darkly, "you outrank me. So we should probably be calling you Great-Grandpa."

At that, Sweeney chuckled. "Not too far off, probably. But like the coach said, we leave our rank at the door. Take care of your mini-platoon, Costa. You've got some good ones." He left, making Brad wonder what the hell that had been all about.

He waited for another few moments at the bleachers, eyes closed, ready to fall asleep on his feet like an elephant. Something freezing cold pressed against his belly, and his eyes widened. "Jesus H.!"

Marianne stood beside him, blinking innocently. "Oh, sorry, should have warned you." She pulled the bag off his stomach and murmured, "Cold ice, coming in."

The innocent mischief that sparkled in her eyes made him want to throw her over his shoulder, drag her back to the training room and spank her—then give the tables a good spin with a workout they were most certainly *not* designed for. "Yeah. Thanks for the warning."

She tilted her head over to where Chalfant was getting Armstrong's number in his phone. "Looks like you'll be spending some quality bonding time with the boys, huh?"

"Like a father on his visitation weekend," he muttered, making her laugh. "I like quiet. I like solitude. Is that so wrong?"

"No, but you're also not an island. You *joined* the Marines. They were here long before you, and they'll be here long after you. And you want to be a part of this team. So spend some time making a difference in something you volunteered for, huh?" She patted his chest. "It won't kill you."

He gripped her wrist for a split second, halting her retreat. But she gave an infinitesimal shake of her head, and he let her go.

CHAPTER

9

Brad let Tressler scoot into the booth before he slid in himself. The younger Marine scowled, but pushed to the end of the bench. The other three Marines slid in across from them, nice and cozy. It was like a group date from hell.

Their server handed out menus, took their drink orders—waters all around—and went off to give them time with the menus.

Chalfant spent approximately seven seconds reading his before he let it fall to the table. "Can you show me how you worked that second combo you used with Armstrong today? The one where you . . ." He threw out his arms and nailed Tibbs in the side of the head.

"Damn, man." Tibbs, a guy who gave Coach Ace a run for his money on size, gave Chalfant a death stare. "Check yourself."

Chalfant blushed, fire flaming under his freckles.

"Sorry," he mumbled. His head drooped and he stared at the napkin roll in front of him.

Brad sighed inwardly. "I'll show you tomorrow. It's not hard, you just have to use it sparingly or else it becomes expected."

He glanced up, and Brad could swear he saw the terrifying hints of hero worship in the young man's eyes.

Their server showed back up with a tray full of waters, then took their orders. She spent more time than necessary coaching Tressler through the finer points of which cut of steak he should get, but seemed amused at his attentions, not offended. Brad didn't bother to stop him from making an idiot out of himself.

When Brad ordered last, and realized he was the only one to order anything remotely healthy, he glared at each of them. "Are you kidding me? Steak? A freaking cheeseburger, Tibbs? And you," he added with disgust to Tressler. "You loaded your freaking french fries."

"They're better that way. Everyone loves bacon and cheese." He shrugged. "I dip 'em in ranch and—"

"Nope. No, stop there." Brad covered his ears with his hands. "I can't listen to the mess you're making of your arteries."

Tressler just smiled dreamily, like he already had a stomach full of fatty goodness.

"So, Coach—"

"Whoa." Brad was nipping that shit in the bud right now. "Armstrong, I'm not your coach. I'm not anyone's coach. I'm a teammate."

"Maybe," Tressler added, and Tibbs made the *dun dun dun* sound of doom. The table cracked up . . . except for Brad.

"I'm just babysitting you until Coach Ace has everyone whittled down to a smaller number. I'm not *coaching* anyone."

Armstrong hesitated only a second, then asked, "But you'll still help me with my block tomorrow, right?"

Tibbs leaned forward, which pushed the table into Brad's chest. "I need some speed, man. Help me out."

Chalfant just watched him expectantly, like he wanted reaffirmation Brad would be working with him as he'd already promised.

Brad's brows lowered, and he looked to his left at Tressler. "Well? What do you want?"

Tressler pretended to consider that for a moment, then pointed. "That. I want that. Can you make it happen?"

Brad turned to see their server bending over another table, bussing glasses. Her ass, covered in tight black pants, was on display for anyone lewd enough to watch.

"No." Absolutely not. He could tolerate being mistaken for a coach, though he didn't like it. But he drew the line at playing pimp. "Get your own ass on your own time. Since you *act* like an ass most of the time, it shouldn't be too hard. Like attracts like, right?"

At that, all four men burst into loud hoots and laughs, Tressler included.

Brad cracked a smile, but held back from a full-blown grin. He didn't want to encourage this bonding any more than necessary.

You want to be a part of this team. So spend some time making a difference in something you volunteered for, huh?

He didn't have to paint their toenails or tuck them into bed with a story and a cup of juice. But it wouldn't be that hard to keep an eye on them and make sure they didn't walk straight into any problems. Or get cut based solely on stupidity.

That was enough. For now.

MARIANNE crossed the final items off her list, satisfied to see she'd managed to work through the entire thing before bed. That only happened once in a blue moon. She was notorious for taking on way more than she could handle in any given day.

Feet propped up on the coffee table, she took a sip of the tea Kara had sworn by for nighttime relaxation and grimaced. It tasted like crushed up dandelions and cinnamon mixed together in tepid milk.

Or, at least, what she assumed those things together would taste like.

So, this tea was not her thing. No big deal. She put the mug aside and closed her eyes. She'd just meditate—aka "daydream"—for a few minutes, then head to bed for a good night's sleep.

The knock on the door jarred her from her meditation two minutes in. Grumbling, she stood and headed to the door. It had to be a mistake. Her mom would have texted before coming over, Kara would never have left Zach so late at night, and nobody else she knew socially lived in the area anymore.

When she saw Brad through the peephole, she sucked in a breath. What the . . .

She started to undo the chain, then remembered she was in her pajamas. She looked down and took in the simple green shirt and *Family Guy* flannel pants. Uh . . . embarrassing.

Undoing the chain and the dead bolt, she cracked the door open enough to stick her head out. "Hi."

Hands stuffed in his pockets, he turned to face her. He wore a light blue, striped button-down shirt, jeans, running shoes and a scowl.

"You owe me." He walked toward the door and she opened it reflexively, though she hadn't intended to let him in to begin with. Mostly because, well, *Family Guy* pants.

"I owe you?" She closed the door behind him and found him prowling her living room. Yes, prowling. It was the only word to describe what he was doing. He reminded her of the caged panthers at the zoo. Restless, confined, agitated by the boundaries their life had been reduced to, they paced from one end of the cage to the other in a fruitless effort to work off some frustration. Brad was doing the exact same thing now, only he was wearing a hole around her coffee table instead of a mock-jungle environment.

"You owe me," he repeated, then stopped dead in his tracks to shoot an accusatory glare at her. "You told me I needed to get to know them. I needed to be a good leader. They look up to me. I should be a part of what I want to join."

She crossed her arms over her chest. "I did say those things, yes."

"You called me a hermit."

"I didn't use the word 'hermit,'" she argued.

"You implied it."

"Maybe."

"I just had the longest dinner of my life. I sat there with a bunch of nineteen- and twenty-year-olds and listened to them talk about scoring ass and getting drunk—not that any of them are legally able to—and the joys of being a general badass." He sat on her couch so hard the frame squeaked. Rubbing his hands over his head, he sighed. "Longest meal ever."

He was weary, and she felt bad about that. But the entire thing amused her. Tickled her, if she were being honest. "You took them out to dinner."

He nodded without looking up.

Gathering herself together, she sat gently beside him on the couch. "You took your group of guys to dinner, and let them ramble on about women and drinking, because they wanted to impress you."

He didn't move, just sighed.

Rubbing his back lightly, she chuckled. "That was nice."

"You owe me," he said, his voice muffled.

"What do I owe you?"

"Decent company. I need a palate cleanser after that. Conversation with an adult who won't talk about a stripper they know in Yuma—though her existence is sketchy, at best, if you ask me—or the last time you puked your guts out from a keg of Bud."

"It was last Tuesday. And the stripper wasn't from Yuma, but Houston." She sighed and leaned her head against his shoulder. "Veronica. God, I miss her. She had this tattoo of a snake on her stomach, and when she did this one move . . ."

He laughed. Laughed, then choked while trying to hold it back and kept on laughing. Leaning back into her sofa, he draped an arm over her shoulder and let the chuckles die down. "I think your debt is already paid, just with that."

"Good." Because it felt so good to snuggle against him, she forced herself to stand up. "Want something to drink?"

"Water, thanks." He propped a foot on her coffee table and picked up her notepad. Since there was nothing of interest on it, she didn't care. Picking up the mug of cooled tea, she went to the sink to dump the failed experiment out. She came back and handed him a bottle of water. He raised a brow at her own drink of choice.

"Beer?"

"Yeah, well, tea wasn't working for me." She took a sip from the bottle and made a refreshed sound. "Screw tea."

He nearly choked on his water in surprise. "Aren't you trainers all supposed to be health nuts with a penchant for making athletes feel guilty about every little thing?"

"Why bother? You'll feel guilty anyway." She took another sip and settled the cold bottle on her stomach. To get her bare feet equal to his on her coffee table, she slumped way down on the cushions so it was mostly the top of her shoulders and her neck resting against the back. Uncomfortable, but a nice place to rest her drink. She tapped one of his running shoes with her bare toes. "I'm not someone who is into the organics, crunchy movement. I respect people's choices. I'm more of the everything-in-moderation crowd. A beer's fine, as long as you're not pounding back a six-pack a night, or driving home."

He glanced at his water, then saluted her with it and took a sip. She did the same with her own brew. "Ah. So good."

"Show-off."

She grinned at his disgruntlement. "Sorry. If you lived in this complex, you could have one and then walk home. Alas, you do not."

"Alas," he muttered, staring at her beer like it was a rabbit and he wanted to reach out and snare it with his bare hands. "I just watched four men devour cheeseburgers, steaks and fries dripping with cheese and ranch sauce. I'm not in the mood to be tempted right now."

"Oh, that's too bad." She took the tiniest of sips. "Tempting is way more fun."

He set the water bottle down on the table in front of them, then reached over for the beer. Since it was half gone, she figured he could have the last of it and still be okay to drive home within the hour. Safe bet. She let him take it from her, but he surprised her by placing it next to his water. "I'd rather just have a taste."

She waved a hand. "Feel free to kill that one."

"Nope, not what I want."

She could get him a fresh beer, but then he'd have to wait at least an hour before going home. It was already . . . She glanced up for the clock, but found him watching her instead. And suddenly, she realized when he said *taste*, he didn't actually mean the beer.

And she was totally okay with that.

BRAD waited for the signal to stop, slow down, back up.

It never came.

So he lowered his body over hers on the couch and kissed her. The taste of the beer on her tongue was nothing compared to the sweet pressure of her lips against his. Her arms looped over his neck and pulled him down over her. He let his tongue dip in farther to explore, and she met him with every stroke. As he turned to fit his mouth better over hers, her hands started unbuttoning his shirt. He had a white undershirt beneath it, but even just the feel of her hands bumping against his chest, knowing what they were doing, kicked his erection from "starting up" to "ready to go" in a second flat. His own hands cupped her head and massaged through her short, blonde hair. She moaned as he did, and he knew without being told she loved it.

Her fingers finished with the buttons and pushed until he slipped the shirt off. But he never broke contact with her mouth. He felt like he would rather give up a limb than stop kissing her. As her hot little hands streaked under his white T-shirt to play over his back, his shoulder blades tightened and danced with anticipation.

Her husky chuckle into his mouth echoed between them. "Like that, huh?"

"About as much as you like this," he responded, scratching lightly through her hair. He pulled back enough to watch her eyes drift closed and her lips purse together with a hum of pure bliss.

"We're a pair. Both of us getting off on scratches."

She cracked one eye. "I like to think it means we're both extraordinarily sensual people who take pleasure in the simple things. It's not a negative."

"Whatever you just said, I like it." He kissed the tip of her nose.

With one knee on the couch and the other foot totally extended to the floor, his balance was precarious at best. And now that his mind wasn't focused on kissing, he realized his knee was screaming. "Not that I don't enjoy a trip back in time to neck on the couch, but can we take this to your bed instead?"

She blinked, and he swore for a second that his balls cried out in frustration. *Please don't let that have ruined everything.*

But she smiled slowly, like a cat who had found where her owner hid the cream, and nodded. "Follow me."

He stood back, fighting the wince as his knee protested, and helped her up. She glanced down at her pajamas and blushed a little.

"Guess I forgot to wear my lingerie." She made a face. "Would you believe it was laundry day, and my usual sleep-wear is in the rinse cycle?"

"If you tell me you have these pants because you watch *Family Guy*, then I'm going to say that's sexier than a nightie."

"Religiously," she affirmed.

"That does it. Woman, I've got to have my way with you." He charged at her and she shrieked and ran down the hall until she hit her bedroom, then flung herself on the bed.

He kicked off his shoes and socks at the door to the bedroom, then pulled his undershirt over his head. When she made a sound, he glanced at the bed before dropping it by his shoes. "What?"

She rolled to her stomach, her head pillowed on her arms. "The way guys do that is just sort of the best."

He looked over his shoulder, then down at his hands. "Do what?"

"Take their shirts off like that. Just gripping it from behind and ripping it over their heads like that. It's so aggressive. Like, *Who cares about being calm and orderly? I've gotta get naked this second.*" She grinned when he laughed at her imitation of a deep voice. "It's just a girl thing we happen to like about guys."

Not one to argue when the odds were in his favor, he shrugged and moved toward her. "I'd do it again, but I'm out of shirts."

"You can borrow one of mine and try."

He looked at her narrow torso in disbelief. "Let's save it for next time."

Eyes gleaming, she reached for him. He prayed his knee would respond better on a well-cushioned mattress and crawled to her. But she flipped the tables on him and pushed him until he was flat on his back. Then she did the sexiest thing he'd ever seen and straddled him, so her ass cradled his erection. Watching his eyes, she crossed her arms and reached to the bottom hem of her shirt. In one swoop of motion, she pulled it up and over her head, flinging it to a corner of the room.

Her breasts bounced free. She hadn't been wearing a bra this entire time. How had he missed that? Thank Jesus he *had* missed that, or he would have been on her from the moment he walked through her door.

"Okay," he said hoarsely. "Yeah, that's sexy. I see the appeal."

"It's all about the rip." She ran her hands down his chest, thumbs dipping into his navel for a moment. "And you've got to be careful. If you get caught up on a boob or an earring, it's game over and you spend the next ten minutes trying to get unstuck or cutting your shirt off."

"You know this from experience?"

"Girls talk." She pressed a finger to his lips when he would have made a joke. "No more talking for you, though." Her hands ran down his chest, nails scratching lightly. "I'm about to tell you something, and I hope you'll understand what it means when I do."

He hissed in a breath when she skirted around, but didn't pull down, the waistband of his pants. "I'm a smart guy . . . most of the time."

"Hmm."

He wasn't sure if that was an agreement or disagreement, but when the button to his jeans popped open, Brad wisely chose to give exactly zero fucks about which.

"You're my first."

At that, his eyes flew open. "Beg pardon?"

"My first athlete," she corrected, smiling a little. Then she bent and pressed a kiss to his sternum. "I've never gotten involved with someone I was working with before."

When she looked up, the teasing light was gone, replaced with a more sincere hope. And he was pretty sure he followed along.

"I get it. This isn't a habit."

She nodded.

Threading his hands through her hair, he pulled her close for a kiss. Of course it wasn't. Nothing about them, about their spark, was normal for him, either. He'd never felt this pull before with a woman. Never realized that there would be a single person on the planet that would call to him without saying a word.

Love? No. There was no love at first sight. He would never buy it. But recognition? In spades. He recognized her, and she did him. They met each other on a level above normal interaction.

Unwilling to follow that rabbit hole any farther while the object of his thoughts was currently topless and straddling him, he pulled back and waved down his torso. "You can continue."

She sent him a saucy grin. "Oh, can I? Maybe I should just get up and get dressed instead."

When she started to throw one leg over him to leave the bed, he grabbed her waist with both hands and held her firmly down. "No way. You've got the anatomy training. Tell me what happens to a man with blue balls?"

"If he's wise, he suffers in silence," she said dryly, but

finished unzipping his jeans and pulling them down. There was little art or grace to the movement, and he muffled a laugh when she nearly stumbled out of bed tugging the jeans over his knees. But he let her do it her way. The look of satisfaction that gleamed in her eyes when she dropped his pants on the floor was more than enough reward.

CHAPTER

10

Without Brad even prompting, Marianne pushed down her pants, revealing she was pantyless beneath. When he raised a brow, she shrugged. "I was going to bed, remember? You're the one who showed up uninvited."

"I did. And you're welcome."

She slapped his thigh as she crawled back up. She tried crawling on her hands and knees like a cat, but the sexy effect was ruined when she let out a horrific snarl and bit at his ribs. He yelped and rolled, which hurt his knee, and he groaned.

"Okay, okay, sorry. Bad joke." Missing that the groan was from pain and not from the bad imitation of a panther on the prowl, she massaged the tops of his thighs for a minute. That seemed to soothe the dull pain a little, though not enough. If she asked to switch positions, he was a seriously dead man.

Toying with the band of his boxers, she let one finger trail down to the fly opening and graze his cock. His entire pelvis twitched with need. She smiled from her perch above him. "You're really at my mercy here, aren't you?"

"Turnabout's fair play," he growled, but let her have her fun. It was more amusing than he would have considered, being in bed with a woman who considered fun to be a part of the pleasure. He couldn't remember the last time he'd been with someone who'd done more than lie back expectantly. "But just so you know, if you've got some condoms in that dresser, you should probably have them ready to roll."

She glanced at the nightstand and nodded absently, pulling his boxers down over his cock at the same time. "Sure thing. They're right . . ." She stroked her fist over him from root to tip once, then froze.

If he hadn't been clenching his teeth against the sensation of her soft hand around his shaft, he might have laughed at the stricken face she made. "What? Jesus H., what?"

"Condoms," she whispered, then her eyes darted around the room. "Where the hell are the condoms?"

"You said they were . . ." He slapped a hand over the top of the nightstand, making the alarm clock rattle. But she was already gone, jackrabbiting off the bed and into the attached bathroom so fast he knew she didn't hear him finish, ". . . right here."

"I'm still not fully unpacked," she said, voice muffled. If he had to guess, he'd say she had her head stuck in a cabinet. "I put most of the stuff away, but the nightstand stuff was in a box by itself, and my mom was over here hovering while I unpacked and I wasn't about to open that up while she was around and . . . *ah!*" Emerging, still naked, she grinned foolishly and held up a strip of condoms. "We are cleared for takeoff."

Jesus H. If the mention of her mother hadn't softened

his hard-on, nothing would. "Get back here and let's put those suckers to good use, then."

She pranced, just a little, but danced out of reach when he tried to grab a leg to pull her back in. "I dunno, you look pretty good there. Maybe we should do some stretches first." Her eyes widened with anticipation. "Oh, some downward dog would be nice. For you, of course." Her face turned serious and she held the hand gripping the condoms over her heart. "I'm just thinking of your own strength and flexibility. Wouldn't want you to pull a hammie while we're doing the mattress limbo."

"I'll risk it." He took one more wild grab for her, managed to connect with her forearm and pulled until she tumbled over the top of him. Her warm, soft skin moved over his so sensually he was ready to burst into flames. "Normally, I'm a lot smoother, but right now I've got to get inside you."

"So much for foreplay," she complained, but she winked to show she was joking.

"Sweetheart, it seems like anytime I'm alone with you, it's foreplay."

Her eyes softened at that. "I think that was really sweet. In a sexual sort of way." She tore one packet off the line, dropped the rest on the nightstand, and handed it over. "I suck at this."

In five seconds flat, he was ready to go. He gripped the tops of her thighs as she maneuvered over him. But when he would have positioned his cock, she shook her head. "Let me. I want to do it all."

Far be it from him to deny her. He raised his arms away, hands laced behind his head, and watched while she rubbed the head of his erection through her slick center. The friction against his sensitive head was exquisite, a stolen moment of foreplay in an otherwise straight-to-the-good-stuff scene. From the way her eyelids fluttered half-closed, he knew she was doing it intentionally.

Marianne Cook knew what she wanted, and was willing to take it, literally, into her own hands to get it.

There was nothing sexier in the world to him at that moment than Marianne Cook.

He felt her body give way as she sank down onto him, pushing his hands back as he tried to steady her. "I've got this."

Realizing she was serious, and wanted no help, he let his arms fall to his sides and rubbed his thumbs over her knees. That, at least, she didn't see as getting in the way.

Back arched, she rolled and flexed her hips until he was fully inside her. He shivered with the delicious feeling. Then she took it a step further and reached behind her, placed her hands flat on the bed beside his calves, and pulsed.

If his eyes didn't cross from the pleasure, he'd have been shocked. He fought hard to keep his body still while she experimented with the rhythm she wanted, then worked it until they were both panting. Her entire body was out of reach except for where they were joined. He watched her breasts bounce gently with each thrust, and his arms flexed with the frustration of not being able to cup those soft mounds, to run his fingers over the puckered tips, to feel how they changed as her breathing became more labored.

Next time, he swore. Because there would absolutely be a next time.

She arched even more, and he admired the curve of her torso, the tilt of her neck, the muscles of her thighs as she held the impossible position like it was nothing.

He took the chance to touch her when he felt his orgasm creeping up. With his thumbs, he opened her top folds and exposed her clitoris. He touched with just the tip of one finger, and she nearly bolted off him from the contact.

"Oh, God, do that again," she panted, her speed increasing, her insides clenching around his cock. "Do it again."

He was a good Marine. He knew how to follow orders.

He pressed and rubbed against that little bundle of nerves until she whimpered, rotated her hips hard around the base of his cock then arched back up like she was ascending through the ceiling with the most magnificent orgasm he'd ever witnessed.

The visual pleasure of watching her come sent him tumbling over the edge of his own climax unexpectedly. And closing his eyes, he released the tension that had been building inside him for months and let go.

MARIANNE waited until he moved first. Or, he was first if you didn't count her not-so-majestic flop over his sweat-slicked body.

How was it she had never felt more sexy, more sensual, more womanly in her entire life than when Brad had been inside her, and then thirty seconds after they were finished, she flopped over like a breaching humpback whale?

Nothing said, *Yes please, do me again*, like imitating the world's largest mammal post coitus.

"That," he said as he shifted a little, "was pretty much epic."

Her hand ran down his chest in answer.

He picked up her hand and wiped it with the corner of the bed sheet. "Sorry. That probably grossed you out."

"What, the sweat?" She propped herself up on one elbow. "Hardly. Sweat's a daily hazard for me, if you couldn't tell. If I hated sweat, I chose the world's dumbest profession."

His lips twitched at that. "That's probably true. Like a doctor who hates blood."

"Or a lawyer who hates liars."

"A teacher who hates kids."

"A Marine who hates guns."

"Doesn't exist," he said firmly, and she laughed.

"You're a different guy here than in the gym," she said after awhile.

"Jesus H., I hope so," he muttered, and she laughed again. He was always doing that, though she was pretty sure he never intended to be so funny.

"Not that way, because, first of all . . . ew. Do you know what kind of germs are on those mats?"

"Don't tell me," he warned when she opened her mouth. "I'll just let my imagination run wild."

"Just make sure you always shower post workout," she warned. "But I mean your personality with the guys. You're so solitary with the rest of them. I know it's not because you're shy, or have the social skills of a tin can. We've never struggled to talk."

"You're different," he said simply, and she had a feeling he considered that to be the beginning and the end of it.

She wasn't going to push. Pushing would be bad. Pushing had no place in their little haven of wonder.

After another few moments, he sighed. "I have to deal with the condom. Don't move," he said sternly as he got up and walked to the bathroom.

She moved. She couldn't help it, it was just too awkward sitting there, buck-ass naked, waiting for him to come back. She didn't even sleep in the nude when she was alone. So she grabbed her pajama bottoms and slid them on. She was still topless when he walked back in, all shiny and muscly and . . .

Bad Marianne.

He scowled at her bottoms.

"I can't just sit here naked." She spread her arms out over the mattress. "This bed isn't a buffet, and I'm not a bucket of crab legs sitting on ice, waiting for you to come back."

He raised a brow at that, but found his jeans on the floor and pulled them on.

Oh. That wasn't the intended purpose. "I can take them back off," she said quietly.

His lips twitched as he buttoned his fly. "I'd say yes, but then we'd just go at it again."

Well, okay then. She lifted her butt off the mattress to wriggle the pants back down, but he just chuckled and shook his head.

"I've got to get back. I just gave four Marines an earful on eating better and getting more rest. And they were already kicking my ass in the talent department. I probably signed my own death warrant with that one. I've gotta get to bed."

She debated playing vixen and suggesting her bed was ready for action—of the sleeping kind. But she could see in his eyes he was earnest in his quest to get a full night's sleep.

And there was no doubt, if they were together in bed all night, rest would be the last thing on either of their minds.

"Fine, fine." She rolled her eyes and groped the floor for her top. "Geez, you'd think you cared about it or something."

He ran his hands down her bare back as she bent to scoop up the shirt. The calluses and rough tips brought goose bumps to her skin. He wrapped them around her front as she straightened, cupping her breasts. With her back pressed to his front, he cupped the heavy weight in each palm, plucking gently at the nipples with his thumbs and forefingers.

He kissed the skin of her neck, just below her ear. His voice rasped, "While you were up there, arched back over me, and these pretty things were straight in the air, I could barely think of anything else but wanting to get my hands on them."

She pressed his hands harder into her chest. "Anytime."

"That would make for an interesting icing session." With a half laugh, he squeezed them and let them fall gently. After she'd put her shirt on, he turned her and kissed her slowly, as if they were about to start the seduction process all over again.

"That arch," he continued, rubbing one hand over her lower back. "Looked painful. But so fucking sexy."

She'd be calling Kara tomorrow to thank her profusely for her insistence on yoga. "Not painful. You'll be having some yoga lessons soon. Maybe you can do it, too."

"I'd rather just watch you bend and twist." With a friendly pat on her ass, he walked toward her front door. When he opened it, he turned back. "This isn't going to be weird tomorrow, is it?"

"What, like am I going to chase you down on the mat to give you a big kiss in front of your teammates?" When he paled a little, she bit her lip to keep the laugh inside. "I'll restrain myself. It'll be tough . . ."

He slapped her ass in mock punishment, pressed a kiss to her forehead, then closed the door behind him.

She waited a second, palm against the door, listening for his footsteps away. But she heard nothing. The man was a ghost.

"Lock your damn door."

She jumped at the sound, then covered her mouth to stifle the gasp. "Go home."

With a laugh, she clicked the dead bolt over.

With a muttered, "Jesus H.," she heard Brad walk away.

She headed to her pad of paper, tore off the day's completed to-do list and wrote at the top of the next day's list: "Yoga."

BRAD and Higgs walked into the gym the next morning to find Marianne front and center on the main mat with Coach Ace and Coach Cartwright. Coach Willis was absent. A few other guys were stretching and talking, but nothing out of the ordinary.

The pile of mats off to the side was unusual, but he ignored that in favor of watching Marianne.

"So Cook's packing a hot body under those baggy training clothes, huh?" Higgs asked under his breath. "Did you know about those breasts?"

"Fuck off," he answered easily, but he couldn't blame the man for looking. Marianne was a compact, hot number, and today she wasn't hiding it under a loose-fitting polo shirt and shapeless shorts or capris.

Her tank top showed no cleavage, and the straps were wide running over her shoulders. The back, as he saw when she angled to point something out to the coaches, was in a racerback style. But it was as tight as a second skin and stopped about two inches above her pants. Those, too, were tight, molding to her legs and stopping mid-calf. And she was wearing flip-flops instead of her usual white socks and running shoes. Her hair, which she normally wore pulled back into a stubby ponytail, was loose but for an elastic headband thingie that ran around her entire head.

"Interesting outfit for icing injuries and wrapping wrists," Higgs said, tossing his bag over to the side with the growing pile. Brad did the same and they headed over to stretch with the rest of the group. Marianne's eyes caught his, and she smiled a little, but didn't acknowledge his presence otherwise. He followed her lead and gave a brief nod before sitting down to stretch out his hamstrings.

"So where'd you go last night?" Higgs asked, sitting beside Brad and pulling his right arm across his body. "You didn't come home before I hit the rack, unless you were ninja-like about it."

"You know me, always the ninja." He debated a moment, then said, "Went out to eat with my group. What'd you guys do?"

Higgs could tell there was more to the story, but—thank

God—he didn't press. "We went out to a movie, gorged ourselves on popcorn—"

Brad rolled his eyes.

"—and then sat in Johnson's pickup truck bed for an hour in the parking lot, bitching about whatever. Came home around ten, shocked to find my hermit roommate gone."

"I'm not a hermit." Why did everyone think he was a hermit?

"Fooled me," Higgs said easily, then bent to touch his toes.

Sweeney plopped down beside them. "What's up?"

Did he have a sign on his back saying, *"Please come talk to me"*? "Stretching."

After waiting a beat, he looked to Higgs. "Forgot to drink his happy juice this morning?"

"Ignore Costa. He's a regular bowl of sunshine, twenty-four-seven." Higgs grinned. "What'd your group do last night?"

"Cookout at my place. I've got a big grill, which I bought before I realized it was pointless to have when I'm only ever cooking for one. So it was good to have an excuse to blow the dust off and use it. Steaks, burgers, corn, and one of my guys made this gooey chocolate dessert thing that cooked in some foil on the grill. It was amazing." He nodded at them both. "You guys should come over sometime so I have another excuse to use the grill."

"Does *anyone* around here stick to a reasonable diet?" Brad wondered out loud.

"Only you," Higgs answered with a dead-serious look. Both he and Sweeney cracked up laughing, until Sweeney's smile faded slowly.

"Who," he asked, voice low, "the hell is that?"

Brad turned to see a woman walking in, a mat under one arm, a tote bag filled with who knew what slung over her other shoulder. Long auburn hair swished from her high ponytail as she walked. She wore an outfit similar to Marianne's, only her top was shorter and bared much more of her stomach. Though that might have been because she was willow-slender and at least five foot ten.

She bounced the last few steps and straight into Marianne's arms. They did the girl-hug thing and chattered at each other, though Brad couldn't hear what they said. Then he watched as Marianne introduced the newcomer to the coaches.

"Cute," was Higgs' observation.

"I'll have one of those" was Sweeney's eye-glazed announcement.

"You're both idiots" was Brad's contribution.

"Marines, on your feet!" Coach Ace barked. They scrambled up and assumed parade rest right where they were on the large blue wrestling mat. "You're going to do a two-lap warm-up, and then grab one of these . . ." He glanced at the new woman, who muttered something in his ear, and he finished, ". . . mats. Grab one of these rolled up mats and spread out."

When they stared at him, not moving, he clapped his hands together and grinned. "It's yoga time, boys."

CHAPTER

11

Marianne struggled to remember the last time her stomach had hurt so much. Not from eating too much ice cream, or from cramps, but from holding in the laughter too long. Oh, God, they were hilarious, bless their sad, inflexible little souls.

They were all struggling through a downward dog—at least two of the Marine infants had snickered at the name—and now most were moaning at the fact that they couldn't do the poses even halfway. Marianne, who had never been fantastic at yoga and only did the poses for the relaxation benefits, was suddenly feeling a thousand times more flexible by comparison.

"Don't overdo it," Kara warned from her mat in the front. She stood and walked around, repositioning men's hands or nudging their feet apart for a better stance.

A voice called out, "Ma'am, am I doing this right?"

Marianne stood up at that, having recognized the voice.

Tressler, in the back, was chuckling like a clown as Kara walked behind him and asked what felt off.

"My hips, I think." He wiggled his ass in the air, which happened to line up with Kara's stomach. "Is this right?"

Marianne walked over and quietly took Kara's hand, motioning for her to be quiet. Then she waved Coach Ace over. The man was a ghost, moving without sound. He shot her an amused grin and gripped Tressler's hips.

"Is this right?" Face still pointing down, Tressler moved his ass up and down.

"I don't know, is it?" Coach Ace asked, and Tressler's arms buckled. He face-planted into the mat and rolled to find the coach standing over him. His face flushed the color of a blood stripe and he stuttered.

Lowering himself to his haunches, Coach Ace said quietly, "Let's let the ladies do their jobs, shall we?"

"Yes, sir," Tressler replied automatically, then scrambled back into position.

"You can keep going," he said, and Kara nodded regally, wandering back toward the front of the group.

"Walk your hands in," she said in a calm, soothing voice that matched the babbling brook CD she'd brought to put in the gym's CD player. "Slowly, slowly . . . If you need to widen your feet more to make it easier, do so. No strain necessary. Just by trying you're getting the health benefits."

Marianne wandered back toward her own mat, passing by Brad's location as she did. She found him already standing, having rolled up as one of the first. "Nice form."

"I catch on." He shrugged one shoulder, but his neck flushed in an adorable show of embarrassment.

"Admit it—you've taken some yoga classes."

"Hell no," he said quickly. "But you know, the instructors are pretty cute when you find one of those classes on TV."

"Uh-huh." She fought against a smile and shook her

head, returning to her mat. She was pleased with the way the morning yoga session had started. Though there'd been some confusion, and more than a few grumbles, Coach Ace had shot them down quickly. From there, the men had joined in without complaint. And although there'd been moments of hilarity—likc when Bailey had fallen like a log during the tree pose—they'd adapted quickly to the program.

"And let's move into one you should all identify with," Kara said, coming back to her mat up front. "Warrior pose."

"Oo-rah!" one of the Marines said, and they all chuckled.

"Oo-rah, indeed. Follow me, men." Striking the pose, she demonstrated. The men followed suit, a little more clumsy in their motions, but not bad. Marianne hit her own warrior pose, and closed her eyes for a nice, deep breath.

When she heard the curse, her eyes popped open again. Toward the back, Brad was sitting down, massaging his right thigh and looking like he wanted to murder someone. She did her best to not be obvious—no helicopter mom jokes for her—and wandered back there. Along the way, she corrected another Marine's form, just to show she wasn't rushing. When she reached Brad's mat, she put her hands on her hips.

"She said Warrior Pose, not Air Force pose."

The joke, which was meant to lighten the mood, did nothing but make him scowl. "I'm fine."

"Doesn't look like it." She squatted down and watched his hands rub over his thigh. "What's up?"

"Just a cramp," he said through his teeth. "Didn't stretch enough before we started."

"This *is* stretching," she reminded him, but knew herself anyone could push too far, too fast, even in something as relaxed as yoga. "Let's go put some heat on that."

He jerked his arm from her grip. "I'm fine."

"Everything okay here?" Coach Cartwright walked up to stand beside her, taking in Brad on the mat. Around them, Marines shifted to the next position. A few glanced their way. And she watched as a flush crept up Brad's neck.

"Everything's fine. Just had a cramp. Probably need some water and to walk it off." Brad's hands continued their steady pressure over his thigh. "No big deal."

Cartwright seemed to take that at face value. "Walk it off, Marine. They're about to wrap up, and then we move on into practice."

Brad waited until the coach was gone, then shot eye-daggers at her. "You can go."

Hurt at his tone, she backed away, hands held up in surrender. "Fine. Do what you need to do." Then she walked back to her own mat.

As they did the final stretch, she blinked hard enough to keep the tears from falling to her mat.

HE was an asshole. Worse than an asshole. A douche bag.

Was there something worse than a douche bag? If so, he was that.

He'd sat there, on the yoga mat, feeling helpless and inept that his knee had completely given out and dropped him like a stone, and she'd done nothing but offer assistance. And for that, he'd snapped.

His pride, and maybe a little fear, had been the leading cause. But after he'd had another ten minutes to cool down, his mind couldn't stop replaying the image of her face as she'd morphed from concern to surprise and to, ultimately, hurt.

He'd done that. To a woman he cared about a great deal. He'd hurt her because he got a boo-boo and wasn't prepared to accept it.

He was an asshole-slash–douche bag.

At the end of the practice, three hours after yoga time had ended, he approached her training room with trepidation.

When he walked into the door, he saw several Marines inside icing various body parts. They draped over the three tables, sat in chairs, and leaned against the wall. One even lay sprawled on the floor over a few towels.

They'd all given up the tough-guy act, he decided with a smirk. Too late now. Walking to Armstrong, he nudged the man with his toe. "What's up with you?"

"Sore wrist." He held up the arm with the ice bag flopped over it. "Wonky punch to the bag. I'll be okay."

"Better be," Brad warned. "I'm not about to be the first guy to lose one of his group members."

"You won't be," Coach Willis said as he walked in with a clipboard. "Just had to let Ciaston go."

"Injury?" Brad wondered. The guy had been a solid boxer. Not at the top, but not clinging to the bottom rung, either.

"Attitude," he answered shortly, then walked to Marianne, who was massaging another Marine's thigh. She glanced over the list Coach Willis held out under her nose, not stopping in her ministrations, nodding and commenting back with him.

Brad's jaw clenched as he watched her hands move effortlessly, competently over the Marine's thigh. He knew exactly what those hands felt like running over his own body, and his jealousy kicked up a notch when he watched them move higher until they were working, thumbs digging, into the area between the other man's thigh and groin area.

It didn't help that, even as the Marine flinched—in discomfort, Brad assumed—she glanced down at him with a smile and a warm word or two to ease the other man's mind.

She looked up then, and just noticed his presence. Her warm gaze frosted over, and she looked back down again. "Nikki, we've got a customer who needs some ice."

"On it!" Hustling over, the female intern who had spent

more time ogling the team as they worked out than doing anything Brad could see as effective, hustled toward him. Her polo, he noticed, was considerably tighter across the breasts than Marianne's was, and her own khakis were short shorts that probably shared a hint of ass cheek when she bent over.

Brad wasn't interested in finding out.

"Ice for you, right?" She put her hands on her hips in front of him. "What ails ya? Hand, shoulder, knee, ankle?"

"Leg," he said, then added, "I'll just take it to go."

"Nope. Sit down," she said, pushing at his chest until he took a step back and fell into a chair that looked like was one of the desk chairs, not meant for sweaty athletes. They'd run out of space on the cheap plastic ones. "I'll be right back. Don't move a muscle, cutie."

"Cutie," he muttered.

"She's hot, isn't she?" Armstrong grinned.

"She's twelve," Brad responded. Though her actual age was probably closer to twenty, she couldn't have been farther from the type Brad would have considered "hot."

"Aw, you're just old," Armstrong said with a moan.

"She's here to work." The other intern, a quiet guy roughly the same age as the girl, let the bag drop on Brad's lap. His scowl told Brad the kid had been listening, and took exception to them discussing the potential hotness of his fellow training intern. "Don't be jerks to her."

"Who's being a jerk?" Brad asked with a shrug, then settled the ice against his knee. "Long as she does her job, I've got no problems."

The intern made it clear he was adding Armstrong to his shit list by scowling his way, then walked off.

"Making friends wherever you go," Higgs said from the doorway.

Brad flipped him off.

"How long you gonna be?" Higgs checked his watch. "I was going to go to Sweeney's for some grilling action."

"So go. I can get home."

Higgs hesitated, then shrugged and took off.

Armstrong asked quietly, "You okay?"

"I'm fine," he snapped, then sighed. The wounded pride strikes again. "Sorry, I'm fine. Just tired."

"It's catching up to a lot of us," Armstrong agreed. In a hushed voice, he added, "I think our group is the best, though."

"Everyone thinks their group is the best. What matters is who's standing here when the team roster is compiled." Brad didn't want this kid to mistake his intentions. "We're here to get a spot. If that means you have to beat out one of our group to do it, you don't hesitate."

Armstrong looked uncertain, but then the young female walked by and tapped his shoulder. "Your time's up, cutie. Off you go!"

Handing her the wet bag, Armstrong waved to Brad and headed through the door.

He could lead without being best buddies with the guys, couldn't he? Hell yeah. It wasn't that hard.

The real problem lay in how to handle Marianne and his injury. Or just handle Marianne, period. The problem was, he liked her. Liked her a hell of a lot.

If he told her about the injury now, she'd insist on examining him further, and he had no doubt that would end badly. He'd be removed from the roster and head back home. He'd be pissed, and it would effectively kill any chance they had of more.

If he kept it from her, she might eventually find out and be even more pissed off than if he'd told her.

Or, option three, he mused as he watched her help the Marine with the pulled groin off the table. She never found out his knee hurt worse than he let on, he got it taken care of outside, away from base, and it was never an issue.

It involved deception on several fronts, but he couldn't

keep doing this every day to his knee. He knew deep down that something was going wrong with it. To wait and see a year from now would be stupid. But the idea of voluntarily walking away from his first—and most likely his only—shot at the boxing team . . . that hurt deeper than any grinding knee pain.

He kept his eyes on her as she moved around the training room, from Marine to Marine, like a bee moving from flower to flower. And hoped, when she caught his eyes again, she would read the apology in them.

THE wounded bear stalks back into the cave to lick his sore paw.

Marianne made a note on her clipboard about the pulled groin she'd just worked on, but her eyes kept darting over the top of the board to watch Brad. He tested the knee, bending it and making it move with slow, measured motions. She focused on his face and saw the lines of tension there.

Much as her pride hated how he'd spoken to her, she understood. By the time they'd wrapped up the yoga session, she'd already moved past hurt and pissed to annoyed and resigned. She understood pride—probably had a bit too much of it herself—and knew what it did to a strong man when he couldn't control what his body was doing with force of will alone. Understood that weakness was not only frowned upon, but not acceptable, and that he must have been raging at himself when she'd walked up.

He could have handled it better, no doubt. But she could have given him the chance to recover more privately. They'd both made a mistake there.

Slowly, Marines filtered through the icing cycles. She'd started making them stay, rather than taking their ice bags and dashing off like thieves in the night. Though there had been some grumbling, they'd done it. Partly, she did it so she could assess injuries.

But the other part of her just loved a full training room. Not due to injuries, of course, but the company. Being around guys who laughed a little too loudly, joked a little too crudely, cursed a little too much . . . was heaven to her. She fit in, and she adored them. It was like being inside the family fold, with two dozen big brothers. Even working in a high school, she'd bonded with what she'd then thought of as her little brothers and sisters. She could put the smack down when she had to, but she liked just hearing about their days and their lives in and outside of the gym and keeping tabs on them.

Levi had scoffed at the new rule, and she was no idiot. The reason why was flitting around the room like a stripper in a room full of men with dollars. Nikki adored the attention anyone paid her, even if it was completely platonic or professional.

And Marianne had to admit, it seemed like all the Marines—even the ones that were right at her age—treated Nikki just as politely as they did her. Maybe more so. As if they knew giving her a side hug wouldn't be misunderstood, but had subconsciously realized early on not to give Nikki the same opening.

Smart men. Using those survival instincts outside the ropes, too.

Nikki tapped Brad's shoulder to indicate his twenty were up, and he stood stiffly to bend his knee. With great care, he made his way to the industrial sink to dump his ice bag out and toss the plastic away. When Marianne expected him to leave without a word, he surprised her by walking to her and sitting on the empty table.

Only a few Marines remained, and Nikki and Levi were handling them. She decided she could break for a minute. She finished her note, then put the clipboard down. "How's the knee?"

"Still attached."

She watched him for a moment, then opened her mouth to apologize.

"I'm sorry."

Her mouth snapped shut again in surprise. "Did you just apologize? Without prompting?"

One corner of his mouth tipped up. "Maybe I'm an evolved version of the male species."

"No such thing," she contradicted quickly. When another Marine got up and left, she made a note on the clipboard by her side. "I'm sorry, too. Let's forget it and move on."

"Sold." He used the toe of his shoe to nudge her calf gently. "I need a favor."

"Hmm?" Watching Nikki and the remaining Marine from the corner of her eye, she looked back to him. "What's that?" Then her mind clicked back into working order. *Finally!* Here was the opening she'd been hoping for. He was going to ask about his knee.

With the soulful eyes of a lost puppy, he said, "I've been abandoned. Can I have a ride back to the BOQ?"

"Oh." Not what she'd expected.

"You need a ride?" Toby Chalfant, the redheaded cutie with a face full of freckles and smiles, walked up. "I'll take you back, sir."

"It's Brad or Costa, not sir," he growled. "And I was just—"

"No, that's great." She cut him off before he could get going. "Chalfant, did you need something?"

"Aspirin," he said with a grim smile, and held up his hand. His pinky was a little swollen, though nothing bad. She grasped it and prodded tenderly. He'd live.

"Don't you have any at your place?"

"Ran out, can't make it back to the commissary tonight before it closes."

"Fine. Here." She bent over to dig in one of the storage

drawers and heard Brad's quiet huff of breath. She could only imagine he was wordlessly commenting on her ass sticking up in the air, but she didn't care. She snapped the drawer shut again and held out some sample packets of aspirin. "Should get you through until tomorrow. But I'm not a pharmacy."

"Yes, ma'am. Cook," he corrected, sensing the warning in her own eyes. "I'll be outside the door when you're ready, sir . . . Costa," he said, flushing with embarrassment at the second mistake in as many minutes, then he fled the scene.

"Kid's jumpier than a flea," Brad said gruffly. "And nosy. I'll get rid of him."

"No, you will not," she said firmly, taking the papers Levi passed her. He was wearing his backpack, which meant he was ready to go. "I'll see you tomorrow, Levi."

"Sure thing." With one last longing glance at Nikki, he left.

"That one's barking up the wrong tree there."

"No shit," she said simply, then grinned at Brad's widening eyes. "I don't use the language often . . . but when I do, it's more impactful."

"I'll say. Maybe I could hear some of that language tonight." He watched as the last Marine left, with Nikki following him out to gather the leftover cups from the watering stations. "Ask me over."

"No." No longer having to keep her voice down, she stepped away from the table and busied herself with filing the clipboard papers for the day. "Not the best idea."

"Best idea I've had in weeks. Months. Probably years."

"Then your ideas tend to suck."

He scoffed at that, then stepped down. Closing in on her, he pressed until his front was against her back and the tops of her thighs were pressed into the edge of her desk. "Marianne Cook, don't be a coward."

"Coward," she sputtered, then sucked in a breath when he squeezed her hip with his big hand. "I'm not a coward."

"You're avoiding the conversation we're going to have, admit it."

"I admit nothing." It was too close to the truth for comfort.

"A coward and a rebel." She felt him shake his head, moving her ponytail slightly. "I'm a doomed man."

He pressed a kiss to the back of her neck and stepped away just seconds before Nikki came back in, lugging two sleeves of unused cups.

"These guys are camels," she complained. "Can't they all come to the one water jug down here? Why do we have to have jugs upstairs too?"

"Because I said so," Marianne said simply as she watched Brad walk out.

Nikki eyed her speculatively. Marianne crossed her arms over her chest and rubbed at her hands. "Is it colder in here?"

"It's because all the hot beefcakes left. They heated the room right up." With a grin, she set the cups down and reached under the cabinet for her purse. "See you tomorrow!"

"Yeah," she said, still watching Brad's retreating back. "See ya."

CHAPTER

12

Chalfant dropped Brad off in front of the BOQ, and Brad waved and waited until the younger man's car was out of sight. Then, sighing, he limped a little to a grassy area and dropped his bag by a bench next to a tree. He'd go inside in a minute. Or two. Maybe tomorrow.

Anything to avoid the third degree from his roommate. Higgs had picked up on way too much, too fast.

To stall, he fished his cell out of his bag and called his sister. She answered on the first ring, because like any other red-blooded American teen, her cell was surgically melded to her hand.

"Brad!"

"Hey, Sarah. What's this I hear about you being old enough for college applications?"

"It's crazy, I know. Can you believe I'm all grown up?" She gave a dramatic sniff, then laughed. "I'm about ready to bust out of this place. Tell me, what does freedom taste like?"

"Disappointment, mostly." She groaned, and he grinned up into the tree limbs above him. "Don't be in such a hurry to cut loose. Mom and Bob are halfway decent parental units. You have no clue how much easier it is when someone else is doing your laundry."

Laundry. Ugh. He had a wet pile of it sitting in his room, just waiting.

"Okay, okay, enough about my prison break. How's the East Coast?"

"Just like the West Coast, only farther to the right."

She groaned again. "Brothers are worthless."

"We practice. It's a fine art. I don't know, Sarah." He ran a hand down his face. "More humid, I guess. I'm here to box, not run around sightseeing. I've barely been off base."

"Any cute guys?"

"I'm pretending you didn't ask that. Because no. Also, no. And for dessert? No."

"The Marines are good enough for my brother, but not good enough for me to date. I see how it is."

"Is that Brad?"

Brad winced when he heard his mother's voice. "I thought you were in your room."

"Living room. Why? And here's Mom . . ." Her voice trailed off.

"Bradley, I'm going gray over here worrying about you. Have you heard of this invention called a telephone lately?"

"No, tell me more."

When his mother sighed in exasperation, he laughed. "Mom, come on. I'm exhausted. Cut a son some slack."

"I heard more from you when you were deployed than I have since you checked in over there."

Brad glanced down at his knee, currently stretched out on the bench. "Not much to tell. Just same old, same old."

"Hmm. How about your roommate? Is he a decent guy?"

"Decent. Talkative. Okay, I guess."

"Well, it sounds like you've made a friend."

Brad winced at that. He wouldn't go so far . . .

"Call more," his mother admonished, then handed the phone back to Sarah.

"I'm hanging up now. I'm waiting on a text."

"From who?"

"Uhhhh. Good-bye, Brad." She hung up before he could pry any more information out of her. He set the phone back in his pack and stood. Sarah, going off to college. It had been a trip to watch her drive the last time he'd visited. Unnatural. His sister was supposed to stay little forever.

And that sentiment only made him feel that much older. *Time for bed, Grandpa.*

THE second his back hit the bed, his door opened. Brad didn't even bother sitting up, just held up a hand with his middle finger extended.

"I'm going to pass on the invitation." Higgs jumped until he bounced on the mattress, sending Brad bouncing until his head hit the headboard. "Whoops!"

"Damn it, Higgs." Rubbing at the bump on his head, he sat up. "What the hell do you want?"

"Can't a guy want to chat with his roomie?" When Brad gave him a bland stare, Higgs sighed. "Fine, I'm here for intel. Give me some info."

"Info on what?" *Why am I not at Marianne's right now?*

"Marianne Cook."

Was the man a mind reader?

"I know you and her are . . ." He held up a hand, tilting it back and forth.

Brad mimicked the gesture. "What the hell does *that* mean?"

"It means I get it. You two are something together. You've got the ka-boom factor."

"The ka-boom factor." It was like talking to a hyper golden retriever. "Use regular words, please."

"You're the gas, she's the flame. You get anywhere near each other and . . ." Higgs slapped his hands together. "Ka-boom."

"That is the most stupid thing I've heard in a long time. And I got to listen to Tressler mouth off about scoring ass and how he mentally rated chicks on a ten-point scale before 'letting them' get with him."

Higgs pulled the fourth-grade move of pretending to gag. Brad couldn't blame him there.

"How are your guys?" his roommate asked, scooting down to the floor and stretching his legs out. He wore athletic shorts—clean, Brad prayed—a simple red USMC shirt and white ankle socks with no shoes. Clearly, he felt comfortable enough invading Brad's room that he didn't need to dress up for the occasion.

"They're okay, minus Tressler." Sadly, the kid was good, and he'd likely be making the cut. "What about yours?"

"Two are decent, three don't stand a chance. Mixed bag." He stared at his feet for a second as he gripped his heels and stretched. "Have you figured out the angle on this whole mini-platoon thing? Sweeney and I talked about it last night, and couldn't get there."

"Well, there are a few theories." Warming up to it, and glad to be talking about something that really mattered— boxing—he rolled his shoulder and let his right leg stretch out, then let the knee bend ever so slightly. It always felt better bent. "Theory number one: the coaches are testing us older guys on our leadership abilities, and want to see if any of us would make decent captains."

"We thought about that," Higgs agreed, bending one leg to stretch deeper with the other.

"Theory number two: it's a test to see how far we'll go to follow Coach Ace's lead. Do as ordered, no questions asked."

Higgs nodded and switched legs.

"Or, in a more Machiavellian plot twist, the unlikely theory number three is they could be testing us to see which one of us is willing to forsake all distractions and focus solely on our own performance to make the team."

"That's cold."

"Boxing isn't a team sport."

"The hell it isn't." Higgs sat up straight, glaring. "I know we go into that ring one at a time, but damn, man. We go to matches together, we wear matching uniforms, and we're all one branch. Marines stand by Marines. Don't act like you're suddenly in the Army."

Brad smiled a little at that. "For what it's worth, my instinct says it's theory number one. He's seeing who will step up to lead." Which frustrated him. He didn't come to lead; he came to box.

Spend some time making a difference in something you volunteered for, huh?

God, would the woman leave him alone, even in his own subconscious?

"You gonna go see her tonight?"

"Nope." No point even pretending he was clueless about who Higgs meant. "Don't need the distraction."

Her ass pressed against his cock, her thighs digging into the desk, her breath panting out in time with his heartbeat . . .

"Cold" was Higgs' final statement as he stood and walked to the door. "I'm pretty sure she could thaw that shoulder of yours."

"Lame" was Brad's comment as Higgs walked out the

door. But it didn't stop him from picking up his cell phone and debating long and hard before putting it back down.

Two minutes later, when he reached back out, he was grabbing his keys.

OF all the places she'd been asked to meet a man, an empty gym late at night had to top the list of WTF moments.

Marianne pulled into a spot two away from the lone SUV idling in the gym parking lot. Her headlights passed over Brad, leaning against the side of the building by the doors to the gym. His arms were crossed over his chest, one foot overlapping the other in a relaxed pose.

But if he was there, then who was in the SUV?

She climbed out and headed toward him, swinging her keys as she walked. "This is weird. You know that, right?"

"What, you don't always meet guys in dark parking lots at ten o'clock at night? What's wrong with you?" He grinned as she reached him, but he didn't wrap his arms around her like she thought he would. "You've got keys to the gym, right?"

"I do, but first I'd like to know why."

"We could do without it, but it's just easier with access to the equipment." When she hesitated, he waved a hand over her shoulder. The doors to the SUV popped open, and she watched as Tressler climbed out of the driver side, with the rest of Brad's assigned Marines piling out of the backseat. It looked sort of like a roll of biscuits pouring out of a popped can. They just . . . tumbled out in a heap.

"Have you named your group yet?" she asked mildly as Tressler yelled at them for sweating on his interior and Chalfant complained that Tibbs was crushing his ribs.

"No."

"The Bad News Bears come to mind." Patting his chest,

she went to unlock the door. Whatever this group was up to, it was harmless.

Brad led them upstairs to the catwalk, where most of the cardio equipment had been moved that week, and immediately got to work. He used tape to mark off a hundred yards, then explained the sprinting drills he wanted Tibbs to run, with Chalfant as his timer. In another corner, he worked with Armstrong on the block, having Tressler throw combinations in random order.

After a few minutes, Marianne set her large tote bag on the ground and walked over to where Brad was observing the guys, hands on his hips. "And I'm here . . . why, again?"

"Well, first off, I needed the keys."

She laughed at that. "You could have done this in the parking lot, and you know it. You didn't need me and my keys."

"True. Which leads me to my second point." He smiled down at her. "I wanted the company."

That made up for having to put on real pants—as opposed to her *Family Guy* pajama pants—and leave her comfortable apartment late at night. "Since they don't have practice tomorrow, I assume that's why you're here so late?"

"Yup. They've got all day to recuperate. And so do I." He watched her for a moment, then turned his head sharply and bit out a command to Armstrong.

"What changed your mind?"

"Mmm?" His eyes stayed on his teammates. "What?"

"Never mind. You do your thing. I'll be over here if you want more 'company' or someone gets hurt." She strolled back to her stuff, slid down the wall, picked her phone out of her bag and started surfing Facebook.

An hour later, something wet dropped on her phone.

"Sorry, Cook."

She glanced up to see Tibbs, his chest heaving, his shirt as soaked as if he'd showered in it, his dark face a cascade of sweat, standing over her.

"No prob." She wiped the screen on the knee of her jeans. "What's up? You doing okay? Hydrating?"

"I'm good." He sucked in a breath. "Just catching my . . . my breath." His face was starting to pale a little, and she popped up.

"Walk with me." He gave her an odd look at the request, but she gestured for him to follow her around the catwalk, away from the others. "I need some company, and Br— Costa's too busy."

"Not for you, he's not." Though he was still puffing, he managed a grin in his wide face. "I didn't say that."

"Say what?" She forced her own breathing to be a little louder, and noticed he unconsciously matched hers in rhythm. She focused for a few minutes on walking at a decent three-and-a-half-mile-an-hour pace and breathing with him. "So how are things with boxing?"

"I'm getting faster, and that's good. The coaches are damn good—sorry, darn."

"Damn right," she said with a smile.

His eyes crinkled in return. "And now we're paired with Costa, I'm feeling extra strong. He's smart, ya now? Knows a lot about the sport."

"And which one of you asked him for this workout tonight?"

"None of us. He just rounded us up and brought us out here. Made Tressler give up a date to come out." That made him laugh, and when he finished, she was satisfied to hear his breathing sound normal. They rounded the last curve of the catwalk. "So he piled us in Tressler's car, since he's got the biggest one, and made him drive us out here."

"That was . . . surprising," she said, going for honesty. That he took the initiative shocked her.

"I think the group leaders are all fighting it out to see how many of their guys they've got left standing. Nobody likes to lose, especially a Marine."

As they approached the first area of the catwalk, Armstrong looked up from the water bottle he was chugging from. "Marines don't lose. We just give everyone else a chance for glory so they'll stop whining about the odds."

"Clever." She left Tibbs to hydrate again and wandered over toward Brad. "Interesting evening. You know, most guys would ask a lady out to a movie, or maybe for a drive, if they wanted to spend time in their company."

Brad brushed that off. "Old-school. I like to impress the ladies with my mad socialization skills. Look at me, volunteering my time with my fellow boxers."

She smiled and patted his arm. "You're my hero," she said in a high pitched, cartoon-female voice.

"Damn right. Another half hour, and we'll be done. You okay with that?"

He was speaking to her, but she saw his mind was already focused elsewhere. The "elsewhere" was with Tibbs, and his attempt at a footwork ladder taped to the floor.

"Go. Help. Do. Wake me when you're done." She returned to her sentry spot on the floor with her phone. But for the next thirty minutes, she couldn't help but occasionally catch a glance at his cute butt while he worked with the guys.

Bad Marianne.

IT was the second time he was standing outside Marianne's apartment in as many nights. He'd left his car at Tressler's when the younger Marine had driven them all to the gym, but he was back to his own devices now. And instead of heading home for some much-needed R & R, he found himself driving toward where he wanted to be the most.

Marianne's apartment.

He knocked, waited then knocked again.

Maybe she was asleep. She didn't strike him as the type to turn in before the late shows started airing, but what the hell did he know? He gave it one more shot and nearly rapped her in the forehead when she yanked open the door.

"I started thinking you wouldn't be coming by," she said.

He blinked. "Were you expecting me?"

"Uh . . . yeah." She gave him a *"duh"* face. Opening the door wide, she let him in before shutting it behind her. She'd changed, this time into an oversized shirt with some high school name on it. If she was wearing shorts, they were tiny enough that they didn't show under the thigh-skimming hem of the shirt. The sight of it made his mouth water.

At least try *to focus on something else for a few minutes before you jump her, Lieutenant Suave.*

"Sorry. If I knew you were expecting me, I'd have texted."

"No big."

"Chalfant wanted one more pep talk. I'm not sure why he doesn't just listen to motivational CDs or something. I've got nothing good to say. But he keeps asking, so whatever." It made his neck burn to think of the way the kid had stared up at him with big eyes as Brad had explained resilience. Like a kid watching a superhero. Scared the piss out of him.

"It's cute. He's enamored with you." She pointed to the couch. "Sit. Do you want something to drink?"

It mimicked their evening from the night before so much, he grinned. "Yeah. A beer this time. My own," he clarified when she glanced back in surprise. "It's my one night off where I'm not going to get up at the ass-crack of dawn for a run. I can live a little."

"Two beers, coming up."

She disappeared into the kitchen, and he sat and picked up her notepad. Again, the day's date was written at the top, and her list of to-dos were all crossed off. It was a pretty simple list, including work and the post office, and a reminder to call some guy about supplies.

He picked up her pen and added one last item to her list just as she was coming out of the kitchen. Two bottles clanked between her fingers, and she handed one to him and sat at the opposite end of the couch.

Disappointment that she wouldn't pull the feminine snuggle trick was short-lived as she poked at him with her toe. "You dragged me out of the apartment at ten at night. You can pay me back now."

"How's that?"

She plopped that foot in his lap and grinned. "Get to it."

Her feet were small and cute, with frosty pink painted toenails. It was no hardship to take a sip of beer, set it on the coffee table and pick up her foot. His thumb pressed into the arch and she moaned in a way that made his cock harden. Then her eyes popped open. "Did you use a coaster?"

He looked at the beer, then around desperately for a coaster. "Uh . . ."

She burst into laughter. "I don't have coasters. Are you kidding me?"

"Tricky witch," he muttered, but kept rubbing, and she kept making sex noises. Eventually, he switched from her right to her left. She slumped back and settled the beer on her stomach.

"I see you scored bonus points for doing your entire to-do list again today."

She nodded, a wistful smile curving her lips. "I was a

good girl. Normally, I write down three times as much as I can reasonably accomplish, but for some weird reason, I woke up with a lot of energy this morning." Her smile turned a little sultry, but she kept her eyes closed. "Fancy that."

"Fancy that," he agreed, though he knew exactly what she meant. He'd woken up that morning, despite having an hour less sleep than usual, feeling like he could climb a mountain. "But you've still got one more thing you didn't cross off yet."

At that, she sat straight up. "That's impossible."

"Nope, it's right there." He pretended to look at the notepad. "Yeah. You're still one task shy of a full day's work."

"No way. I just looked at that myself." She pulled her foot from his lap, leaned over to grab the pad then froze when she saw his handwriting at the bottom. "Do Brad." She raised one brow and gave him a sardonic look. "You can't be serious."

He held up his hands in a *What can you do?* gesture. "Well, if that's what it says, I won't stop you from completing your assigned duty. That would just be wrong."

"*You're* just wrong," she countered, but she was laughing. She tossed herself at him, the pad flying from her hands as she landed against his chest and kissed him. She peppered his lips, jaw, cheekbones and nose with the innocent pecks, then returned to his mouth and made the kiss longer, hotter. When her tongue darted inside his mouth, he opened easily for her. Let her lead the way, set the pace.

Fortunately for him, she set a pace he would have agreed to no matter what. She hummed against him, ground her pelvis down against his rigid cock, and let her hands roam over his upper body.

God, she had good hands. Strong, firm hands, but still with a hint of softness to the touch. When she let them drop down to the waist of his shorts, he sucked in a breath. Then, in another moment, his cock was free between them, and she used those soft-but-firm hands to stroke him until he was nearly out of his mind.

"You know," she said, pulling back to take a quick nip of his bottom lip. "Since I've met you, I've had this sort of fantasy. But I'm not sure if I should tell you."

At this point, Brad wasn't sure he could do anything more than sit there while she had her way with him. "If it involves carrying you around, I'm out. I've had a long day of training and I'm pretty positive I'd drop you. That's not the way we want to start this."

Her laugh was husky, like smoke. "No. In fact, you don't have to move a muscle." She slid down until her knees hit the carpet between his spread legs. Then she gripped his erection firmly at the base and gave the head a teasing lick. "I'm not sure why, and I'll deny it if it's ever brought up in public, but this position always made me curious."

"Mmm," was all he could strangle out, as she licked a long path from root to tip, the edge of her tongue tracing the slit at the head of his cock.

"Maybe it's that whole AT-athlete thing. You know, like a student-professor fantasy, only more specific." She engulfed his penis, sucking hard once, then pulling back. "I just let my mind wander, imagine some little fantasy scene where you come to me so I can tape your ankle, and I'm down here, eye level with your waist, and your erection, and I just can't help myself." Another long suck.

"God, you're good." His voice was embarrassingly hoarse at this point.

"That probably makes me sound dirty, but I can honestly say it never occurred to me, ever, until you."

"Glad to hear it." His hands cupped her chin, thumbs pressing up enough to have her looking into his eyes.

"And I just can't get it out of my head." Her teeth grazed up and over the sensitive head. "So I figure I should just excise the image by fulfilling it, and see how that works."

She quieted down as she took him again fully inside her mouth.

"You don't have to finish. I'm about five seconds away from tapping out here."

She grinned. "Then I'm not stopping." Eyes still on his, she engulfed him with her mouth, worked down as much as she could, and rubbed up to meet her lips with her fist. The wet heat, the suction and the friction of her twisting hand were more sensations than he could handle at once.

"Coming, baby, I'm coming . . ." Jaw clenched, body straining not to thrust upward, he felt the orgasm build in his balls until it released in the most intense moment of his life.

CHAPTER

13

Marianne licked her lips, feeling quite pleased with herself. She was the one down on her knees, but if she had to guess, she'd say that Brad was the one who was ready to fall over and worship her. That was the true fantasy. The power switch, the feeling of ultimate supremacy. This unbelievably strong man, consumed by her, at her mercy, and willingly giving up the moment to her own hands.

She wasn't exactly into power play or anything like that. But every so often, a fantasy was nice to indulge in.

"Now that," she said with a smile as she stood, "was a nice training session. Do you need me to stretch you out now?"

"I need you to go grab a condom and get your sweet ass back here," he growled. "I'd do it, but my legs seem to have stopped working. You can give me an exam when I'm through with you."

She grinned, hustled to her room and came back with

the handful of condoms. When she tossed them on her coffee table, they scattered. A few fell to the floor. He raised a brow.

"How many times do you intend on using me tonight?"

"As many as I can." She made him lift his ass and she pulled his shorts off his legs to give her better access. Then she pulled her own pants down. Straddling him, she kissed him again. Hard this time. No slow seduction, just a tough, primal meeting of two people whose sexual needs matched each other's.

"The second you're recovered, I want you inside me," she whispered. He groaned, and she knew then he was a man who wanted some dirty talk. She wasn't exactly a pro at it, but she wasn't squeamish, either. "I'm wet for you," she tried, gauging his response.

His cock twitched against her thigh. On the right track.

Kissing her way to his ear, she murmured, "I need you thrusting inside me. So hard, you can't stop or slow down, even if you're going to beat me to the next climax. I need you helpless with wanting me. Unable to see straight."

Two fingers speared inside her, surprising her into a quick gasp. She hadn't felt his arm move. But *now* she did. His fingers worked her inside, his thumb massaging her clit until she was moments away from her own orgasm.

Then he pulled back and reached around her for one of the condoms. Quick work to don one, and he gripped her hips to lift her up and settle her back down over his erection. They both sighed with pleasure when she was fully around him.

She started to move, but he held her still.

"Just . . . sit with me. For a minute, just sit with me."

The peaceful request was another surprise. He lifted her shirt up, but not over her head like she'd assumed. Just enough to bare her breasts. He palmed her back and urged her into him until her nipple fed into his mouth. He sucked, nipped and played lazily, like they weren't actually already having sex. As if they had an entire day free to do nothing but play with each other.

And they did, sort of, didn't they? Neither of them had work in the morning, and nobody had a curfew. They could take as much time as they wanted with each other.

Brad nuzzled his way to her other breast and worked the tip until she was panting and trying desperately to move her hips. But he held her firm. If anything, it felt as though his cock was still swelling inside her, with no friction at all.

"I could spend hours on these babies." He cupped them both, brought them together like she was wearing a push up bra, and kissed the warm flesh. "You probably know you've got a great rack, right?"

She snorted out a laugh. "I've never thought of it quite like that, but if you say so." His hands kneaded her breasts, and then finally—*finally*—his hips thrust gently against hers. "Thank you, God."

He chuckled and held her tight to him, kissing her as their lower bodies worked together. She threw in a hip swivel every so often to mix things up, and he held her down a few times to keep her from moving too fast. He wanted it to last, he said. Make it last.

And maybe she hadn't been the one in power after all. When she thought she'd gained playful dominance, he'd turned the tables on her and controlled things, even from the bottom. He manipulated the pace to keep them both wanting, panting, desperate for more. The man's self-control was legendary.

But like a shaken bottle of soda, there came a point where her orgasm wasn't going to hold off any longer. "Brad, I can't . . . I can't stop it."

Her shaky tone must have registered because he let her

fly. Let her work the pace she needed in order to pull the cork and let her climax free. Head back, hands clutching his shoulders, she surrendered to the orgasm she'd been waiting for.

He suckled one nipple while he came again, prompted, she knew, by her own finish.

As she slumped against him, her breathing still irregular, she knew whatever they had had long since moved past being about sex.

BRAD watched as Marianne slept. She wasn't what he'd call a sleeping beauty. He grinned at that. Come to think of it, she was more like a sleeping disaster. Her ice blonde hair was draped half over her eyes, her face bore creases from the pillow and she was drooling, just a little.

The fact he found it endearing more than horrifying was a good sign shit had truly changed for him.

And speaking of that change . . . they needed to talk.

He caught a glimpse of the clock on her nightstand. It was still not quite six in the morning. She'd probably murder him for doing it, but he craved her enough to take the risk.

And his craving wasn't just for her sweet body.

"Marianne," he whispered, hoping to slowly drag her out of sleep. "Come on, sweetheart, time to talk."

She mumbled something and turned away from him.

"Oh, no you don't." He pulled on her shoulder until she was flat on her back. "Open up those beautiful eyes for me."

He bent down to nibble at her neck, and she swatted him in the face. "What the hell?" Rearing back, he realized she was still unconscious to the world. He grumbled about uncooperative women, then made her sit up. "Up and at 'em, sweets. We need to chat."

"Die."

The word came out like gravel run through a coffee grinder. He couldn't help but laugh. "Sorry, no can do. I'm pretty sure even your stellar training skills can't bring a guy back from the dead. Just chat with me a bit."

Eyes still glued shut, she slapped at his hands, which were pulling the sheet away. "Die," she said more firmly. "It's not even light out, and it's our day off. What the hell is the matter with you?"

"How can you tell it's not light out when you won't open your eyes?"

"There's no light bleeding through my eyelids. I need more sleep."

Smoothing down one side of her messy hair, he dodged another elbow. "We can talk and go right back to bed."

"How about we skip the talk and you take a long walk off a short bridge?" She kicked at him and tried to lie back down, but he caught her and kept her upright.

"Nope, not happening, Naps McGee. Come here." He made space for her in the crook of his arm, and she snuggled there like a contented kitten.

"You're an ass," she said on a sigh.

"Probably. But give the ass a minute before you kick him out, would you? I want to talk about how we're handling things outside of the bedroom."

"I thought we made my couch very proud." A tiny smile kicked up the corner of her lips. He kissed the corner. She'd yet to open her eyes.

"No doubt there. But I meant more generally, how we're handling this in public. As in, what are we disclosing to people?"

She tensed up, and he hated to lose that loose, warm, snuggling Marianne. But in an instant, the no-nonsense athletic trainer Marianne took her place. She eased out of his hold and rubbed at her eyes with the heels of her hands before blinking them open. It was sort of like watching a mole emerge from being underground for three weeks or something.

"Okay." She blinked rapidly, then focused on the clock. "You're a dead man when this is over."

"Understood."

She ran her fingers through her hair, looking disgusted when they caught on the snarls. "Oh, that's lovely," she muttered, but kept thinking. "Okay. I guess the real question is, what is there to disclose?"

She said it in a businesslike tone, as if she were asking him for expense reports from last quarter. He knew that wasn't how she viewed them and their situation, but it was still a tad unnerving how she was able to shift back and forth between the lover and the trainer so quickly. "Well, we're having sex."

"We are." She looked at the two dented pillows behind them. "Good sex."

"No arguments here. But," he said firmly, and took hold of one of her hands, kissing the palm, "I'd like more than that."

She watched her hand as her fingers curled slowly over the area he'd kissed. "So would I."

"Two for two there. Sounds like we've got something to disclose. I'm not sure who your supervisor is, but I would assume you have one."

"I do. Several, in fact."

"Sounds familiar." He thought back to his chain of command at his home base and smiled. "There's never a lack of leadership in the military, is there?"

"Brad, it . . ." She sighed and rubbed her hands over her arms. "It worries me. I've got plans for after this. I'm really trying to lead into a career with a professional team. How's it going to look that I'm known for sleeping with the athletes I'm working with?"

"You're not sleeping with me, you're dating me. We're

a thing. And unless there are others—which you said there weren't—"

"There aren't," she agreed quickly.

"Then I'm a one-off. I'm your special snowflake." He grinned when she groaned, grabbed her pillow and hit him with it. "And besides, if we're dating, then that means you're not exactly available to be hanging all over pro athletes, doesn't it?"

"Women cheat."

"Not my woman," he said firmly, and she groaned all over again. "Sorry. Had to."

"You can just 'had to' right out of here."

"No way. You said we could sleep in."

"And you woke me up. You broke the Day Off rules. On purpose. To talk about serious stuff, no less. You don't break the Day Off rules unless someone's life is at stake."

"Day Off rules . . ." he said slowly, a question in his voice.

She held up a fist, started ticking off numbers with her fingers. "One, you don't set an alarm or get out of bed until your body has caught up on as much sleep as it can stomach. Two, you spend as much time being as slothful as you physically can be. Three, you don't cook elaborate meals. PB and J are your best buddies on your day off. There are more, but you get the idea. You woke me up. You broke the rule."

"I'll make it up to you." He eased her back, and her eyes drifted closed again, as if she were a doll whose eyelids were designed to close when flat on its back. "Just lie down, and dream of admitting to others you are sleeping with a god."

She pinched his stomach, and he yelped. But then she settled back against him and sighed with contentment.

He knew the feeling. With a kiss to the top of her head, he let himself drift again. Now that they'd taken care of the whole "disclosure" portion of their relationship, they could move forward.

Because with Marianne Cook, forward was exactly where he wanted to go.

MARIANNE tossed the knife in the sink and smiled at her PB and J. Her one regret was that Brad had left and wouldn't be sharing her sloth-like lunch with her. He'd had errands to run, as well as wanting to check on Tibbs and make sure he was feeling okay after his additional workout the night before. He promised to come back later, though, this time with a pile of laundry.

Just like a little domestic couple. Doing laundry on a Sunday evening while watching a movie or TV. The thought should have made her gag, but it only made her grin wider.

For now, she had two choices. Eat her lunch of a sandwich and a bag of chips at the coffee table while she watched some of her DVR'd shows, or take it back to her bedroom and surf Facebook and Pinterest while she ate.

Pinterest won. She loved finding inspirational quotes and pictures. When she had her own training room again— a permanent space—she wanted it decked out in quotes for the athletes to read through while they iced or got their massages or just hung out, talking.

She had just set the plate down on the comforter when she heard her front door open. Since she'd locked it after Brad, she knew the only other person possible was . . .

"Marianne! Your car was in the parking lot."

"Be there in a sec, Mom." She grabbed the lunch and headed back out. Looked like she'd be eating on the couch after all. Her mother was standing in the living room, waiting. When she saw Marianne enter, her eyes widened.

"Oh, my Lord. What in the world have you done to yourself?"

She glanced down at her sweatpants and tank and shrugged. "Woke up?" She sat on one end of the couch, legs curled under her, and took a bite of her sandwich.

"It's noon, sweetheart. You just woke up?"

"Day off." Marianne took a big bite of her sandwich and grinned around the flopping crust. Her mother winced.

"You look a bit . . . rough, sweetheart." Her mother sat more delicately on the opposite end of the couch. "There are adorable Marines all over this apartment complex, you know."

"And none of them are looking in my window, so no problem." No way in hell was she going to mention she'd just had an adorable Marine in her bed not three hours ago, and he hadn't minded her being "rough" at all.

In fact, he might have liked her even more when she was rough.

"Marianne, what's that smile for?"

"Hmm?" She glanced up from her plate to find her mother staring at her. "What?"

"Nothing. I came by to . . ." Mary trailed off, and she glanced down under the coffee table.

A moment too late, Marianne realized what her mother was reaching for. "No, don't. I'll get it . . . later," she finished as her mother pulled two condom packets from under the table and held them with two fingers.

"Do I . . ." Her mother cleared her throat and set them on the empty table. In the middle, as if they were a freaking home decor item. "Do I want to know?"

"Probably not."

Her mother stared at them for a moment. "Will you be embarrassed if I say I'm glad you're having some fun?"

"Yes," Marianne said immediately. Shut it down, shut it down. Abort. Abort. "Yes, I absolutely will."

Mary shot her a disbelieving look. "You know that won't stop me. So, who is he?"

Marianne rolled her eyes and settled back against the armrest.

"Have we met him before? Old friend from high school?"

In response, she smiled blandly and took a large bite of her sandwich. Couldn't answer with her mouth full, could she? No. That would be rude.

"He's not a Marine," her mother mused, using one finger to spin one shiny foil packet like it was a freaking top. "You were never really into that type. Maybe—"

"Please, God, strike me now."

"Fine, fine." Her mother huffed. "Just thought we could have a nice conversation."

"Could it not involve those?" Marianne asked, and pointed at the table.

"If you insist. Though I must commend you on your safety."

"Okay!" Marianne popped up and snatched the condoms, crumpling them in her fist. Her neck burned. "How about I shower, and we can go do whatever it is you came over here to drag me out for?"

"Shop. I wanted to know if you wanted to run down to Wilmington to shop." Her mother stood and glanced around the room. Marianne could all but see the wheels churning in Mary's head. Her mother was trying to place where they'd had sex for them to need condoms under the coffee table. The sooner she shuttled Mary out of her apartment, the better.

"Sounds great. I love shopping. Shopping is good. Shopping, shopping, shopping!"

Mary eyed her curiously. "Are you sick?"

"Nope. I'm just excited to spend time with you, you know, shopping." Honestly, she hated shopping. It wasn't fun, she never found something that fit her short frame without being tailored, and she'd rather spend her money on other things. But at this point, anything to get her mother out of the porn palace.

"I'll just wait at the table. Can I get a glass of water?" Her mother was still watching her, as if concerned for her welfare.

"Sure. Great. I'll just . . ." Marianne's eye caught on one more wrapped condom on the floor, and she snatched it up too. "I'll . . ." Damn, another. And another. She sucked at life. "I'll be back." There was no way she was playing Find The Condoms on the floor of her apartment while her mother watched. Resigned, she tossed the lot of them in the fruit bowl next to the apples and left her plate in the sink before rushing to the bathroom.

"Is he at least cute?" her mother called out as she reached the bathroom door.

"Cute? No," she said after a second's hesitation. "He's sex in shorts."

Her mother's airy laugh followed her through the closed door.

CHAPTER

14

The instant Brad hit the parking lot of the BOQ, his phone beeped with a text.

Mom stopped by. Surprised me. She's taking me shopping. Feel bad for me. I should be home by six.

So there went his plans to take a quick nap and head right back over to her place. With a sigh, he put the phone in his pocket and headed inside.

He passed by Higgs on his way into his room. The man's laundry basket was filled to the brim.

"Heading to the Laundromat. Wanna grab a load and come with?"

Brad shook his head. "I'm doing it tonight."

"Better with company to keep you from going nuts sitting there."

He debated a minute, then held up a finger. He changed quickly from the clothes he'd worn to the late-night workout into cargo shorts, a polo and running shoes, then grabbed his sunglasses and met Higgs at the door. "I'll keep you company."

"Just bring your laundry, man. If you're going to be sitting there, then you might as well be productive."

"I'm doing it tonight," Brad repeated, and closed the door to their joined rooms behind him. This was as good a time as any to try out the whole disclosure thing. "I'm doing them over at Marianne's place."

"Marianne's place, huh?" Higgs' voice took on a speculative, teasing tone. "So it's like that."

"It is." He waited for Higgs to load the basket in the back of his car and get behind the wheel. "And it's not just sex. We're . . . dating," he decided on. It sounded a bit high school, but what else could he call it? "So we're not sneaking around."

"Anymore. You forgot that important word. You're not sneaking around . . . anymore."

"Shut up," he muttered, much to his roommate's delight. "I wasn't sure how to handle it. But we're just going to be upfront and go from there."

"Mature," Higgs said with a nod as he pulled out of the parking lot. "Not as much fun, though. There's something about sneaking around, even if you don't really have to, technically. Adds to the excitement, you know? It's like, pseudo role-playing."

"I don't need to know about your role-playing." Brad held up his hands in an effort to make it stop. "Really, I don't."

"Ah, you don't know what you're missing. But anyway, she's cool. And you could probably be cool, if you let yourself. She must see some redeeming qualities in you, so hey." He shrugged his shoulder and grinned. "Mazel tov."

"Gee, thanks. Your blessing means the world," Brad said dryly.

"This doesn't explain the real question, though."

"What's that?"

"Why are you coming with me to the Laundromat when you could be spending an entire Sunday with the hot trainer?"

"She's out with her mom." Unfortunately. Otherwise, his plans would have been just that.

"So I'm second place in the company department."

Brad scoffed. "To Marianne? Hell yeah."

Higgs laughed. "Beat out by a pair of breasts. The world has become a sad place."

"Higgs, the day a pair of breasts *don't* beat you out, the world has taken a turn for the worse."

MARIANNE set her bag down in her office and watched as the Marines stretched on the mats. She'd been at her supervisor's office early that morning to explain her relationship with Brad, and had prayed that meant she wasn't about to get canned.

On the contrary, her supervisor had been welcoming, and said as long as she treated him the same as the others, there wouldn't be a problem. He thanked her for the honesty up front, and that was all.

For something she had been dreading for two days, the process had been relatively painless.

Now she had to handle the real problem: introducing the poor guy to her parents.

That, however, could wait. At least until they were more settled, and probably not until the tryouts of this team had concluded.

What if he doesn't make it?

The small voice had a chill running down her spine. If he was cut, he'd head straight back home to his home base.

That was across the country. How the hell would they get to know each other from across the country?

Borrowing trouble. That's all she was doing. There was no point in wishing for or worrying about things that would work themselves out later.

She unlocked the door to her training office and flipped on the lights. The sound of pounding feet outside, along with the coach's shouted instructions, told her they were off on a quick warm-up jog.

Since it seemed as though both Nikki and Levi were running behind, she started getting the water jugs ready to take upstairs herself. Just as she had the first one full and placed on the rolling cart, the two students walked in. Nikki was chattering up a storm, and Levi just looked dazzled by her presence.

She resisted rolling her eyes. Barely. "Hey, guys. Someone needs to take this upstairs."

Nikki pounced on the opportunity. Now Marianne did roll her eyes. But who was she to care? She didn't have to lug the thing up there. The beauty of minions.

"I thought I'd study for a bit, if that's okay," Levi said quietly, holding up a textbook. "I'm struggling a little in anatomy and we've got midterms coming up."

"Sure thing. Long as you're prepared to toss the book aside if I need you." She walked out to the front door of her office and saw the group of Marines heading up toward one of the stairwells, which told her they'd be doing up-and-downs as part of their warm-up.

Coach Ace wandered over toward her, his large arms crossed over his chest. "Morning, Cook."

"Good morning, Coach Ace. Have a nice day off?"

"I did. You?"

She debated saying something now about her relationship with Brad, but hesitated. Maybe Brad would want to be the one to do it. They had to tell him, though it probably wouldn't make much of a difference. She'd wait and check with Brad first.

"Not too bad. Headed down to Wilmington and . . ." She trailed off as she heard what sounded like several pairs of running shoes squeaking on concrete above and some curses. She wandered out onto the gym floor so she could look up at the catwalk. But the overhang kept her from seeing anything. Coach Ace followed.

"Is there a problem up there, men?" he called out. His voice was so deep it echoed and sounded like the voice of God in the huge gym.

"Yeah," one of the Marines said, peering over the rail. "Coach, you should come see this."

With a glance at her—Marianne shrugged and indicated she'd follow him up—Coach Ace headed for the nearest stairs. The man, for all his weight and age, was quicker than he looked, and she had to jog to keep up with him. When she walked up onto the catwalk, she immediately saw the problem.

Across one wall, near where their conditioning equipment sat, were the words "Eat Shit And Die, Jarheads," spray painted in deep red. The paint had been done so heavy-handedly, it dripped from the edges of the letters, like a bloody warning written on a mirror in a horror movie.

Tressler approached slowly, reaching out to touch it.

"Don't touch," Coach Ace barked.

Tressler shook his head as he took a few steps back. "It's dry. You can't smell the paint at all. Wasn't done recently."

"It wasn't here Saturday," Chalfant said, then flushed when people turned to look at him. "Well, it wasn't."

"Back downstairs. Now. Wait for me there." Coach Ace waited until the Marines had jogged back down the stairs they'd come up, then leaned over the railing. "Willis, need you up here."

"What do you need me to do?" Marianne asked quietly.

"Nothing. Willis will handle it." With one more dark look at the ugly words, he headed back down, Marianne trailing behind him.

She met Nikki and Levi at the bottom of the stairs.

"What's going on up there?" Nikki asked. She kicked at the full jug. "I got halfway up lugging this big-ass thing, and saw everyone heading back down. Should I take it up there still?"

"No, nobody goes upstairs." She had no clue what the MPs would make of this, but it chilled her bones a little, remembering the words written as they had been, dripping red like blood splatters. Would they chalk this up to annoying teenagers, too? Or would they see it as more of a threat? "Wait in the room. I'll be back." She wandered over to where the coach stood. Her eyes couldn't help but find Brad in the mix of Marines. He stood out to her, more so than anyone else. That was probably her heart talking, though.

"We'll head over to the track by CEB. Conditioning day." When a few Marines groaned, Coach Ace's mouth split into a wide smile. "I'd save your breath, men. You're going to need it. Grab a ride if you didn't drive. I'll see you over there in fifteen."

"I've never been over to the track before." Marianne walked alongside Coach Ace as he went to his small office on the opposite side of the gym from her training room.

"Do you know where the combat engineer battalion is?"

"Vaguely."

"Then head that direction. You can't miss the track."

"Should I bring anything special?"

"Your usual should be fine. Do you need a ride?"

"I'll drive my interns over with me. Thanks, though." She hesitated a second. "Actually, you drive a truck, right?"

He nodded absently as he bent down to open a file cabinet and grab out a folder marked, simply, "Hell." She had a feeling the Marines were in for quite the treat with their conditioning.

"Let me toss my water jugs in the bed of your truck before you take off. We've got to pack up some supplies to bring, and then we'll follow. I can lock up if—"

"No, Cartwright is going to stay here. He'll be talking to the MPs and the supervisor about that mess upstairs. Goddamn kids, they say," he muttered. "Kids don't pull shit like that." He looked up then, his dark eyes blazing with fury. "That's a problem. I hate problems. I don't accept problems. So they better not try to act like it's no big fucking deal again. Pardon the language."

"It's fine." She nodded once. "Okay, I'll have my guys toss the jugs in your truck, and then we'll follow." She left him to his mutterings and file shuffling and walked back to find two very confused, slightly intimidated interns bouncing on the balls of their feet.

"So, what's up?" Levi asked, hands in the pockets of his cargo shorts.

Nikki clapped, more excited than her counterpart. "Are we going somewhere?"

Marianne nodded. "Prepare the fanny packs, kids. We're going on a field trip."

BRAD'S left leg ached for compensating, and his right knee was crying. It had long ago left behind screaming in pain. It now just whimpered in agony, as if it knew there would be no respite anytime soon and there was no point in wasting energy.

The running sucked. But it was the stairs that did him in.

Two hours into their conditioning, Brad was ready to rip the head off whatever fucker had spray painted their catwalk. And he had a feeling almost any one of his potential teammates would hold the bastard down to give him the opportunity. They were all a hot mess. Dripping with sweat, shirts long-ago abandoned on various parts of the stadium steps and baking in the sun. They were all drooping. Shoulders were slumped and chests were heaving in an effort to keep up. "Drooping" was the only word for it.

Marianne and her interns had their hands full. They hydrated, they took temperatures and they stretched. Every time he caught sight of her in his peripheral vision, she was on the ground pulling some guy's arms up, or hovering over a guy pushing his leg to his chest, or standing over some prone guy, massaging his calf.

What he wouldn't give to feel those hands on his legs right now . . . .

His lungs were still going strong. His mind was ready to do another lap.

But his legs . . . His legs told him if he ran one more flight of stairs, they were going to give up and let him roll back down to the bottom, headfirst.

"Water break!" Coach Ace bellowed from the base of the stadium steps. They all moaned in relief. Brad let a few pass him by in order to give his leg a few extra minutes to get down without sobbing.

It worked. Barely.

He had to get it taken care of. Maybe, just maybe, he could ask Marianne to help him out quietly. If she thought it was in his best interest, and that it would keep them together—because getting cut meant he would be heading back to Twentynine Palms—then maybe she'd be willing to work with him outside the gym.

Even as he thought it, he rejected the idea. It was playing her emotions against her career. It was a shit move, and he knew it.

He'd just have to work this out on his own, without her.

He couldn't ignore the pain any longer. So he'd figure out another way.

They gathered near Coach Ace, who was on his cell phone, ignoring them. Tibbs stood next to him, practically hyperventilating, his dark face a fast-moving river of sweat.

"I don't think," he gasped out, "my conditioning is working, sir."

"Costa," Brad corrected. "And it's been one day. You can't build conditioning in one day, Tibbs. That's absurd."

"How the hell are you not breathing hard?" Tibbs squeaked out in one quick sentence before sucking in another breath.

"You keep doing that, you're going to pass out," he said mildly. "And I've always been good with distances. I'm not fast, but I can keep going."

"Do your girlfriends all call you the Energizer Bunny?" Tressler asked from behind.

"Your mom did last night," he shot back, causing several Marines to make the "ooooh, *burned*" noise.

Tressler glared at him, but kept his mouth shut.

Coach Ace finished his call and put his phone back in his pocket. "Marines, listen up."

Automatically, they all moved to parade rest.

"That was Coach Cartwright. The MPs are coming over to chat with you about anything you might have seen in the last week or so with regards to the vandalism today, and with the training room earlier. Cooperate, don't give them any reason to hate you and we can move on. We'll break here for lunch, and meet back at the gym at three."

The news of the extra-long break had most of them sighing in relief. Brad's eyes tracked to Marianne, but she wasn't focused on him. She was in the small stretch of shade the bleachers had to offer. She was crouching beside a Marine who was on the ground, a washcloth draped over his forehead, his eyes closed. She was taking his pulse, and though he couldn't hear what she said, he could see she was on her phone speaking to someone.

She was in her element. Damn, she even made that huge black fanny pack look cute.

Kind of. Okay, not really. Nobody could pull that ugly thing off; not even her.

"What the hell do you think the problem is?" Higgs asked as they walked over to get their bags. He glanced around and sighed. "Shit. Where did I leave my shirt?"

The female training intern waved her hand. "I draped them all over the fence there, so they'd dry." She batted her eyelashes. "But if you just want to keep it off, you know, for ventilation purposes, that would probably be best."

Higgs smiled absently, then walked with Brad to get their shirts. "Is it a bad sign that she makes me feel old? It's like jailbait or something."

"Technically, I doubt she's jailbait. She's gotta be at least twenty, but I know what you mean." Brad grabbed his shirt, but didn't put it on. The thing was still wet. All draping it over the fence had done was to make it wet *and* hot. He grimaced as he balled it up and tossed it in his bag. He was definitely going to need another laundry night sooner than later.

Of course, with the way he and Marianne had used the washing machine when it hit the spin cycle the night before . . . laundry was hardly a burden. He grinned at the thought.

"Wanna grab some tacos?" Higgs asked as they walked to the stadium benches. The MPs were there already, speaking to the first two Marines. "This shouldn't take long. I was hoping to eat at least seven of those, then take a good two-hour nap."

"The nap sounds good. Tacos, though, sound revolting."

He gagged as Higgs made a sound of deliciousness and rubbed his stomach. "Seriously, we just ran like nine miles, and you're going to throw taco meat in that gut?"

"Tacos are a gift from God. Don't judge." Higgs let his bag drop to the ground. "I'm about to lose another one." He nodded toward the Marine by Marianne, who was now draped with several more washcloths, over his shoulders and neck. She was speaking to the male intern, who nodded rapidly and sprinted for the gate.

"One of yours, then?"

"Yup. He wasn't going to make it either way. His attitude sucked and he cut corners. But that doesn't look good."

Even as they watched, the Marine slumped farther until Marianne called Nikki over to help lay him flat out. The stadium bleachers grew quiet as they watched Marianne dunk a full towel into one of the tubs of ice water—which had been refilled at least once by the interns—and drape it over the Marine. Another quiet minute passed while she repeatedly dunked washcloths into the icy water, then placed them under his armpits and around his neck, even stuffing a few down the guy's shorts.

He heard the distant ambulance wail, and he wondered how they'd gotten there so quickly. The hospital was at least ten minutes away—maybe six or seven minutes with no traffic and traveling with their lights running. Then he realized she must have called them before just now. She knew what she was doing. She'd seen the heatstroke coming before it hit.

The entire group, coaches included, watched while the medics hopped out, loaded the Marine onto the stretcher, and took him. Marianne sent Levi on with them, shouting a few instructions before watching them leave, hands on her hips.

He could see, even from behind, that her posture spoke of anger. He wasn't sure who she was angry at, though.

"Damn," Higgs whispered. "Hope he's going to be okay."

"Yeah," Brad murmured, but he acknowledged even then, he was hoping just as much for Marianne's sake as he was for the Marine's.

CHAPTER
15

She fought back the tears. For an hour, while she spoke to the MPs, while she spoke to the coaches, while she spoke to her supervisor and finally while she made the call to the base hospital to check on her heat-stroke Marine.

But the moment she heard he would be okay, she'd gone to her car, driven three blocks away, parked at the back of the commissary parking lot, and let the tears flow freely.

She let herself jag for a good ten minutes, then ordered herself to dry it up. He was going to be fine, and this was a hell of a learning experience—for her, and for the coaches and the athletes, too. As much as she hated thinking of it like that, she knew watching one of their own struggle with the heat would make the lecture she planned to give that much more impactful. She drove back to the gym, knowing she would find Coach Ace there. It was time to have a bit of a come-to-Jesus with him, and to accept part of the responsibility herself.

After a quick check in the flip-down mirror of her car and another minute spent with a cool water bottle over her eyes, she was ready to enter the dragon's lair. She knocked on the door frame and waited until the large man's head lifted. When he motioned her in, she sat down and waited for him to finish scribbling.

"Damn paperwork," he muttered. "Every time I lose one, I've got reams of paperwork to shit out and hand back to someone. Makes me want to keep all of them just to avoid it." When he put the final period on whatever form he was filling out, he did so with a vicious jab of the pen. When he looked up, he looked amused. "That's a total lie. I wouldn't keep some of these guys even if I had twice as much paperwork. So, Cook, I assume you're here about Johnson."

"Yes, Coach, I am. First off, I spoke to the hospital, and he's doing okay. His temp is stable and his vitals are normal. They're going to observe him a few more hours, keep him on the IV to make sure he's hydrated then let him go."

"Good, good." The chair creaked under his weight as Coach Ace leaned back and laced his hands over his stomach. "And I can tell there's more."

"There is." She took a breath; let it out slowly. "I made the mistake of not checking with you on the plans for the day. I know they were changed at the last minute, and that was unforeseen due to the . . ." She waved her hand in the general direction of the catwalk and the blood-like threat. "But the instant you made new arrangements, I should have asked you details on the location. If there was shade, if there was a place to refill our jugs. And, barring that, I should have asked for another fifteen or twenty minutes to load up a tent to bring with us. That's my mistake."

She waited, and he nodded. "I assume you're going to tell me my mistake now."

"Let's just call it . . . What Would Cook Have Done Differently?" She smiled, hoping to soften the blow. But she'd say what she had to anyway. "The temp was way too hot to pull off the conditioning exercise you did. I should have stopped you sooner, and again, that was my error."

"Seems you made several today."

That stung. But she wouldn't let it deter her. "I did. That doesn't change the fact that I'd like to work *with* you in the future on conditioning and outdoor workouts. Inside, we're shaded from the sun, and—pathetic though it feels sometimes—there's air conditioning. Plus, the training room is inches away. Out there, in a different location, I'm limited. I could have helped him better if I'd had more equipment. And he might not have needed help to begin with if you hadn't pushed them all to that point. I have no doubt that another ten minutes and I would have had four or five more Marines handling heatstroke. As it is, I think many of them will be running at half speed, max, for this evening's program."

Coach Ace watched her with his dark eyes, not moving a muscle. He really was like a ghost, as she'd heard some of the guys say in her room.

"So you want to tell me how to do my job."

"Not even a little. I want to work with you to keep your guys healthy. I think you do, too. Your openness to try things like yoga and stretching was so encouraging. I want to keep moving along that train of thought." She gave him her sweetest smile. "And think of this . . . the more Marines you keep, the less paperwork you have to do."

He barked a laugh out at that. "You've got a point. Fine. If you want to take on the extra work, check with Coach Willis tonight. He's got the list of workouts we plan before each practice. Though I'll warn you, we go off script from time to time, when an ass-kicking is warranted."

"Totally understood. I just want to be kept in the loop, that's all. And I'd also like to have about ten minutes this evening before practice begins so I can give the guys the

---

warning signs of heatstroke. Just things to look out for so they can come tell me if they're feeling any of it."

"That I can do. Ten minutes are all yours, when we start back up after break."

She stood, then sat when he waved her back down. "Yes?"

"Got a call a few minutes before you arrived from headquarters. We're normally assigned a liaison that keeps track of our business stuff when we travel. They're usually not assigned until closer toward tournament time. But with this second . . . issue," he said, eyes glancing up for a moment toward the defaced catwalk, "the brass want us to start meeting with her now. Since your room was trashed, she'll likely be coming to see you later this evening. So there's your warning."

"Sure thing. No problem." She hesitated. "Are these two incidents linked?"

"If they're not, then my mama can't cook." He winked. "And my mama's Betty Crocker's first cousin."

That made her grin. "Lucky you. I'll see you later, sir." She stepped out of the office and nearly ran into Brad. "Oh!"

"Hey." He grabbed her upper arms and squeezed lightly. "You okay?"

"No harm done." She smiled, but he kept watching her with those careful eyes, and she felt her lip start to tremble.

No, no, absolutely unacceptable. Pull it together, Cook.

"I'm fine. Johnson will be fine, and that makes it easier. I made mistakes, though." And part of her wondered why she'd made them. Was it because she was distracted? Had the spray painted catwalk been to blame? Or Brad?

No, as far as that was concerned, she knew without a doubt that Brad, and their relationship, had nothing to do with the mistake. She'd made the error, no question. But not because of Brad.

"That's good, that's good." He rubbed her arms and shoulders lightly. "We all need to be more careful about getting overheated. It's not your fault."

Just then, Marianne wanted nothing more than to let her forehead drop to his chest and give herself five minutes of relief from the negative thoughts still swirling around in her mind. But here was definitely not the place, and now wasn't the time. So she took a steadying breath instead and stepped back. She started to offer to eat lunch with him in her training room, but caught sight of two more Marines over Brad's shoulder, heading straight for them.

"Okay, so, I'll see you later."

"Later tonight?" He watched her intently. She nodded. "Okay. See you later." He stepped around her and knocked on the coach's door, asking if he had a moment. As Brad stepped in, she took another deep breath.

"Hey, Cook." Higgs stopped beside her, with another Marine whose name she struggled to recall. The dark hair and tanned skin hinted at a Greek ancestry, though she wasn't sure his last name had sounded too Greek.

"Hi. Here to see me, or Coach?"

"Neither." The darker-haired one smiled, and she swore her own heart leapt just a little. Good Lord, he was handsome. As if understanding she was struggling to place his name, he added helpfully, "Sweeney."

"Sweeney, right. Sorry." She fought for a self-deprecating grin. "I suck at names. I'm just enjoying being able to yell out 'Hey, Marine!' and have an entire roomful look my way. Quite an ego boost."

They both laughed, but she noted both their eyes strayed toward the coach's door.

Then it hit her.

"You're here for Brad. Costa," she corrected quickly. Not quick enough, though.

"He's in there, talking to Coach. We just thought we'd

be here to take him out for lunch afterward." Higgs stepped aside. "We won't keep you."

So polite. She nodded her head a little in acknowledgment. "Have a good break, boys. See you later. And make sure you rehydrate and stretch!" she called out over her shoulder.

BRAD walked out of the room, rubbing a hand over his hot neck. The coach had been pretty laid-back about the whole thing—even appreciative that he'd come straight out and explained it rather than sneaking around like moronic teenagers playing at *Romeo and Juliet*.

Coach's words, not Brad's. Apparently Coach Ace had a pair of "moronic teenagers" at home and knew the damage they could inflict.

He caught sight of Higgs and Sweeney hanging by the coach's door in the gym. "What the hell are you guys doing here?"

"Moral support," Sweeney said simply. "We weren't sure how that was going to go, so we thought we'd be here to put out any flames."

Higgs walked a circle around him. "No smoldering clothes, no obvious burn marks. Must have gotten out unscathed."

Brad pushed at Higgs' shoulder. "I'm fine. It was fine." Then he blinked. "How do you both know what I was about to do?"

"I'm a genius," his roommate said. "And Sweeney there's a mind reader."

"Uh-huh." He started for the door.

"Mostly," Sweeney said, falling in step with him, "I just wanted to be here to say it was cool, in case it was necessary. I mean, I doubt our input matters that much to the coach, even if he made us group leaders. But if he started pulling some *This is an unfair advantage* crap on you, we were ready to go in and back you up."

"Like a couple of Beyoncé's backup dancers." When Sweeney and Brad both halted to stare at Higgs, he grinned. "'All the single ladies, all the single ladies.'"

Sweeney reached around Brad's back and kicked Higgs' knee so it gave out and made him stumble. "Don't say stupid shit like that again. That was awful."

"I appreciate the support," Brad said, putting the conversation back in perspective, "but it didn't come to that. He knows both Marianne and I are mature adults and can handle ourselves."

They were both quiet a moment. "That's all we get?" Higgs asked.

"Yup." That's all it really was, truthfully. Coach Ace had had very little to say on the subject.

"Come on." Higgs slung his arm around Brad's neck so he couldn't escape, and started walking toward the parking lot. "We're going to Sweeney's for lunch and a nap."

"You're kidding me."

"Do you know when the last time I had a good couch nap was?" Higgs sighed, like he was thinking of a long-lost lover. "I miss my couch. Napping on a bed isn't nearly as restful. Wonder why that is?"

"Your body's conditioned to think it's settling in for eight hours of REM-cycle sleep. So when you get up after an hour, it feels cheated."

Higgs and Brad both stared at Sweeney. "No shit?" Higgs asked.

Sweeney shrugged. "I don't know—I just made that shit up."

"Lawyers," Higgs muttered. "You're lucky you've got a house with a grill, or we could never be friends."

"Thank God," Sweeney said dryly.

"Could you two Golden Girls knock it off? We've got

less than three hours before we have to be back. No way in hell can we waste that on a freaking nap."

Higgs got to his car and pushed Brad into the passenger seat. Sweeney crawled in the back. "Why not?" Sweeney's head popped between the two front seats. "What else were you gonna do? Go running in this heat?"

"Watch training videos, or . . ." Brad ran out of options. The other man was right. It wasn't like he could safely work out in the heat. He'd be exhausted for evening practice, which was the opposite of the point. "I don't know. Hit up a salad bar or something."

"I've got lettuce," Sweeney said. Then he glanced to the side, mentally considering the contents of his fridge. "I think."

"Let's try an easier one. Do you have a frozen pizza?" Higgs asked as he started his car.

"Well, duh."

"Then we're good."

"I'm surrounded by children. Children who can't eat properly without Mommy or Daddy forcing vegetables down their throats."

"We could put olives on the pizza," Sweeney suggested. "I might have a jar of olives somewhere in my pantry."

Brad let his head fall into his hands as the other two laughed. But he was fighting back a smile himself as they pulled out of the back gate and headed toward Sweeney's house.

CHAPTER

16

"So, in closing," Marianne said, lifting the last sheet of her poster board back to the chair she'd set up as a makeshift easel, "if you feel any of these symptoms, stop what you're doing and immediately come to me. I'll be able to work with you and determine whether a headache is just a headache, or the start of something more serious. Heatstroke is no joke."

She grinned when a few of them groaned good-naturedly at her lame rhyme. They'd really love the fact that the pamphlets she'd created during her break had "*Heatstroke Is No Joke*" as the title. A pamphlet could be funny and informative at the same time.

"I'm not a poet. But I'm here to support you all, and I'm not going to let you down. I'm doing my best, so give me some help and don't make me look bad in front of the boss." She nodded to Coach Willis, who stood off to the side. "There are going to be some heatstroke pamphlets sitting on the stool outside my office. I say this because I know you will all be dying to get one. You love my pamphlets. Don't lie."

A Marine in the back made a gagging motion. She ignored that.

With a sigh, she added, "Anyone who can recite the preventative measures outlined in the pamphlet to me tomorrow morning gets a cookie."

There was enthusiastic cheering at that.

Sometimes, you just had to bribe a guy.

"Thanks, Coach. I'll get out of your way."

She started to pick up the poster boards, then a few of them scattered. She bent to pick them up, and the nearest Marine also bent over to grab a few. It was Higgs, and he waited until she was ready to carry the ones he'd picked up, then handed them over with a wink.

That was no ordinary flirtatious wink. That was *I know about you and my roommate, and it's cool* code.

Or it was *I'm being a good guy and helping you out* code and she was being a freak.

"Higgs," Coach Willis barked. "Help Cook carry those posters to the training room, then get your ass back here. We've got work to do that doesn't involve pop quizzes and cookies."

Marianne ignored the sarcasm. Coach Ace had seemed okay with it, but the other two coaches acted like it was a waste of time. Such was her life. People either thought she was a waste of oxygen and athletic funds, or that the fate of the entire world depended on her fixing a broken leg with Scotch tape and toilet paper during halftime. There was no middle ground.

Higgs gathered the last of her poster boards, then waited for her to pick up her tote bag.

"Nice presentation." Higgs looked down at the boards. "I haven't seen these things since I did my last science project in high school."

"I'd have had something better, but it was sort of last-minute." She had a gorgeous PowerPoint presentation—animated with GIFs, even—that she'd used in one of her final projects in college. But where the hell she was going to project that in the dim gym, she'd never know. So she'd resorted to scurrying over to the exchange, begging the Marine she'd recognized in the parking lot to help her purchase the boards and Sharpies since she didn't have a military ID, and then hurrying back to scribble down the bullet points. Nikki, though, had been *super* helpful when she'd come in half an hour ago. The presentation wouldn't have been complete without those little flower doodles in the corners.

Nothing said *Please take me seriously* quite like flower vine doodles.

"I just wanted to say," Higgs started as he followed her into the room, "that Sweeney and I know about you and Costa. But we're not saying anything. Your business is your business."

She froze, then turned to look at him. "You know . . . what?" How much did they know?

"That you guys are . . ." He held up his hands, as if embarrassed that she was making him say it. "I don't know . . . together. An item. A thing. Dating."

"He told you this?" That surprised her. For all that Brad was now more open and relaxed with her, he didn't seem to have reached that same level with his teammates.

"He told me nothing. But I figured it out. I'm a quick study." He winked again, then turned and almost ran into a woman. "Whoa, sorry, ma'am."

"That's okay." She took a step back quickly out of his steadying grip and tugged on the jacket of her suit to straighten it. "No harm done."

"Later, Cook. Ma'am," he said, hand to his forehead like he was pulling at a hat. Sarcastic cutie.

She gave him a dry smile, and Marianne waved before

sliding the poster boards behind a file cabinet to keep them out of the way, then went to start filling the jugs. Levi wasn't coming in, and Nikki had jumped on the chance to help a few Marines stretch, so she was SOL on grunt work. But first, she had to deal with the suit.

"Can I help you?"

"Marianne Cook?"

She stopped filling the jug with ice and glanced up. "Yeah, that's me."

"Hi." The woman's smile warmed a little and she walked forward. Marianne wanted to warn her not to come closer in those kick-ass high heels. The laminate was often wet in patches and a serious hazard to anyone not wearing grip soles. But she was already across the room in three long-legged strides. "I'm Reagan Robilard. Team liaison for the duration. I wanted to introduce myself and talk about what happened here last week."

"Oh, right. Of course." She grabbed a towel, wiped her hands down and shook hands. "Sorry, Coach Ace warned me you'd be coming in and it totally slipped my mind. Rough day."

"Yes, I heard. I also heard the Marine was going to be fine, thanks to your quick work."

Marianne fought to blink back the tears once more. What the hell was wrong with her? She'd never been this emotional about work before. "Honestly, I feel a little guilty about it. But that's not why you're here. What's up?"

She nodded, as if accepting that Marianne wasn't ready to talk about it. Then she started wandering the room slowly. Marianne let her, but kept an eye on her. If she started touching things or moving stuff around, game over.

"I'm here to see how you've coped with putting the room back to rights. But frankly, it looks like nothing ever happened. You've done well."

"Maintenance did the majority of the work. I just restocked. They deserve the credit. It was a bitch to clean."

She nodded absently, stopping to view a few motivational quotes Marianne had printed off on pretty stationery paper and taped to one wall. "Cute. I needed to know if you were capable, but from today's events, I'd say yes. I'd also say you cared very much about this job, and about the guys you were tasked with watching over."

"I always care about doing my best work." She scooped another load of ice into the bucket. If she didn't get this done soon, it'd just be tepid water. "Is there anything specific I can answer?"

"I'll be honest. I didn't mean to, but I overheard your conversation with the man who was just in here."

"Higgs," Marianne said, as she scooped more ice in. "That was Higgs."

"Hmm. And he was referencing you dating someone else. Another Marine?"

Marianne's arm slowed for a few seconds, but she forced herself to keep scooping. "Bradley Costa. He's a member of the team."

"Potential member."

"Okay, yes. Potential member." She tossed the scoop back in the plastic sleeve on the side for drainage and let the ice machine's lid snap closed. "Is there a point?"

"I assume you've disclosed this relationship?" The woman's smile looked concerned, a little strained, like she was fighting to keep it in place.

"I did, with my supervisor—who I assume is also your supervisor—and Costa has spoken to Coach Ace. We've addressed it, and have been assured by both sides that it was not a problem."

"I understand. And I don't want there to be a problem, either." Suddenly, the woman's icy cold demeanor seemed to slide away, and she slumped in Marianne's rolling desk chair. The chair skidded a foot away and she grabbed for the desk to steady herself. "I'm sorry. I'm doing a real shit job here."

Marianne snorted at that. The polish rubbed away, revealing a slightly frazzled young woman in a really killer outfit. Marianne hopped up onto the nearest table and let her legs swing. The heels of her running shoes bounced gently against the side. "First day on the job?"

"I wasn't supposed to start for another three weeks. I got called off vacation. This is my first time doing this and . . ." She scooped a stray brunette wisp of hair back behind her ear. "I'm lost. Can I say that to you?" She looked up with big brown eyes a little wild with confusion.

Marianne laughed and nodded. "Yeah, you can. I'm a little lost too, on some things. Nice shoes, by the way."

Reagan held one foot out to study the black shoe with silver filigree swirled around the heel. "They hurt like hell, but I wanted to look good for my first day." She grimaced and looked up at Marianne's outfit. "I think I overdressed."

"I think you look nice. But . . ." She took one last look at the shoes, then the tidy, perfectly tailored suit. "Maybe. If you're going to be around here, walking around the gym in those things is going to kill your feet. Should we discuss the effects of high heels on your arches? I have a pamphlet I could bring you."

"Let's not and say we did. My world without high heels wouldn't be worth living." She sighed and settled back. "Sorry I came on so bitchy earlier. I've got nerves, and then resting bitch face added to it."

"Resting bitch face?" She couldn't help but laugh, then hopped down and started filling the jug with water to go with the ice.

"Yeah. You know, when your face just naturally rests in a scowl, but you're not actually thinking negative thoughts? So people automatically think you're making a pissed-off face, when you're not doing anything but considering whether to have steak or seafood for dinner." Reagan let her face smooth out, then her brows naturally drew down a little. "See?"

Marianne snickered. "Sorry, but that's sort of funny."

"Funny for you, maybe. Not funny for me, when everyone assumes I'm a bia!" She sighed. "Okay, so you've got everything under control here. Nothing odd to report, or any suspicions on who wrecked the training room?"

"It was kids, I thought." Not that she'd fully bought the theory, but it helped her sleep at night. She lugged the jug to the cart, faltered, then breathed a sigh of relief when Reagan reached the other side and helped her slide it on. "Thanks. And . . . that's why you should probably pick a new outfit tomorrow."

Reagan glanced down to see a big water spot on the front of her jacket. "It'll dry. The MPs said it was kids when it was just a big mess in your training room. Now they're thinking it might be tied to whoever left the nasty note upstairs."

Marianne raised a brow. Reagan shrugged. "I saw photos. My job is to keep things running smoothly and make sure none of this crap gets leaked to the press. It can get ugly quickly. People have a hair trigger when the more physical sports are mentioned to begin with. You add in the military, and protesters start rubbing their hands together, salivating."

Marianne understood that one. She'd lived in Jacksonville long enough to have seen her fair share of protests outside the front gate. Some had been small, barely worth mentioning in the local paper. Others had been national news.

Levi walked in at that moment. Despite the fact that he wasn't scheduled, Marianne gladly waved him over. "You've got mail." She rolled the jug toward him, and he caught it easily. "Push that out there, would ya?"

He grunted a reply, tossed his book bag down on a bench, grabbed a sleeve of cups on the way out and left.

"How about your interns? How are they?"

"Your average college students. Little bit of focus, lots of daydreaming and—for Nikki—ogling. Pretty standard."

"I was a college student until like a month ago," Reagan said dryly.

Whoops. "Sorry, you look older."

"Six-year plan, and then some. Not the point." She tapped her toe on the ground for a moment. "Guess I'm off to the races to figure out where to go from here. Thanks for taking the time to talk to me."

"Have fun," Marianne said with a wave. "Resting bitch face," she said to herself with a laugh and went to create a new pamphlet about the effects of alcohol on an athlete's body.

"FAVORITE color."

Brad didn't hesitate. "Green. You?"

"Tied between blue and turquoise."

Brad's spoon halted halfway to the bowl of ice cream they were sharing. And in this case, *"sharing"* meant Marianne was eating most of it and pushing his spoon out of the way for the good chunks with the cookie dough in them. It was cute. "That's the same color."

"No it's not." She knocked his stationary spoon aside and dug out another bite with chocolate chip cookie dough in it. "They're completely separate things. Check a crayon box sometime."

"Your leading argument is based on a three-year-old's craft supply? Weak." He snagged a good bite for himself and ignored her pout. "You were the one who didn't want to get your own bowl. Suck it up and share like a big girl."

"You're in training. Why are you even eating ice cream?" She took up a spoonful too big for her own mouth, and pointed it at him. "I offered to split a bowl because that's what girls do. We offer to share food because it makes us feel more delicate and dainty. Then you were graciously supposed to say no, you couldn't, but go ahead and have some anyway, please. And then I would have my bowl to myself and not worry about feeling fat. *Everybody* knows that. But you ruined it by agreeing to share. Then I was stuck sharing. You locked me in and broke the rule."

"Who the hell made up that stupid rule?"

"God."

"Jesus H.," he muttered, then took another bite, even though he was full. Just because. "Don't offer if you don't want to share."

"Have none of your other girlfriends trained you yet?" She took the bowl from where it sat between them on the couch and held it in her lap, conveniently out of reach from his own spoon.

"I've never had a long-term girlfriend."

She looked horrified at that. "Did I pop your girlfriend cherry?"

He laughed so hard at that his stomach cramped.

"Wasn't meant to be funny. I don't have time to house-break you, you know. Nobody told me I'd be starting from scratch with you." She stared at the wall in wonder. "Seriously, a relationship virgin? Why am I being punished?"

"I'll do my best to keep up to your standards," he managed to gasp. God, she cracked him up. "Brothers or sisters?"

"None." She looked sad for a moment. "I wanted them. Not sure why my parents didn't have any more. But it's not my business to ask, so . . ." She shrugged. "You?"

"I've got a younger brother and a younger half sister.

Brother in college, sister—because the *half* never really mattered—in high school." He held out a hand for the bowl; she studiously ignored him. "You can take them both, if you want. I'd love to be an only child for a while."

"Grass is greener," she sang and took another spoonful. "I'm sorry, did you want to share this?"

"We already established—"

"That you aren't housebroken yet, I know." She patted his leg gently with a sad look. "We'll work on it."

"No, honey, you go ahead. I don't need to share your ice cream," he said robotically. She rewarded him with a tiny spoonful.

"Perfect." She ate the last bite, then placed the bowl on the coffee table and reorganized herself so her back pressed against his chest. He wrapped his arms around her, hands resting comfortably on her stomach. "We could watch a movie."

"It's getting late. I won't last through an entire movie."

"It's barely nine," she said, then sighed. "Forgot. Sorry. Early conditioning."

He rubbed a circle over her stomach, his hand grazing the tops of her thighs, then lightly running over her groin until he squeezed. "You could always tuck me in."

"I could do that." She sat up. "I think I've got a CD with some lullabies somewhere in one of my boxes."

"Smart-ass." He blinked. "You've still got boxes? I thought you were done unpacking."

"I always think I am, then I find another one. I've just stuffed a lot of them in the second bedroom closet, or in random nooks and crannies. I don't know how long I'll be here anyway, so . . ." She shook her head to end the thought. "Come back. Let's get in bed."

Now there was an idea he couldn't dismiss. He stood and followed her back. As she walked, she loosened the string to her pajama bottoms and walked out of them, leaving them in a pool on the hallway floor. Her panties followed, then her shirt, until she was totally naked in her bedroom. "You forgot to strip down, too," she chided as she pushed his shirt over his head.

Her breasts pillowed against his chest, hard nipples poking into him. He kissed her, running his fingers up her neck and into her hair. He loved how light it felt, like feathers in his hands. He loved the way she tasted. The way her body responded automatically to his, softening for him.

He felt the softness as his hands parted her thighs, then her sex, and dipped two fingers in. She was ready for him. Marianne moaned into his mouth, her hips jutting against his hand to make him go faster. He didn't; he just kept a slow and steady pace. His forearms were sore from the bag workout earlier, but the burn as she moaned and clenched around his fingers was only more erotic.

He walked her backward to the bed, pressing her down and resting on top of her. So far, she had taken charge in their sexual exploits, and he'd let her. Mostly because he loved watching her on top, exerting her control and doing whatever the hell pleased her the most in that moment. Watching her ice-blue eyes haze with climax was one of the sexiest things he'd ever witnessed.

But tonight, he needed to be in charge.

He removed his shorts and boxers, coughing to cover a hiss of pain when he twisted his knee in the wrong direction. She didn't notice and instead kept doing that wonderful thing where she smoothed her hands over his back, scratching every so often. He grabbed a condom from her bedside drawer, put it on and plunged in. His arms burned from holding him up; his knee screamed from the constant motion. But there was no switching now. No way in hell.

She arched into him, rolled left and right between his arms. Her breasts press into his forearms before she raised her hands up to cup them and toy with her own nipples.

"Aw, Jesus H.," he muttered. That was the end of his plan for endurance. In the sack with Marianne, apparently, he was doomed to endurance failure. The woman turned him inside out.

"I'm coming," she warned with a whisper, then fisted around him until she cried out.

He followed her into his own climax, nothing but grateful for having her reach her peak seconds before him. Pure luck.

The second he was finished, he half collapsed on top of her. His arms were jelly.

"Brad!" she shrieked when he blew a raspberry against her neck. "How the hell do you get so sweaty after ten minutes?"

"You light me on fire, baby."

She groaned at the horrible line, and he smiled against her skin. "Just call me a furnace. Can't help it. I'd sweat sitting in a walk-in freezer."

"Well, Furnace, your ass is still in the air. Toss the condom and let's snuggle."

"Can't. Arms are immobile. Speed bag did me in tonight."

She huffed. "You can't stay here forever. I'm rolling you over."

He grunted. "I've got it. Damn, woman, give a man a minute to recover from mind-blowing sex, why don't ya?"

"Mind-blowing, or arm-blowing?" She grinned up at him as he struggled to his hands again. He watched her for a moment, smiling up at him, her cool blonde hair bed-rumpled behind her, ice-blue eyes shining, and fell headfirst in love.

Unable to say anything past the lump in his throat, he kissed her nose. Later. When he didn't have a spent condom to deal with.

He went to straighten his legs and hop off the bed when

his right knee locked completely. Having already distrib-
uted his weight to step down, but unable to fully straighten
his leg to put his foot on the floor, he collapsed off the side
of the bed.

Jesus H.

"Brad?" Marianne's voice was questioning, and maybe
a little amused. "Are your legs jelly, too?"

"Apparently," he muttered, trying to straighten his right
leg. It only worked about ninety percent. The last ten wouldn't
budge. It was as if there were a roadblock in front of his
kneecap preventing him from straightening completely.

"Brad?"

"Just gimme a sec. Sore," he said through gritted teeth.
He removed the condom before he made a mess and tied
it off just as she popped her head over the edge of the bed.

"Problem?"

"Hit my funny bone," he lied without hesitation. The
fact that he still didn't hesitate to lie made his stomach roil.

"That sucks. Want some ice for it?" She grinned. "Look
at that. You're getting preferential treatment after all." She
jumped down and raced to the hallway buck naked. "I'll
bring back a baggie!"

With her out of the room, he shot to his feet and hobbled
to the bathroom and closed the door behind him. He
debated for a moment, then sat on the toilet seat and turned
the shower on. She wouldn't bust in on him taking a
shower. Wasn't her style.

Brad stepped in and let the hot water beat down on his
knee. After five minutes, he was able to slowly bend it all
the way back, then straighten it fully after a sharp pop. He
massaged the thigh just above, shifting his kneecap a little.
The grinding, clicking sensation was back again, and
worse than ever.

There was no way he could let this go on any longer.
He had to make an appointment off base. Maybe it was

nothing and a round of cortisone shots would clear him up. If that was the case, he could "admit" to the pain, let her diagnose him, and they could all move on.

He heard her reenter the bedroom with his ice and, knowing she would be waiting for him with a smile and a soothing touch, he dunked his head under the water and prayed that was all it would be. He'd started the journey toward the team risking only his chance to box. Now, he was risking his heart, too.

CHAPTER

17

The next afternoon, Marianne met up with Kara for lunch. Her friend had brought over bagged lunches to eat in her training room. Grinning, Marianne hopped up on a table and opened the bag with glee. "You coming over for afternoon yoga with the guys is the best thing that's ever happened to me."

"Oh, is it?" her friend asked with a laugh, sitting more delicately on the second table and opening her own bag.

"A healthy, hand-delivered lunch, girl talk, and the knowledge that I get to watch a bunch of Marines struggle through yoga poses in a couple hours?" Marianne held the Saran-wrapped sandwich aloft. "Hell yeah!"

"You're supposed to keep them healthy, not laugh at them."

"Laughter is good for the soul."

"I don't think laughter is what put that happy glow in your soul." Kara leaned forward. "Something else is up. What is it?"

Thank God they were alone in the building—minus Coach Ace in his office, which was on the opposite side of the gym. "I think I'm in love."

"Think?" Kara sat back and wrinkled her nose before picking out a baby carrot. "Wouldn't you know?"

"It's too soon to say for sure. I've known the guy for like two weeks!"

"When you know," Kara said in a singsongy voice, "you know."

Marianne sighed. "Fine. I know I'm in love. I just didn't want to say it in case my mother heard and busted through the wall like the Kool-Aid Man. The woman can smell potential romance in the air like a hound dog chasing after an escaped convict."

Kara laughed at the imagery. "That's quite the picture you've painted for Mary."

"Mary is a woman all to her own. And at least here, I know she's not going to walk in and catch me with my proverbial pants down." She told her friend about the scattered condoms in her apartment, which sent Kara howling with laughter.

"Oh . . ." Kara wiped tears away with her knuckles. "Oh my . . . I have no words."

"I believe the word you're looking for is 'horrified.'" Marianne bit into a carrot with an extra vicious snap. "I have to keep her far away from Brad as long as possible. The instant she hears I'm dating a Marine . . . *bam*." She smacked her hands together. "In comes Mary to tell me how to handle it. *Wear this outfit, don't wear that. Sweetie, do you think a stud like that would care for your hair all pulled back like that? How soon do you think you'll start having gorgeous babies? Your eggs won't stay fresh forever.*"

"You do look nice with your hair down," Kara conceded, then held up her hands in surrender when Marianne gave her a death stare. "But I understand it's practical to keep it up at work. No arguments." She glanced at Marianne's baggy outfit. "Is this assigned wear, or do you dress all mannish on purpose?"

"I have to wear the shirt. It was the smallest size they had." A unisex medium, which was more like a medium-large for a woman, swallowed her, especially when she usually wore a women's small. "The pants are just . . . what I wear. They make it easy to bend and move around without showing off any butt crack. That's a real deal breaker."

"I can imagine." Kara brushed at her own yoga pants, which molded perfectly to her long legs. "And I suppose something tighter—"

"Wouldn't be appropriate for the training room," Marianne finished. "If I'm not doing yoga, I shouldn't be wearing yoga pants. How's Zach?"

Kara's eyes clouded. "Another week, another late call from the sperm donor. He's crushed, and pretending not to be, which is almost as heartbreaking as if he'd just had a good cry on my lap. But he's '*too old*' for that now." She used quote fingers for emphasis. "He's got Man of the House complex and thinks everything is on him. We had a leaking sink—just a drip. I was going to go out and buy a new washer to replace it, but he was convinced he had to do it himself."

She sighed and ran a hand through her hair. It was still down, flowing beautifully around her shoulders, though Marianne knew she'd tie it up with the hair tie around her wrist once their class started. "Part of me wants to be proud he's reacting so maturely, and the other half wants to shake him and say, *You're still a kid, so act like it. Get in trouble, get dirty, come home late.*"

"Ah, all the things I would have loved to hear as a child." Marianne sighed wistfully. "He'll be okay. He's got you to watch over him. Any word on the egg test?"

"Failed," Kara said simply, crumpling her lunch bag. Marianne didn't push. Allergies were rough for her to handle. Not as the mom, because Kara managed to go with the flow on all her son's dietary restrictions. But Marianne knew, with every failed allergy test, she hurt for her son. The more restricted his diet, the more difficult it was for him to have normal experiences in everything from birthday parties to a simple afternoon snack at a friend's house.

Reagan Robilard walked by at that moment, did a double take and knocked on the door frame. "Okay if I come in?"

Marianne waved her in. Today, Reagan wore kitten heels, which made Marianne shake her head. But they were paired with simple tan pants and a button-down shirt with more airy cap sleeves. The look was still business-appropriate, without being as stuffy. Definitely more comfortable for the hot, humid gym.

"Good timing." Marianne introduced Reagan to Kara. "Kara here is leading the guys in some yoga before the afternoon practice."

"Pilates today, actually." Kara stretched her legs out on the table. "Coach Ace called yesterday and asked if I could handle the switch. Said he wanted to show the guys some moves so they could work on them at home."

Reagan rubbed her hands together. "Perfect! I'll take some photos to have ready. Marines doing yoga and Pilates? Gold mine for good press." When Kara blinked, Reagan explained, "I'm the team liaison."

"Oh." Kara said it simply, though Marianne could tell her friend had no clue what all that encompassed. "Well, if you want to stick around, that's fine. You could join in, too, if you wanted."

Reagan looked down, then back up with a smile. "I think I'll pass this time. Maybe with some extra warning." She waved and headed out again.

"She's going to break an ankle," Kara said.

"Yup."

"Have you warned her about that?"

"Yup."

"Given her the 'High Heels Ruin Feet' pamphlet?"

"Offered."

"Guess it's on her, then."

"Yup."

AS Marianne made the rounds at the back of the room, adjusting positions along with Kara's directions, she passed by Coach Willis. "By my count, we're down two Marines. What happened?"

"Ambrois went home this afternoon. Tapped out himself."

"Oh." She made a mental note to hand his file to Coach Ace after practice so he could include it with the final paperwork. "And Costa?" she asked, praying her voice sounded casual.

If Coach Willis thought it was odd she didn't know where her own boyfriend was, he didn't act like it. "Said he had a dental appointment that couldn't wait. Toothache or something. He'll be around later."

"Right, okay. Sure." Coach Willis moved on without another word, and she breathed a sigh of relief she'd escaped that without any questioning stares.

But why hadn't Brad texted her to say as much? That's what people in a relationship did, right? They told each other things like, "Hey, won't see you later, got a dentist appointment." Even with something that benign, he had to know she'd wonder.

A Marine torquing his spine in a dangerous position forced her mind back to the present. "Whoa there. That's not the way."

She pushed Brad from her mind and focused on the task

at hand. She could handle twenty Marines now, and one Marine later.

BRAD stared at the handout on his lap. "Exactly what does a torn meniscus mean?"

"It's a guess, not an official diagnosis. We'd need an MRI for that, and we can't do one until the day after tomorrow. But between feeling the click just now and hearing your symptoms . . ." The doctor sat down on his stool to scribble a few notes. "It's fairly textbook. If it were an ACL tear, I'd be more concerned. But the meniscus might be rehabable without surgery."

No surgery was a good thing. A great thing. "So what, keep icing and all that?"

"For starters, you'll need six weeks of rest, no strenuous physical activity. Then we've got to deal with physical therapy for a few months, in addition to the rest. We can go from there, monitoring how you feel and—"

"There's no way," Brad said firmly. "I work out every day, heavily. I can't rest. Not now."

The doctor sighed and rubbed at his forehead, and Brad knew exactly what the older man was seeing. Some arrogant son of a bitch who came in for an opinion and was throwing it back in his face, wasting everyone's time.

"Look, doc." Brad stepped down from the exam table gingerly. "I'm in the middle of important tryouts. I don't have the option of postponing. This isn't like being a runner, where there's always another marathon somewhere a month from now. This is it. My only shot. I need something to just get me through. Cortisone shots or whatever."

"Then . . ." The doctor waved him back and stared at the wall for a moment. "You understand this isn't my first recommendation. That what I'm about to say is not my first choice in treatment."

"Yes." This sounded promising.

"After the MRI, we'll get you fitted for a knee brace, put you on light exercise and—"

"Light won't work."

"If you're not willing to follow orders, then I'm not entirely sure what I can do for you." The doctor stood, sending the rolling stool across the room. "Good luck to you."

Brad leaned against the exam table and let his head fall back. He was in too deep. He couldn't handle this himself. He had to call Marianne. She'd know what to do, who to send him to so he could get this taken care of.

But then he'd be putting her in the middle of something ugly. *Hey, I know we've been dating like two weeks, but please straddle this shady line of workplace ethics and keep this secret from your boss for me. Okay, thanks.*

Thanks, life, for the impossible choice.

Be honest with her, and ask her to be dishonest at work. Or lie to her, but give her the deniability.

Or the third choice: be honest with her, and let the chips fall where they may.

Was he ready for that yet? Ready to accept that he would willingly be putting this dream of his in her hands?

Maybe. Maybe he was. But he'd still have to think about it.

A cute nurse walked in then, flipping through the clipboard that held the thin sheets of paper that made up his file. "Mister . . . Costa." She glanced up and gave him a once-over. Despite being in full civilian attire, there was no way she didn't recognize him as a Marine. She confirmed it when she asked, "I don't see your insurance information here. We do accept Tricare. We just need your military ID and the name of your primary care manager and we can work that out."

"Paying cash," he said shortly, which made her blink. But she didn't miss more than a beat.

"Then I'll lead you up to the front office to check out."

He stopped her with a hand on her arm as she started to walk out. "Where would I go for physical therapy?"

THE couch remembered her.

It was the most ridiculous thought, but it made Marianne smile anyway as she sat down in the same spot on the same couch she'd spent a great deal of her high school years using. Whether she'd been reading, studying, playing around with her laptop or watching a movie with her father, this had been her spot. Just like her father and mother both had their own spots in the family room.

"I think the dent's still there," her father said from his position on the recliner. The leg rest was popped up and the back reclined until he was nearly horizontal. Just like always.

She wriggled her butt a little on the cushion. "Feels like it."

"Oh, stop that," Mary said as she passed, swatting at her daughter's arm. Then she handed her a mug of coffee—lightened just how she preferred it—and a small plate of homemade cookies. "Now what made you stop by tonight?"

"She wanted to steal some food and use her dent," her father filled in. "Don't you remember us popping in unexpectedly to see your parents when we were hungry and poor?"

"Okay, first off, I'm not poor," she corrected.

"Mary, take those cookies back. The girl's not poor."

Marianne wrapped her arm around the plate balanced on her knee. "My cookies."

Her father grinned. Her mother just rolled her eyes.

Marianne took a big bite of a cookie. Around the mouthful, she reiterated, "Not poor. But I'll admit to hungry. Store-bought cookies are no substitute, Mom."

"So come get them more often, sweetheart." Mary leaned forward. "How's work? Meeting anyone?"

Oh, so they were going to play *that* game. The "I Didn't Catch You With Condoms" game. Mary liked to consider herself a modern woman, but knew Marianne's father would hate hearing his little girl was getting some on her own time. "I meet anywhere from ten to twenty someones regularly. I ice them, stretch them, wrap them . . ." When her mother scowled, she blinked innocently. "Not what you meant?"

"I meant anyone to date. With all that delicious eye candy at work, I find it hard to believe you haven't jumped on the chance to score one of those for yourself."

She nearly swallowed the second half of the cookie before she'd chewed. It was rather scary how close her mother was to the identity of her condom-user. "'Score one of those.'" She turned to her father. "Really, Dad? This is the stock I come from?"

"Genetics are a mystery," he said, and turned the TV on. Marianne hoped that would be the end of that, but he muted the damn thing.

"Ignore him, and keep going." Mary touched her daughter's knee lightly to indicate she was listening.

"Work's really interesting, actually. The coach is down for alternative workouts, like Pilates and yoga. Kara's been helping me. You remember Kara, right Daddy?"

"Sure do. She's got a son . . . Dax."

"Zach, but yes to the rest. She comes in and does yoga with the guys. It's pretty hilarious, to be honest."

Mary grinned at that. "All those yummy butts in the air for downward dog? I can imagine it's more than hilarious."

"Mom. Dad's right there."

"I'm immune," he said, waving it off with the hand clutching the remote. "They might have yummy butts, but she comes home every night to me."

Mary reached over and patted her husband's knee.

Marianne wasn't sure whether to be encouraged at her parents' love and affection or to mime gagging, like Zach would. Fine line. "Anyway, I was just feeling a little restless, and it's too late to head to Kara's. Zach's got a strict bedtime."

"So interesting, that your high school friends are becoming parents now," Mary said, not at all smoothly.

"Yes, so interesting that *one* friend from high school—who was two years ahead of me—is a mother." Marianne rolled her eyes and picked up another cookie.

"Children are such a blessing. And when you get to share those children with a man you love . . ."

"Mmm, so good," Marianne broke in, moaning loudly. "These cookies are amazing."

"Marianne."

"They're delicious. So yummy."

"Mari—"

"I'd have a baby with this cookie."

"Marianne!"

Her father wheezed out a laugh, causing the recliner to heave him forward. Mary shot her an irritated look.

"Sorry, Mom. But come on, you're coming on a little strong." *Especially when I'm trying to hide from you that I'm in love already.* "Just let me do my own thing, like an adult, and stuff will fall into place."

Maybe it already had.

Then again, maybe not. Brad had shown up just after yoga hour had concluded, given her a quick smile, then went straight into his workout. She hadn't expected a long, drawn out explanation of where he'd been. She wasn't his parole officer. But a simple "Sorry, forgot to warn you" or something wouldn't have been missed. After practice, though, had been the icing on the snub cake. Ignoring her rule of icing in the training room, he'd come in, charmed Nikki out of a bag of ice and left without a word.

That she wouldn't let fly. If he intended to stop by later for a booty call, she'd just be unavailable. And she'd taken herself out to her parents' house to ensure that was actually true.

So maybe she was using her parents as an excuse to not deal with the issue. But it was only temporary, and only until she figured out how much she wanted to push Brad for answers.

Why, oh why, had she fallen for one of her athletes?

Bad Marianne.

SHE was nearly home when her phone rang. She hesitated, then, when she hit a red light, pulled her phone from her cup holder to check the readout. *Brad.*

Two choices. She could ignore it and talk to him tomorrow—he'd blown her off, and she could do the same. Or she could be the bigger person and answer.

Before she'd reached a good stopping place, the phone stopped ringing. She calmly pulled into an Applebee's parking lot, picked the phone up and made a call.

"Hello?"

"How old are we?"

Kara huffed out a laugh. "Please don't make me say it. No matter how old we get, you'll always be younger, anyway. I'll never win this game."

"Why does my brain want to revert to middle school tactics?"

"Because at the end of the day, we're all thirteen forever?"

Marianne groaned.

"Do you want a pep talk, or a suck-it-up talk?"

"The second."

With the ease of old friendship, Kara said, "Suck it up, buttercup. Whatever it is you're trying to avoid, get out of doing or give up on, just do it and get it over with."

She let her forehead fall to the steering wheel. "Life was so much easier when we were thirteen. Nobody expected us to be mature."

"But we couldn't have a nice glass of wine to get us through life's curveballs, either," Kara pointed out.

"Okay." With a slow breath, she forced herself back up. "Here we go."

"Whatever it is, good luck."

She waited for her phone's screen to clear, then called Brad. "Hey."

"Hey. You still awake?"

"Was on my way home, actually."

He didn't ask where she'd been. Which made her wonder if it was just a guy thing to not wonder, and not explain. Had she overreacted from the start?

"Want a hot date with a badass Marine?"

That had her smiling. Slowly. "Oh, don't you know it."

"How about five badass Marines?"

Her smile turned from sultry to amused. "Sounds like more than I can handle, if you want the truth. But for you and your Bad News Bears, I'll make an exception. Gym?"

"Twenty minutes."

"See you there."

CHAPTER

18

"If you're going to swing like that," Brad said, ducking easily as Chalfant threw a pathetic hook, "you're going to have to stop telegraphing. Otherwise . . ." He threw a one-two punch into Chalfant's stomach that sent the man stumbling back until he tripped and landed on his ass.

Brad used his teeth to rip off the Velcro and tossed his right glove away to help Chalfant up. The man stood, face red with embarrassment.

"Cheer up, Chalfant." Tressler, ever helpful as he leaned against the railing of the catwalk, grinned. "You could always be the water boy."

Chalfant growled and advanced, gloves up by his shoulders. Brad stepped between them and shouldered Chalfant back. Tressler barely moved, just laughed softly.

Tibbs ran by, huffing a little as he made another lap around the outer circle. He punched Tressler lightly on the shoulder as he passed by. "Don't be an ass," he managed to gasp.

"Don't bust a lung," Tressler shot back.

"Jesus H.," Brad said to the ceiling, ripping his other glove off and letting it fall.

No divine assistance was forthcoming.

Armstrong managed to keep his fat out of the fire by focusing on the bag Brad had set him up with in the corner. It probably helped that he'd taped his left arm up to resemble a block, so he had no choice but to keep it up. Muscle memory would make it difficult for him to lower it next time he had the choice.

"You," he said to Chalfant as the younger man started forward again, "go take a drink and cool off. Tibbs!" He cupped his hands around his mouth and yelled. "Walk it out for a bit!"

The large man held up a hand in acknowledgment from across the gym and slowed his pace.

"And you," he said, pointing to Tressler. The man's shit-eating grin slowly faded as Brad walked up. He leaned in, lowering his voice until it was just above a whisper. "Go downstairs, into the hallway by the main doors, and study the team photos."

Tressler pulled back and blinked in surprise. "Seriously?"

"Yeah, sure." Arms crossed, Brad stepped back. "You're hot shit, right? Don't need the extra practice?"

Tressler made a huffing sound and looked to the left, over Brad's shoulder. As if he couldn't quite make eye contact.

"There are guys up here who want it. Not need—want. You don't want it. So, get out of the way. Go study the photos. Read the names. You can tell me what you've learned when we get done up here."

Tressler scoffed, pushed off the railing and walked to the stairs. Either he'd take Brad seriously and give the photos of boxing teams of old a real study, or he'd take a nap.

Either way, he was out of their way upstairs, where Brad could focus on the Marines who actually wanted the help.

Tibbs ended up back on their side of the catwalk, and Brad clapped once to get his and Armstrong's attention. "Take a break, guys. Grab some water, rest your eyes a minute, take a leak, whatever you need to do. Come back ready to go in ten."

Tibbs looked like he wanted to fall over, but he walked toward the stairway that led to the head, and Chalfant followed. His head was dropped low, shoulders up high.

The posture of a resigned man.

Before they left, Brad was going to fix it. Either he'd walk out ready to win, or he'd walk out ready to fake a winner's posture. Sometimes, there wasn't a difference.

He walked to Marianne and slid down the wall beside her. His knee locked for a moment when he went to straighten his legs out, then popped out.

After a few moments of silence, she glanced up from her phone. "Do you think anyone would be interested in a pamphlet on the effects of alcohol on an athlete's body?"

He snorted and leaned over, resting his temple on her shoulder as she made notes in her cell phone's notepad app. "I'm guessing that's a no. No offense."

"I'm sensing a pattern with my pamphlets." She said it good-naturedly, then set the phone down in her lap. Her arm came around his back and she rubbed her palm in slow, soothing circles. He arched away.

"Don't, I'm sweaty."

"So? You're sweaty in bed, but I like it."

He nuzzled into her neck for a moment before pulling back. Sitting with her was one thing. But he'd be damned if the guys caught him necking with the trainer. They weren't playing secret agent spy anymore, but there were still standards.

"How's your tooth?" she asked, picking her phone back up.

His tooth . . . aw, shit. "Okay. Preventative. I'm good."

"Mmm." Her thumbs flew over the screen, typing away.

It occurred to him belatedly . . . "Should I have mentioned I'd be MIA for yoga? I told the coach, but—"

"It's okay. I worked it out myself."

She still wasn't looking at him. "I left pretty fast after practice, too. Look, I'm sorry. It was a bad day for me and I just . . . didn't handle it well."

She glanced up then, no recrimination in her eyes. Somehow, that made it worse. "Okay."

"So . . . we're okay?"

"Mmm." She picked her phone back up and kept typing. "Maybe something on steroids?"

"Probably not an issue. We get piss tested more than any other kind of athlete."

"Good point. But it never hurts to have more information, just in case anyone gets any ideas." She looked up and smiled. "Right?"

He pressed a kiss to her forehead. "Right."

A noisy bang preceded Chalfant into the gym. He walked over to his bag and started rifling through it, pulling out another shirt.

"Why are you working with them so much?" she asked quietly. "You were so against it to start with."

He took a deep breath, then let it back out. Felt good to cleanse the lungs. "Your little quote about doing something good for what I volunteered for? That was the start. But the more I work with these guys, the more I hate the thought of them failing. It'd be like me failing . . . only worse."

"Worse, huh?" She grinned. "Sounds like you've grown just a little attached to your Bad News Bears. For a guy who wanted to go it alone, that's a big step."

"I'm attached all over the place." He watched as her

eyes softened and her grin changed into a sweet curve. He knew she'd taken his meaning the right way.

MARIANNE rolled onto her back after a heavy workout. "That," she said, breathing intensely, "was insane."

Brad leaned over her, his face split wide in a Cheshire cat smile. "That was nothing."

"You're insane."

"It wasn't insane."

She tried to raise her head, then realized her neck wasn't going to cooperate. "Nope. I'm done."

He slid his hands up under her workout tank. She slapped his arm away before he reached the sweaty band of her sports bra. Now that would be horrifying. *Hey, not only am I not nearly as in shape as I thought I was, but here, have some boob sweat.*

"You asked me to show you a workout, and I did."

"I didn't think you actually *would*." She raised her head an inch—all she could manage—to find Higgs and Sweeney walking into the gym. She kicked at Brad ineffectively with a noodle-limp leg. "I thought you said nobody was coming back here for lunch."

"They weren't." He sat on his haunches as the two other Marines approached.

Higgs nudged her foot with his toe. "Problem, Cook?"

She pushed at the bangs that had flopped over her eyes in a sad imitation of hair. They were soaking wet, like she'd just showered. "No. No problem at all. I've just lost function in most of my extremities. I'm sure that's normal."

"I gave her a workout," Brad explained.

"Dude, over-share," Sweeney said with a wrinkled nose.

Brad lunged and tackled him around the knees. They both wrestled to the ground over the mats that covered their area of the catwalk.

Higgs sat down beside her, wrapping his arms around his knees to watch. "Children."

"I'm sure you're so much more mature," she said dryly.

"Oh, yeah. Of course I am. Ouch," he said with a wince as Sweeney landed a decent elbow to Brad's kidney. "That's gonna hurt."

"Stop it, both of you!" she yelled to the ceiling.

They ignored her.

"Don't make me come over there!"

They called the bluff, and she wasn't prepared to stand yet.

"Either cut it out or I'll have Higgs sit on you while I wrap you together with tape."

That seemed to get their attention. They pulled apart, with Sweeney sitting back on his hands and Brad crawling over to flop on his stomach beside her.

"Don't you get enough of a workout during, you know, your workouts?" she asked him.

"Ah, but haven't you heard?" Sweeney grinned at her, his teeth a white flash against the swarthy skin of his face. She just bet he was the kind who could go outside for ten minutes and come back in with a gorgeous golden tan. Jerk. "Costa is our endurance man. In fact, we've been meaning to ask you—"

"No!" Brad yelled, facedown on the mat.

"How's the training business treating ya?" Higgs added to change the subject.

Brad held up a hand tiredly. Higgs slapped it in a pathetic high five.

"You're all children." She struggled to roll over, accidentally kicking Brad in the shin in the process. She'd apologize later, when she could feel her lips again. With Herculean effort, she managed to get to her hands and knees, then stretched her back like a cat. "There's a reason I'm a trainer and not an athlete. That . . . was a killer."

"Now, give yourself a rest and do it again in an hour," Higgs advised.

She flipped him off, then stood on wobbly legs. "I immediately regret this decision," she said, mimicking Ron Burgundy.

"C'mon, Training Princess." Higgs took her arm and walked her to the stairs. Brad followed behind, clearly not concerned that another man was taking care of his girlfriend. She liked that. No need to thump his chest and freak out about it. He was secure in their relationship. Nice.

They made it down the stairs and she grabbed her bag from the training room. "Go get some rest," she said, pointing to all three of them. "And food. And water."

"Yes, ma'am," Sweeney and Higgs said in unison, the cheeky nerds. She shooed them away. Brad waited until they were gone, then leaned in for a kiss. "After practice tonight, you okay with meeting upstairs for my group's training?"

"Sure."

"And after that, your place?"

"You got it. And this time," she said, digging through her bag and finding her flip-flops for the locker room showers, "I'll be the one giving *you* the workout."

He winked, then kissed her again, his fingers tunneling through her short ponytail and dislodging the band. She went up on her tiptoes to meet him and make the kiss last longer.

"Oooooooo."

She heard the mocking, high-pitched male sound and broke away just before Brad cursed under his breath. He turned and she saw over his shoulder Higgs and Sweeney waiting for him by the door, making kissing faces at them.

"I've gotta go kill someone. I'll see you later."

"Don't leave any evidence!" she yelled at him as he sprinted for the two other Marines. Her trainer's eye couldn't help but notice the hitch in his step as he took the five stairs to the door to catch up with them. He still heavily favored his right knee.

Tonight, she'd work on him. Subtly, nothing obvious. But she had to get the full story sometime soon. If he messed up his knee permanently, she'd never forgive herself.

MARIANNE waited for Brad to finish giving last-minute advice to Chalfant, Tibbs and Armstrong before walking with them back downstairs. She hung back, following at a distance. He sent them off to their own cars—though it appeared they had all carpooled in one car, with Tressler's SUV being the other. Then Brad turned to her. "Wait for me?"

"Sure." She waited to see where he was going, then left her bag by the doors and snuck on quiet feet behind him. He turned into a hallway where she knew several trophy cases were held. He walked up to Tressler, who was sitting on the ground, arms draped over his knees, head bent as if in a nap.

For the second night in a row, Brad had sent Tressler downstairs to the hallway containing photos of Marine Corps boxing teams of old. Marianne had no clue why, and clearly, neither did Tressler.

Brad kicked one of his feet, and the younger man struggled to right himself before face-planting.

"Nice nap?"

"You said it was my choice. I could come down here and study or nap. I napped." Tressler stood, leaning back against the wall. His attitude screamed *defiant teenager*, though he was at least twenty-one. Everything in him was rebelling against Brad's authority—whether the authority was perceived or real didn't seem to matter.

"Yeah, I did, didn't I?" Brad wandered around, and Marianne shrank back into the shadows when he pivoted and turned her direction. But his eyes were on the walls, holding year after year of team photos, with plaques to indicate the year the team competed.

"The Marine Corps has put out some damn fine boxers over the years, haven't they?" Brad's tone was casual, his posture relaxed. But Marianne had a feeling nothing about their conversation would be restful for Tressler.

The younger man shrugged one shoulder and stuffed his hands into his sweatshirt pocket.

"Couple of these guys have gone on to the Olympic teams, even. You know?"

At that, Tressler straightened. "Yeah, I know."

"Something weird, though." Brad made a slow three-sixty turn. "None of those guys are up here."

"Yeah, they are." Tressler pointed to one team photo, though Marianne couldn't see the year. The colors were faded, though, indicating it wasn't a recent one.

"That's a team photo."

"But there." Tressler pointed out an individual. "He went."

"Where's his own photo?"

Tressler stopped searching for the other Olympians and looked around frantically. "I dunno, another hall?"

"This is it. So, where's his photo proclaiming him an Olympian? One of the chosen few? A special snowflake individual."

"It's . . ." He did another quick spin, like a drunk ballerina. "I . . . don't know."

"Doesn't have one," Brad supplied. "Why?"

"Hell if I know."

"He already had a photo. He was with his team." Brad palmed the brass plate holding the team's year on it at the bottom. "This was his photo. He didn't need the individual recognition. He made the Olympic team, sure. But he got there with his guys. His one achievement was no more or less important than what they all accomplished together."

Tressler sulked. "That's bullshit. He was the best. He wouldn't have made it to the Olympics if he wasn't."

"Maybe. But how many tournaments would the team have won with just him fighting?"

"You can't have just one guy. You've got someone from every weight class."

Brad rocked back on his heels and remained silent.

"He was still the best," Tressler insisted.

Brad shrugged.

"It's bullshit," he said again, quieter now.

"Think about it." Brad slung his arm around Tressler and led him back toward the gym.

Marianne ran like hell to beat them back to the main doors. She had just barely thrown herself against the wall, ankles crossed, looking at her nails as if she'd been waiting there the whole time, when they approached. "Ready to go?" she asked, fighting to keep her heavy breathing from showing.

"Sure thing. Thanks for waiting."

"No problem."

He pushed Tressler out the door, then waited while she locked up. "Hear anything interesting?"

When she looked up sharply, key still stuck in the lock, he grinned. She scowled at him. "How'd you know?"

"First off, you're too curious to let that opportunity slide. And secondly, you're terrible at hiding. But thirdly," he said, kissing her lightly on the nose, ignoring Tressler's groan from across the parking lot, "you were sucking wind like a half-dead racehorse when we came back."

She rolled her eyes and finished locking up.

"Can I bum a ride?"

"How'd you get here?"

"Made Tressler pick me up. He's got the Compensation-Mobile, so I figured I'd let him waste the gas."

"A ride back to your place, or mine?"

"Yours, if you'll let me bum a spot in bed, too."

Tressler's headlights flashed over them as he pulled out of his parking spot. He honked a few times, rudely, then disappeared.

"Little shit," Brad muttered without heat.

"Like you're one to talk. You came in with a nearly identical attitude, Mr. I Work Solo."

"I didn't have nearly as pissy an attitude."

She said nothing.

"I wasn't so arrogant."

"I'll agree with that one." She poked him on the shoulder, then walked to her car. "Is that where you dug that cute speech up from? The depths of your forever-changed soul?"

"Don't make it any deeper than it's supposed to be." He opened her door and waited for her to slide in. "I watched a ton of movies in the last week in my spare time. All the inspirational sporting greats. From *Hoosiers* to *Coach Carter* and up to *When the Game Stands Tall*, I made the rounds."

Waiting for him to sit in her passenger seat, she started the car. "I've seen all those movies. Most of them more than once. That speech wasn't in any of them."

"I modified."

"You ripped off Hollywood," she clarified. "You plagiarized your most important motivational speech."

He shrugged. "Whatever. It worked."

"Maybe."

"If he's still a little shit in the morning, I guess we'll know."

CHAPTER

19

Later that night, with Marianne curled up against his shoulder, Brad tried to imagine returning to California without her.

It hurt. The thought of it alone sucked his breath away. The thought that it could start tomorrow made him want to punch a wall. He wasn't ready to lose her—lose *them*—yet.

As if sensing his inner thoughts, Marianne slid her body more firmly over his. She'd slipped on a shirt and underwear—"I can't sleep naked!"—but there was enough skin-to-skin contact that his body hummed in response. It seemed like a never-ending condition, this constant state of desire around her.

"Why'd you join the boxing team?"

Her voice surprised him. He'd thought she was asleep. "Hmm?"

"Why boxing instead of, say, wrestling or baseball?"

He fidgeted with her hair a minute, letting the nearly

colorless strands flow through his fingers. "I started with karate early, like a lot of kids. But that became less cool the older you got. So I dropped out for a while. Played typical team sports, but wasn't great at them."

"The lone wolf and his need for solo sports," she said with a grin. She eased the joke with a kiss. "You could have tried golf, or tennis, or even bowling. Why boxing, specifically?"

"I'm getting there." He tugged gently on a lock of her hair in mock reproof. "I tried other team sports, but failed miserably at them. My hand-eye coordination when it comes to flying balls, or even stationary ones, is subpar at best." When she laughed, he squeezed the area between her neck and shoulder, making her squeal and squirm. "Thanks a lot for the boost to my manhood."

Her knee rubbed suggestively where his half-erect cock lay against his thigh. "I think your manhood's doing just fine, with or without my laughing."

"Not wrong. So, my mom asked if I wanted to try karate again when I hit high school. I was burned out of trying other sports, but I wanted to be active. I said no to karate. Been there, done that. Needed something new. So she took me to boxing instead."

"You said your mom, *she* took you to boxing. Did your dad not agree?"

"He was gone by then. My biological dad, I mean." His hand stilled in her hair, but he forced himself to continue, clogged throat and all. "He was in the Marine Corps, too. Did the cross-country team thing. Was all set to compete in the All Military games, when . . ." His lips felt a little numb, like they had the day the CACO guys showed up. "He and the cross country team had been out on a run. Sideswiped by a car going too fast. Several other guys were hurt, mostly minor stuff. Dad was the only one who died."

Her head dropped to his chest, and he felt her lips press

a long kiss to his skin, just above his heart. "I'm sorry. That sounds so inadequate, but—"

"It's not." He smoothed a hand over her hair. He didn't want her thinking it haunted him day after day. "It was awful, and I'll never forget the sounds my mom made when they told her. The way she just sort of . . . crumbled, and those two Marines in their dress blues kept her from hitting the ground. You can't forget stuff like that, even if you're only eight."

"Eight," she breathed, and hugged him a little tighter.

"Almost eight," he qualified. "God, my brother was a baby. He doesn't even remember Dad. I still think about that day on the few times I've had to put my dress blues on. It hurts. I actually cried when I tried them on to make sure they fit for the first time."

"Oh, baby." She held him tight, rocked a little, and pressed her face to the crook of his neck.

"They don't wear the blues anymore for notifying family. It's service alphas." He lifted a hand to rub at the hollow of his breastbone. "The ache eases each time I put them on, though."

She just linked her fingers with his over his chest. That silent connection encouraged him more than she could know.

"So, I guess, knowing I wasn't going to be a runner—because that was my dad's thing, and I wasn't touching that—I went with something that I was good at. I inherited his endurance, apparently, but not his speed. So I went with boxing, because hitting things felt good by the time I was a teen. I was a bit of an angry shit."

"I can't imagine why," she said dryly.

"I think most people assumed I was fine. I got through the initial pain of losing Dad without too many problems. Life went on. Mom married Bob—my stepdad, Sarah's dad—and he was great. No transition problems there. I think if my dad could have handpicked a husband for my mom, he wouldn't have done a better job."

"That's good. Lucky."

"Very," he agreed. "But as hormones kicked in, so did the anger. Despite having a really good guy for a father figure, I guess residual pain started showing up. So I channeled it in boxing. I was able to wear my opponent down, thanks to that endurance. I rarely get a knockout, but I'm usually the last one standing anyway. It's just they get taken out by their own lack of energy."

"Did you go into the Marines because of him?"

"Not really. The military is a decent fit for me, though eventually I'll get out and do other things. I wouldn't have chosen an entire career path based on making my dad proud." He hesitated continuing from there.

"But the boxing team is different."

"It is," he admitted. "It feels like, by getting to the All Military games, I'm somehow fulfilling his dream for him. It's my dream, too. I want it. I need it. But for him, I might just want it a little more than someone else. Maybe that sounds creepy—"

"I understand." She rubbed her hand up and down his arm, from shoulder to wrist. "I think it's nice, not creepy. I feel like I understand your dedication more now."

"I'm not just some crazy guy who loves boxing?"

"Oh, you're that, too." She laughed when he poked her ribs, then they subsided until their breathing evened out, mellowed, and eventually aligned so that when he breathed in, she was breathing out. The pattern was so relaxing, his eyes drifted closed without him even realizing it. And he was close to drifting under, his hand sliding from her back down to her side, when she whispered, "I love you."

It was all he had in him to not react, and to keep his breathing even. Because what was he going to say—*I'm lying to you?*

He could be honest and say he loved her, because he did. But an admission of love might only hurt her more if she found out about his going behind her back later.

Oh, what a tangled web you've woven, Costa.

BRAD sat on the floor of his room, working on the thigh strengthening exercises the physical therapist had shown him during his lunch break. It had been touch and go on being able to get out to the therapist's office, put in a good forty-five minutes and make it back for the second practice, but he'd done it. And now he was freaking exhausted. He'd even told Marianne he wasn't coming over tonight.

And that, if nothing else, said volumes about how fatigued he was.

His phone rang, and he checked the readout. His mother. He silenced it and set the screen facedown. Just what he didn't need when he was feeling his lowest . . . his mother's worrying nature kicking in and beating him into a guilty pulp.

Right after another fifteen-second leg lift, he let his right leg fall to the carpeted floor with a soft bounce. He could bench nearly two hundred pounds, squat close to four hundred . . . but lifting his own leg six inches off the ground while sitting straight up was killing him.

Hello, Pussy Police? I'd like to make a report . . .

After a quick knock, his roommate stuck his head in. "Decent?"

"If I wasn't, would you be staying to watch?" Brad rested his back against the side of the bed, resigned to company, but mentally rejoicing at the break. He'd finish his exercises later. Right now, Higgs was the perfect distraction. "What's up?"

"Just curious why you weren't with the hot AT, and seeing if you wanted company or to be left alone." Settling in a chair, Higgs scanned the room. "So, are you sticking it out?"

"I'm still here, aren't I?" He thought back to their first conversation. "How about you? Thinking of bailing?"

Higgs shrugged, looking unconcerned. "More fun than hanging out back at my own battalion. Here, I get to punch things." He grinned, then his grin faded as his eyes caught on something sitting to the side of the bed. "Wanna talk about that?"

Brad knew what it was before he even looked. It was the knee brace the physical therapist had badgered him into getting, which he knew he'd never use but got just to get the therapist to shut up about it. He had a childish second of debate over whether to shove the brace under the bed, then realized how stupid that was. He rolled his eyes, making light of it. "That's nothing. Overcautious docs."

"Overcautious doc, or idiotic Marine?" Higgs scowled. "Dude, what's going on? And don't give me shit about it not being my business," he said, cutting Brad off before he could speak. "I'm part of this team, and we're both group leaders. Just tell me straight."

Half his career had been about making last-second judgment calls. It had served him well up to now. He'd just have to keep going. "Just a small knee thing. Nothing big." He looked at his phone as it rang again. His mother . . . again. He silenced it and put it aside.

"So what, Cook prescribed the brace? Why aren't you using it?"

"Just got it today." Truth. "And no, she didn't. A PT did. Don't worry about it, Mommy," he mocked. "I'm fine."

Higgs stared at him for a moment, then shook his head in disbelief. "Cook doesn't know, does she? She'd be all over your ass for it if she did. She'd be shoving pamphlets down your throat about knee exercises and proper brace etiquette. You're keeping it from her."

"There's nothing to keep from anyone. It's no big deal."

Jesus H., would everyone just drop it? "I'm taking care of it, so don't freak out."

Higgs stood, still shaking his head. "Man, you need to get your shit sorted out. Is boxing worth busting your knee up? Is it seriously?"

"You don't know anything about what this means to me, so don't throw that pile of shit my way." Angry now, he worked on standing as effortlessly as he could. His knee clicked viciously, but held him up. "You want to play the judgment card, then go right ahead. But I'm making the goddamn team. That's the end of it."

"Maybe it will be the end of it." Looking disgusted, Higgs closed the door behind him.

What, so now you're a comedian? Pride dented, Brad walked over and kicked the knee brace. It flew into the wall with a dull thump and landed, no worse for the wear.

"No, you know what?" Higgs reentered the room as if he'd never left. "You need to tell Cook. Tonight."

"Or what, you'll do it for me?" Brad picked up the brace, dusted it off—the thing had cost him a freaking car payment out of pocket—and set it on the chair. "I thought making the team wasn't that important to you."

"You jackass." Giving him a pitying glance, Higgs sat on the corner of the bed. "Push me away all you want, but I live here, so I'm just gonna keep coming back. You can't get rid of me. I'm your personal circle of hell."

"Goody." Brad picked up his phone and set it on the nightstand by the alarm clock.

Higgs studied him a minute. "Tell her."

"I will." *Eventually.*

"Tell her now. She'll be pissed, but Cook doesn't strike me as the kind of woman to hold a grudge."

"Lot you know." *All* women held grudges. It was coded in their DNA. Having a younger sister had taught him that one fast enough. "And pissing her off isn't what I'm worried about."

"What is?"

Making her give up on me.

He scoffed, tried to play it off. "I've got an easy thing with her. Don't wanna blow it, right?"

His roommate blinked once, twice, then laughed. Laughed until his sides apparently hurt, as he doubled over and grabbed his stomach. "Oh . . . oh my God . . . Oh, that was a good one." Higgs knuckled a tear away. "Do it again. Do the *I'm Benny Badass Womanizer* again. Wait, let me get my phone first so I can record it. I wanna show Sweeney."

"Kiss off."

"I'm going, I'm going." He shook his head, chuckling as he walked to the door. "You've got an easy thing with her, that's for sure. But it's not about the sex. Or not just about the sex," he corrected as he closed the door.

"Guy thinks he's a fortune-teller," Brad muttered as he studied the brace. He grabbed his phone from the nightstand, unsure whether he should call Marianne or his mother first. Mom, probably, to get that over with. Then Marianne.

But the thought of hearing her voice put a little jump in his throat. He set the phone back down. No need to call her tonight; he'd just talk to her tomorrow.

When it rang a few minutes later, he jumped, thinking he'd conjured Marianne's phone call. When he saw Tressler's name, he nearly ignored it. But something told him not to.

"What?" he groaned into the phone. Then he sat up. "Son of a . . . yeah. Gimme ten minutes. I'll be there."

MARIANNE'S to-do list resembled a forest of hearts and stars. She'd been sitting on her couch, in her favorite

Family Guy pajama bottoms and threadbare cotton T-shirt, doodling around the edge instead of actually writing her dang list for tomorrow.

And why? There was no question about that. She was in love, and had no clue if the guy felt the same thing. Of course her mind was in another territory.

She'd said it. In that weak moment, after the heat of passion had cooled and left them comfortably snuggled together under the blankets, with his arm a dead weight over her and his skin so warm against her cheek, she'd let her defenses slip and had whispered those three secret words she'd been planning to save.

He hadn't heard her, though. Or he had, and hadn't reacted.

No, better to think he'd already been asleep. If he heard, and didn't respond, it meant he wasn't traveling down the same path. And that would be . . . hard. So hard.

She looked down at her doodles and scratches. The last heart looked a little . . . well, a little squashed.

Screw you, symbolism.

At the heavy knock on her door, she sighed and turned the pad of paper upside down on the table, then placed a book over it. Odds were, at this late an hour, it was Brad. No need to see her scribbling in her notepad like a seventh grader bored in geography class and writing "I heart One Direction" all over the margins of her folders.

A quick look through the peephole had her swallowing a curse instead of a greeting and wrenching the door open. She cursed out loud this time as the chain at the top halted the progression and nearly swung it closed again.

"What the hell happened?" With shaking hands, she got the chain undone and swung the door wide, letting in Brad—his shirt, neck and jaw covered in blood—with a large black man draped over his and Tressler's shoulders. The man in the middle's head was down, his neck swinging with each step. They half walked, half dragged the man to her kitchen, then unceremoniously dumped him on the ground with a loud *oof.*

"Are you hurt?" Hurrying to Brad, she ignored all protocol and grabbed his face between her hands to examine him closer. Turning his chin in a firm grip, she looked for a wound, dilated pupils, a dented skull . . . and found nothing. "Where's the injury?"

Brad pointed down to the prone man. She looked at him, then Tressler, who held up his own hands—also covered in blood—and said nothing.

Since the man was groaning pathetically, and moving a little, she knew he wasn't dead. Maybe halfway there, but he'd wait two damn minutes while she caught her bearings. Hands on her hips, she backed out of the tiny apartment kitchen. Time to triage the idiocy. "What the heck is going on?"

Brad glared at Tressler, who shook his head and pursed his lips together as if zipping them shut. Mature.

With a heavy sigh, Brad nudged the prone man over onto his back. He rolled, ungracefully, until she could see it was one of the boxers. One of Brad's group members, as it turned out. Tibbs, the Marine who always running laps, building up his speed and endurance. But what the hell happened to him? Had they decided to hold a late-night practice without calling her?

"Tibbs, here," Brad said, answering her unvoiced questions, "decided to play crash test dummy with a friend's crotch rocket. The moron wasn't wearing a helmet, went flying ass over elbows and caught himself with his face."

Hence the blood. Head and face wounds, even the non-fatal kind, bled like stuck pigs. She looked to Tressler, who only nodded and kept silent. She had a feeling there was a reason for his uncommon quietness, but wasn't in the mood to figure it out.

Stepping around Brad, she knelt down and gave Tibbs'

face a cursory exam. Broken nose, no doubt about it. Concussion was probable. She worked her way down his shoulders, his arms and his legs, feeling no fractures. Nothing that made him hiss in pain. Just the same dull groan when she found tender spots and road rash. "You brought him here. Why here? Weren't the police involved if there was a crash?"

"No cops. It was in an apartment complex parking lot. No other cars. Just an idiot who had no right playing on a machine he wasn't familiar with." Brad said the word "*idiot*" a little louder than necessary, leaving no doubt as to his feelings on the situation. "Can you help?"

Did she have a choice? She couldn't just let the man bleed on her kitchen floor while she went to take a bubble bath. With a sigh and a nod, she ran to gather her supplies.

CHAPTER

2 O

Twenty minutes later, Marianne emerged from the kitchen, wiping sweat from her brow with her forearm. Brad and Tressler stood up from where they'd been sitting in stony silence on her couch.

"Broken nose for sure. His limbs seem fine, and he doesn't say anything else hurts. My guess is, based on how you say he landed, there's no internal bleeding, though I can never be one hundred percent without testing. The concussion is more concerning to me than anything." It worried her a great deal. "I'm sorry, guys, but he's got to go to the hospital."

Tressler stood, hands fisted at his side, his face a white sheet of pure anger. "You promised you'd handle it."

"I promised I'd *help*. And making sure he gets the right treatment *is* helping." The young man vibrated with frustration, and she could understand. But there was a responsibility to the man still propped up against her kitchen cabinets, moaning quietly, that overrode his friend's loyalty. "I'm sorry, but a concussion is not something to mess around with. Plus, there's no way to check for additional internal injuries. He's probably fine," she said quickly when Tressler's eyes widened in concern. "Probably okay. But it's better to play it safe."

Brad stayed suspiciously quiet the entire time.

Tressler folded his arms over his chest, his body positioning still defiant. "We can drive him there ourselves, can't we? Just take him over to the hospital, get him checked out and take him back home? We don't need an ambulance or anything?"

"I don't see why you wouldn't be able to just drive him over and walk him into the ER. They'll be able to do a CT and maybe some X-rays, just to rule out everything." After a moment's hesitation, she left it at that. There was no point in telling him they'd likely admit Tibbs overnight for observation with what was, to her, a clear and undeniable concussion.

Brad exchanged a look with Tressler. "Naval hospital is closer, by far."

"Closer is better. Tomorrow's Sunday, so we're off." With a relaxed breath, the young man sighed and let his arms drop. "Okay, can he walk downstairs?"

"Half walk, half drag is more likely." She went back to kneel by Tibbs' side. "Tibbs." When he didn't open his eyes right away, she snapped her fingers in front of his nose. His eyelids shot open. "Tibbs, where are you?"

"Hell," he muttered, then blinked rapidly and gave her a loopy grin. "Hey, it's the trainer. And it's my group leader," he added when Brad crouched beside her. "Did that pussy Chalfant knock me out?"

Brad gave her a look that clearly asked, *Is that normal?* She gave a short shake of her head and then smiled gently at Tibbs. "C'mon, big boy. Up and at 'em. Let's walk down to the car."

He grumbled, but stood when Tressler and Brad wedged their shoulders beneath his armpits and rose. The man outweighed both of them, but they bore up under the weight well enough.

"Let's go, buddy." Tressler helped guide him through her living room and out the door. She followed, after grabbing her purse and locking her own door. Then, after a moment's hesitation, she ran back inside and threw a sweatshirt on over her shirt. She wasn't wearing a bra again, but the loose, thick fabric of the hoodie concealed it well enough. Plus, it wasn't like she was trying to make a fashion statement.

They'd reached the bottom of the stairs when she arrived, and they got him into Tressler's backseat without much problem. She pointed to her own car. "I'll follow. You keep him talking, even if it doesn't make much sense, okay? Keep him talking." Brad gave her a curt nod, then sat in the passenger seat while Tressler took the driver's position.

She followed them on base and to the hospital, considering herself lucky they hit very little traffic due to the hour. Parking her car, she raced to the front just as they eased Tibbs into a wheelchair at the ER's front doors. A woman in mint-green scrubs smiled at her. She probably looked like hell, with her hair in a now-falling-down ponytail and a sweatshirt she had grabbed from the dirty laundry pile over the top of her faded pajama bottoms.

"Are you with this guy?" the nurse asked.

"Sort of. Friend," she clarified when the nurse arched a brunette brow. "He's got a broken nose and I'm about ninety-seven percent sure he's got a concussion."

Tibbs took that moment to roll his head back and look up at the nurse upside down. He grinned, and leered, as much as a guy with bloody gauze and a half-swollen-shut eye could leer. "Heeeeeeey, pretty lady. Did you come to watch me box?"

The nurse muffled a laugh, then winked at Marianne.

"I think your ninety-seven percent was conservative. Let's go," she added to Tibbs as she competently wheeled him through the doors. "There are plenty of pretty ladies in here for you to charm."

Though he was probably double her weight, she had no problems wheeling the chair with ease. Tressler tossed Brad the keys to his SUV and followed, giving the nurse the description of the crash.

Marianne started to walk in after them, but Brad caught her arm.

"Are you going to ruin this for him?"

"Ruin what, his CT scan? I don't think that's possible." She watched as frustration rolled over his features. "Oh, I see. You mean, am I going to play tattletale and call the coaches this instant about this? No, I'm not."

His relief was palpable as he let go of a long breath.

"I'm waiting until Monday. Brad," she said, cutting him off when he got ready to argue. "You can't possibly think I'd let a Marine who just had a concussion step into a boxing ring, do you? I'm not bound by the 'first do no harm' oath like a doctor, but I'm still a decent person. That's insanity."

"Don't you have patient confidentiality?" he argued. "What about Tibbs' right to privacy?"

"Much like I don't have a Hippocratic oath to worry about, I also don't have patient-client confidentiality. My job is to keep everyone healthy. That includes knowing when they've gone too far, and pulling the plug when they do!" Her temper was boiling now. How dare he try to tell her how to do her job?

"What about his dreams?" Brad shot back. "Do they mean nothing?"

"I'm pretty sure Tibbs is a rational guy, and would rather choose a life without permanent brain damage." And if he wasn't, then she'd work it so he didn't have the choice. "This is my job. If you don't like it, tough tits."

At that, Brad's mouth quirked, but he firmed it again quickly. "I don't like it."

"Then I'm glad you're not the one who gets to pick my career. I would never forgive myself if I let him get back in the ring Monday morning, whether everything turned out okay or not. It's my job to tell the coaches the truth about their athletes. End of story. I care about *all* of you guys." She poked his chest, and he grabbed her finger. "Even you, when you're acting like a jerk."

"You care about me, huh?" When she scoffed, his lips lifted in a ghost of a smile. "Even when I'm acting like a jerk."

"Apparently," she muttered. He pulled her close. She squirmed, but didn't break his hold.

"But do you like me more than just one of the Marines you watch over?"

"Well, I didn't let anyone else in my pants yet," she said sweetly, and grinned when he growled. "You know I do. God knows why, but I do." *I love you. You just don't know it.*

"So we're just at an impasse on this."

"You like him." She shook her head when he would have spoken. "You'll deny it, but I know you like all the guys in your group. Even Tressler."

He groaned.

"But as much as you identify with their dream to be on the team, I also know you'd be devastated if something did happen to them. So while you're all hot under the collar about it now, I'm guessing when you've had a day to cool off, you'll see I'm right."

BRAD let Marianne go home and waited on a bench outside the entrance to the ER. He could have gone back with her, left Tressler to handle it. But he was the group leader, and he'd be damned if he gave up his responsibilities to someone else. He just wasn't ready to go in there yet. Not when he knew he was going to be facing a man whose dream had just ended.

Not when he knew it would be like looking at his own future.

He let his head fall back to the rough brick, closed his eyes, and fought for a little rest. It was fitful, at best, with cars pulling in to pick up patients, people walking by for visits or the occasional drop-off with a mild emergency. But he managed to squeeze some sleep out of it. He wasn't sure how much time had passed when he felt something settle beside him. He cracked one eye open and found Tressler, hands covering his face, elbows on his knees, beside him.

"Tibbs?"

"Making the nurses all want to run away with him." His voice was muffled by his hands. Tressler sighed, his back moving with the heavy sound. "He's awake, and alert, and knows the president's name. He's shaky on details from the fall, but they said that's not uncommon. Past that . . ." He lifted one shoulder without changing positions.

Brad took a chance and patted Tressler's back a few times, then let his arm fall to his side. "Did he call you first? I never asked why you were there before me."

"I already was. That was my friend whose bike he got on. We were hanging out and he got the brilliant idea. I should have stopped him."

The last came out on a torn, harsh breath. Brad knew if he didn't get it under control, he'd be a mess in a minute.

"Cut that shit out, right now," he said, using his best platoon commander voice. Tressler's back stiffened and his shoulders lifted a little from their hunched-over position. "Tibbs shouldn't have gotten on the bike. You shouldn't have egged him on. Oh, like I didn't put two and two together," he added when the younger man looked at him warily from the corner of his eye. "The choice was his, and he made a shitty one. Now he will end up living with that choice."

"He's going to be okay." Voice firmer, Tressler sat back and stared off into the dark. "He's going to be fine. He's not going to look any prettier . . ."

Brad snorted at that.

"But he'll be okay. So, he wears a face guard for a few weeks at practice and—"

"He's not going to be at practice."

The other man watched him for a moment, then his mouth dropped open. "You're not kidding. You're going to pull him? That's such bullshit and you know it."

"It's not my call, it's Marianne's. Cook's," he corrected when the other man's eyebrow winged up. "And I'm not going to ask her to make a different choice. That's her job on the line."

Letting loose a heavy breath, Tressler slumped a little again. "Damn."

"I know." He waited a moment. "Starting to get it now?"

Without missing a beat, Tressler picked up where the conversation had flowed. "Be a team player, don't be a show-off, yadda yadda."

"Yadda yadda," Brad muttered, but nudged Tressler with his elbow. "Close enough. It took someone else reminding me I joined a team, despite the individual way the sport plays out. So you needed a reminder, too. We all do, from time to time. Just don't be a jackass about it."

"Same goes," the younger man quipped, then danced out of range when Brad took a half-joking swing at him. "Old man, you couldn't catch me if you had a net and a head start."

"Drive me home, punk. I forgot to take my nightly prune juice."

The entire way home, he debated, he bargained, and he fought against the need to tell Marianne about his knee. But he saw exactly what she did for Tibbs in his very near future. If he could just get through tryouts and claim an official spot on the team . . . maybe then. Maybe. They wouldn't be so inclined to turn and burn the Marines who were officially on the team. They'd let him practice with the brace, get through the All Military games, and then see about more intense therapies from there.

So he was still stuck with another week of subterfuge. There was a reason he wasn't special ops . . . this secretive crap was over his head. He didn't like it. It gave him pre-ulcers just thinking about it. Were pre-ulcers even a thing? Hell, he couldn't even ask Marianne something stupid like that.

Forget the pre. Thinking about lying—by omission—to the woman he loved was going to give him real-deal ulcers.

He had to tell her. He couldn't wait any longer. It was bullshit otherwise, to keep holding back.

"Hey, Grandpa. We're here." Tressler nudged him on the shoulder. "Did you fall asleep on the way back to the nursing home?"

Brad swatted at the badgering hand. "Stop that. I'm up, I'm going." He raised up and watched as Tressler checked the clock on the dash. The first hints of watery dawn light were creeping in through the trees, over the BOQ roof line, in any stray crack it could find before it muscled its way into official daylight. "Thinking of going back to the hospital?"

"I, uh . . ." Tressler's ears reddened, as if he realized he'd been caught caring about a teammate. A very non-loner thing to do. But he caught himself, scoffed and blew that off. "Nah. He can harass nurses all by himself. I'm more of a naughty teacher kinda guy, myself."

"Uh-huh." He climbed down from the Compensation-Mobile and started to close the door. Just before it shut, he added, "Tell Tibbs I'll see him later today."

"Roger." Then Tressler scowled. "Damn you."

"Go be with your teammate, Marine. Not an order, just a suggestion." He closed the door, then watched the younger man peel out of the parking space and head out to the main road, slowing down enough for traffic laws. Brad grinned when he saw that Tressler turned left to head to the hospital, instead of right for the barracks.

Some guys were easier to read than others. If only women were so transparent.

He'd take one more day. One Sunday to be with her, absorb her and—hopefully—crawl just a little more permanently under her skin, so when he fessed up, she'd have a harder time pushing him away.

As plans went . . . it sucked.

THEY had developed quite the routine, Marianne mused as she rested her feet on a pillow in Brad's lap. Her laptop, sitting on her lapboard, obstructed most of her view of him while he watched a UFC fight. He was only visible from the nose up. But even that small sliver of him gave her so much insight. He watched the fight with true intensity, not missing a single kick, a single punch. But she knew he was cataloguing every single move for future use.

He wore one of his olive green undershirts and a pair of red mesh workout shorts. And she, feeling comfortable enough to have given up caring, wore a pair of bikini bottoms with a flimsy tank top. She'd given about seven seconds of thought toward wearing a bra, then had decided against it.

It had been like this for most of their Sunday off. The

last Sunday before the final team was announced. Despite the fact that she could feel the low-level vibration of stress and worry hum through him, he'd kept it light. Even knowing that if he didn't make the cut, they'd be separated almost immediately by an entire country, he'd managed to wake her up in a good mood.

The reminder of exactly *how* he'd woken her up—from behind, with a gentle sliding into her—made her smile a little before resuming her work. There was something to be said for sleeping naked, like he preferred. It wasn't her first choice, but it was definitely becoming a new favorite.

A long finger tapped on top of her screen. "What's that secret smile about?"

"Oh, nothing. Just remembering something about waking up this morning." She glanced up, and found heated eyes watching her carefully. "You know, when you played alarm clock and got me up way before I was ready."

"I was already up."

She chuckled at the sexual innuendo. "I know. That's why I didn't complain." She poked him playfully in the ribs with a toe. "Watch your fight. I'm working here."

"What pamphlet is it this time?"

"What makes you think it's a pamphlet? I could be writing an email, or buying shoes." She smiled wickedly. "Or sexy lingerie."

He eyed her with an *Is that a joke?* face.

She grinned. He knew her too well. "Well, for your information, smarty-pants, it's not a pamphlet."

His brows rose in surprise, but his eyes didn't leave the TV screen.

"It's a brochure."

He snorted and settled her feet more comfortably in his lap. One hand ran light fingertips up and down her shins. Just to her knee and back; nothing sexual at all. He probably didn't even sense he was doing it. But the touch charged her more than it probably should have.

"A brochure for what?"

"It's for Kara, actually. She's a blogging queen and can change out the skin of her website in ten minutes flat, but never gets the proportions or margins right on promo items." She spun the laptop on the board and showed him. He spared it a three-second glance—generous, given his interest in the fight—before turning back to the screen.

"She needs to get some new yoga and Pilates clients. I'm helping her gear this one toward potential military clientele. Adding in some key phrases that might attract a jarhead's attention."

"'Yut'?" he asked in a primal, caveman voice, and she laughed.

"Exactly." A few more clicks, then she saved the presentation and emailed it to Kara for first-round approval. Closing her computer with a quiet snap, she set it on the coffee table and picked up the pad with her list on it. She realized, with a flash of embarrassment, she'd never torn off the doodle-hearts page. Before he had a chance to glance her way, she ripped it off, crumpled it up and stuffed it down the couch cushion behind her.

He didn't even blink.

As she made out her to-do list for the next day, she asked, "Are you still mad at me about Tibbs?"

He was quiet for a while, then a commercial came on. He muted the TV and turned to her with her feet still in his lap.

"I'm sad. I'm sad for him, and for our group, because he's the first to go. But I get it. And I'm not going to stand in the way of your job. Me telling you how to be an athletic trainer would be about as useless as you telling me how to be a Marine."

She smiled a little at that. When he kept watching her, she raised a brow. "What?"

"Everything good?"

She nodded, then sucked in a breath. Time to try again. Be bold. "Brad?"

"Yeah?"

"I love you."

He blinked, and for a second, she wondered if he actually heard her wrong. But then he set her feet down gently, covered her body on the couch and kissed her. He kissed her with such passion, she knew he'd heard her this time.

It didn't occur to her until later, when they were tucked in bed and he was breathing deeply beside her, that he hadn't responded in kind.

CHAPTER

21

"Look over the list of travel dates, make any arrangements you need to, and we'll be set." Reagan set the sheet by her paper, started to leave then thought better of it and spun on her heels to come back.

Marianne couldn't help holding her breath until the woman was firmly standing still again.

"You really have to stop wearing those death traps on your feet. You never know when there might be melted ice that we missed mopping up."

Reagan looked down, brows raised in question. "These are kitten heels. They're practically the same thing as flats."

"Oh, yeah. Twinsies. Except for the heel and flat part." Marianne sighed and settled back in her chair. She held the paper up. "Anything else?"

"Yeah, what's wrong?" Propping the hip of one business skirt–clad hip on Marianne's desk, Reagan studied her closely. "You're all upset today. What's going on?"

Gee, I dunno. The guy I'm seeing is in pain and won't confide in me about it. I'm in love with him and have no clue how he feels. I lost another guy this morning to an injury, which was my call, and now all the Marines are staring at me like I'm Public Enemy Number One?

"Just a lot on my mind."

Reagan huffed and shook her head. "That was pathetic. If you're going to lie, at least do the job some justice, please?"

"Hey, pretty lady." Kara halted at the entrance to the training room, hand clutched around her yoga tote. "Oh, sorry . . . pretty ladies."

Saved by the friend. "Kara, you remember Reagan, right?" She stood as the other women acknowledged each other. "Reagan has a date with an orthopedist in about ten years to have her knees replaced from wearing all those heels, and we have a lunch date." She nodded to Reagan, who was smiling smugly.

"But they're so cute," Kara said. She looked down at her own flip-flops, which Marianne knew for a fact she'd gotten for one dollar at the Old Navy flip-flop sale.

She knew, because she'd been standing with her, buying a few pairs of her own.

"Thank you," Reagan said, and held out a foot delicately. "I'm really getting into this whole 'working woman' thing. It's fun."

Kara snorted at that. "Right. I think I'd drown myself if I had to wear a suit every day."

Marianne started packing up her own bag. "And that's why you're good at what you do, Kara. You're working in your own talents, at things you're passionate about."

"Yeah." Reagan watched Kara for a moment as Marianne searched her desk for her cell phone. "You run your own blog. I found it. It's cute. The layout, I mean, not the subject." Her eyes widened and her jaw slacked a little.

"Oh my God, that's not what I meant. I'm so sorry. I know you talk about your son and—"

"It's fine." In that soothing, maternal way she had, Kara laid a hand on Reagan's forearm and rubbed gently. "I know what you meant."

"Okay." She breathed out and brushed hair back behind her ears. "I'm good at writing official copy for media, but I wanted to actually keep a blog, connected to the team's website. Just good little bits for the media to snatch up, photos, that sort of thing. But the whole idea of knowing how to format it gives me the willies. Think we could get together and you could give me some pointers from that aspect?"

"Shouldn't be a problem." Kara glanced over her shoulder as Marianne grabbed her wrist and tugged. "I'll talk to you about it later. After yoga?"

Reagan called out a good-bye as Marianne steered Kara out the door and into the parking lot.

"Geez, Cook, where's the fire?"

"I get two hours, and you were fifteen minutes late. I want to eat without wolfing the food down. You know that's bad for your digestive system." She hopped into Kara's car—the Mom-Mobile, as she thought of the compact SUV, with its kid-friendly radio stations programmed and the juice boxes at the ready. "I'm not going to join the yoga session today. Too much paperwork."

"Hmm." Kara pulled out of the parking lot and into base traffic, doing her best to drive as slowly as humanly possible. "Too much paperwork, or too many repressed feelings?"

"You've been watching *Dr. Phil* again, haven't you?" She sighed as Kara took a turn at the speed of a sea slug. "Okay, I'm cautious about the MPs, too, but this is insane. Why are you driving like this?"

"Oh. Right." She picked up the pace marginally. "Mom habit. He's noticing my driving more now, making comments on stuff. Won't be much longer before he's in the front seat, learning from my moves. I've been hyperaware of my own driving for a while now. Practice what you preach, and all that jazz. I've had to hide my cell phone in my purse on the floor of the passenger seat so I'm not even tempted to check messages at red lights."

"Sounds like hell. Grinders or salad bar?"

Kara snorted. "You know I'm going to pick the salad bar, and I know you want me to say grinders. So why don't we grab you a grinder, then swing by and pick out my salad from the grocery store, and we can park and eat in peace?"

"This is why we are friends. Sold."

Ten minutes later, Marianne sat in Kara's car as her friend ran into the grocery store to grab her salad. Kara had left the car running so Marianne would have AC and the radio, but there was nothing remotely appealing about the kids' music playing. After studying the radio controls for a few seconds, she gave up. Just her luck, she'd hit the wrong button and screw up the car, leaving the radio stuck on death metal or something.

So instead she people-watched. The strip mall where the grocery store was located was full of thriving businesses. A shoe store, a party supply store and a physical therapist's office lined the left side.

Physical therapy. She'd considered being a PT for a bit in college. Smiling at the memory, she watched as a mom held open the wide glass door for her limping teenage son to walk through. Probably a football injury, given the kid's size.

She'd have never been happy in an office all day. Serving athletes, definitely. But not nearly as close to the action as she wanted to be. No, she'd made the right choice, even if it wasn't as profitable as . . .

She sat forward, squinting. Was that . . . No. No way.

Apparently, yes way.

Brad—her Brad—paused at the door, opening it wider for the teen who was still hobbling his way up to the front door from the parking lot. Probably because the kid needed crutches to match the ACL brace he was sporting, and was too stubborn to use them.

Speaking of stubborn.

Brad gave the mom a little salute—probably in acknowledgement of a thank-you, though Marianne couldn't hear anything from this distance—and headed out to the parking lot, favoring his leg. He was nearly to the first row of cars when he turned back. Marianne's eyes darted to the door and saw someone wearing the typical PT uniform of khakis and a polo shirt running out to catch Brad, holding a knee brace in his hand. Brad accepted the brace and headed back to his car.

He was getting physical therapy on the side. And had a knee brace he wasn't using.

The sound of crinkling paper assaulted her ears, and she glanced down to see what was left of her grinder balled up in her fists. Her stomach roiled at the thought of eating, and she tossed the sandwich in the backseat.

He'd been going behind her back from the start, seeking outside medical attention, and deliberately not telling her. Why? Because he didn't trust her judgment, or her abilities? Or was there something else to it?

The driver side door opened and Kara slid in, her plastic bag squeaking as she set it on the center console. "Sorry, I had to wait for them to refill the green peppers, then there was a line at checkout. Where do you want to park and eat?" She glanced over, noticed Marianne's attention was focused elsewhere and followed her line of sight. "Oh, is that Brad?"

Marianne nodded numbly.

"Well, that's a fun coincidence." In her cheerful way, she grinned. "Let's nab him and make him our lunch prisoner. I can quiz him on which yoga positions he thinks have been the most beneficial for the team."

"Don't," she said weakly as Kara started to roll the window down.

Her friend froze, finger still on the button. "What's wrong?"

Marianne waited until Brad got in his car and drove away. "He was here for an appointment," she murmured. "He's in pain, hurting, potentially injured, and won't tell me about it. Won't let me do my job."

"Oh. Ohhh." She settled back in the seat, the red bun of her hair bobbing gently against the headrest. "So . . . what do we do now?"

She took a deep breath, then bit down hard on her bottom lip to keep the tears from coming. This hurt way more than she'd imagined. Like she'd been slapped, then punched in the gut then kicked off the side of a building. He'd had hundreds of chances to be honest with her. And instead, he'd sat there and listened to her say she loved him . . . and hidden the truth.

A truth that could wreck her career, and his leg.

"Maybe . . ." Kara's voice trailed off, then she just reached over and squeezed Marianne's knee. "Maybe he's going to talk to you today. It could be a brand-new development?"

Marianne pasted on a smile for her friend and nodded. And kept nodding, because her throat had closed up due to emotions she wasn't ready to unpack in public.

As if understanding she couldn't talk, Kara started the car and headed for the back of the grocery store's parking lot, where the employees parked. They ate in silence, the only sound the low volume of Kara's radio and her occasional texting to her son, who was at the babysitter's. Then she drove them both back to the gym.

They sat in the car for a few minutes in understanding silence. Brad's car was there, empty, so he was already inside. Marianne stared at the doors with dread.

"You could call in sick," Kara murmured quietly. "I have to go set up now. I could tell them you felt sick during lunch and went home."

"No." Feeling a little stronger, she shook her head and grabbed her bag. "I have to go in there. I'm going to give him the chance to come to me. If he's not willing to talk about it . . ." She slapped the dashboard, watching dust motes sprinkle the air, twirling around in the sunlight.

"If he's not . . . then you'll come out here and dust my car?" Kara asked hopefully.

Marianne laughed, though it wasn't quite to her normal level of happiness. "Thanks." She took a deep breath and let it go slowly. "Here we go."

She walked into the gym with Kara, parting ways at the door of the training room. She set her bag down, said hello to Levi and Nikki, then settled in for some paperwork. When Nikki asked if she was going to join them for yoga, Marianne waved her off and kept working.

If she was going to be fired soon for failing to aid a Marine with an injury, she needed to have her paperwork up to date for the next trainer to come in.

But curiosity got the better of her, and she peeked in to watch the Marines turn and twist themselves into pretzels. Kara was truly wonderful. Going at a three-quarter speed to give the novices a chance to keep up, she picked positions that worked best for loosening the muscles they needed. Not exactly a cardio workout, but important all the same.

But Brad, she noted with some concern, was not among them. His roommate was, as were the rest of Brad's group. But Brad was absent. She checked the water stations, but no dice.

Probably in the locker room, she told herself. He'd driven here after his appointment, so clearly he was around somewhere. And he had to come see her afterward for ice, anyway. She'd give him his final opportunity to fess up at that time, and then . . .

Well, she had no clue what then. But a very big part of her was already tightening up against the knowledge that she'd have to let him go. Even though she didn't want to.

Bad Marianne.

"COACH, can we talk?" Brad knocked on the open door with his knuckle and waited for Coach Ace to look up. He didn't, but waved Brad in without glancing away from his computer.

"Fucking machines," he muttered while Brad took a seat and set his bag by his feet. His thick finger stabbed at the mouse with vicious intensity, repeatedly, until Brad wondered if the thing would just collapse under the pressure. Another minute of moving the mouse around and intense clicking grated against Brad's nerves before Coach gave up and pushed away with a disgusted snort.

"Used to be, we could just scribble down our thoughts on a sheet of paper. Or, hell, tell someone. Now I've got forms spilling out from every which way, and half of them have to be done online, and the system hates me, and my computer hates me . . ." He sighed and glared once more at the mutinous computer before giving Brad his attention. "Losing Tibbs was a blow, but the paperwork is the real bitch. What do you need, Marine?"

"It's about my knee, Coach." Brad dug through his duffel and pulled out the brace his PT had insisted on. "I just saw a physical therapist and they want me to wear this."

Coach held out a hand and Brad willingly passed the brace. He studied it for a moment. "Torn meniscus, right?"

Brad nodded, a little surprised he'd guessed.

"I had one myself, maybe a decade ago." When Brad raised his brows, the coach scowled. "Fine. Two decades. The surgery was no biggie. The exercises during recovery were from hell, though." He winced, as if imagining having to do them today. "Is there a reason Cook didn't come talk to me about this? She's usually more on top of things than that."

"Ah, yeah." Here came the tricky part. "She didn't know. I hid what I could from her so she wouldn't have the chance to kick me out before the team was final."

"And yet you came to me with this anyway," he said quietly, handing the brace back. "Team isn't final, you know. Why tell me now?"

"Because I didn't want you to think she was covering for me. You know we're . . . well." He felt heat creep up the back of his neck and he rubbed at it. "Together. So I didn't want you thinking she was giving me preferential treatment. I'm sure if she knew, she would have walked the steps with me to get me healed up."

The coach nodded, then sat back and laced his fingers over his stomach. "Sounds like we have a problem. Several problems, really. If you can't be honest with your trainer, then how do we know you're not going to keep hiding injuries until you get yourself killed or permanently injured?"

He started to speak, but Coach Ace cut him off.

"And if she couldn't see you were hurting, despite you insisting you were fine, then maybe she doesn't have quite the backbone for this job I thought she did."

"No, that's not it at all." Aw, hell. He'd come in here to prevent her from getting fired, and now he was walking the entire conversation in that direction on accident. "She pushed me to talk about it, but I chose not to."

"And she didn't come to me with her concerns. That's a problem."

"I'd rather you take that out on me, Coach. But even if you think there's a conflict with our relationship, the solution is simple." With a deep breath, he stood. The ache in his chest bloomed like a wound. He wondered whether, if he looked down, he'd see a puddle where his dreams had bled out of him. "I understand this is the end of the road for me, but I hope you'll let me talk to my group before I go."

"Where the hell do you think you're going?"

Brad's ass hit the chair before his brain clicked. "Uh, back to my home base, I assume."

"I didn't dismiss you, Marine." Coach leaned forward, elbows hitting the desk with twin thuds. "You've gotta be shittin' me. You're ready to give up?"

Give up his dream? No. Sacrifice for Marianne's sake? Brad debated how to phrase it without sounding sanctimonious . . . and found there wasn't one. So he simply shook his head.

"But you'd rather walk out the door than have me ask for Cook to go."

He nodded, figuring words weren't required.

Coach made an inarticulate sound. One of those neutral sounds that could mean things were turning around for the better . . . or that shit was about to get really bad.

"Why are you so sure you're done here?"

"I was dishonest." The situation was pretty cut and dried to Brad. "I should have spoken to Ma—Cook when it started hurting, and I shouldn't have hidden the prognosis."

"So instead of letting the heat come down fifty-fifty on her head with yours, you'll just take it all, pack up and go. Marines," he muttered. "White knights, every one of them. How about," he continued in his normal tone, "we choose to not look at it as dishonesty, but rather as a mistake."

Brad sat at the edge of the chair, feeling suspiciously like a rabbit surrounded by traps. Some were real, some were fake. And he had no clue where to place his next step. So he just sat, blinking, like a genius.

"Some might call it grace," Coach went on, as if not noticing Brad's sudden lack of speech. "It's not an ideal mistake, I'll grant you. But I have a feeling this isn't a mistake you'll be making again. *Ever.* Is it?"

Brad shook his head at that.

"Besides that, I think you do more good to the team than harm, even if you've got a semi-bum leg. Come with me."

Brad followed him to the door of the office, looking out over the gym. The team was all in a forward fold, with Marianne's friend Kara leading them through a transition to a half moon. Kara demonstrated both the beginner positon and what Brad assumed was the actual regular position.

Instinctively, Brad's eyes sought out Marianne. But her compact body wasn't mixed in with those of the rest of the athletes. She wasn't there.

"See Tressler?"

Brad fought the urge to roll his eyes. Pavlovian response to the younger man's name. He glanced through the rows and found him at the back. "Yes, sir."

"Watch."

Beside Tressler, Chalfant wobbled, then nearly collapsed on the next transition. Brad winced. The guy had come a long way, but he still carried the heart of a klutz around with him. And falling on his ass in front of Tressler was the worst-case scenario.

To Brad's surprise, Tressler waited for Chalfant to stand, then nudged him with an elbow, and pointed to his own feet. He was demonstrating a better way to position his lower foot for the pose to make it easier. Chalfant grinned and followed suit, hitting the next pose with more confidence, if not grace.

"Two weeks ago," the coach's deep voice said over his shoulder, "Tressler would have been mocking Chalfant for a week for landing ass over elbows during yoga. Now he's helping out, without any of the coaching staff watching to suck up to. That change in his spirit wasn't from us. It was you."

"Me," Brad said in disbelief. "He doesn't even like me."

"This is exactly why we chose you to be one of the group leaders. They want to please you. Impress you. You've done something to earn his respect, enough that he's starting to emulate you." Coach laughed a little. "There are worse guys to pattern themselves after."

"Uh, thank you." *I think?*

"Just promise me there will be no more dumbass stunts like this again."

"No, sir."

"Later today, we'll bring Cook in and talk about a game plan to deal with the knee. Make sure you give her the paperwork from the physical therapist and we'll meet here after practice to discuss it."

"Actually . . ." Brad cleared his throat. "Coach, I was hoping I could discuss it with her privately first. Given the, um, situation. I'd like to just have some time to talk it out. Could we meet before morning practice instead? Half an hour before warm-ups, maybe?"

Coach raised a brow at that, but smiled. At least, Brad thought it was a smile. The older man's lips twitched upward for at least half a second. "Tomorrow morning is good enough."

Brad stood and held out a hand. "I apologize for—"

"Just go play yoga," Coach grumbled. As Brad hit the door, he swore he heard the Coach mutter, "Good luck with that, kid."

He was going to need it.

CHAPTER

22

Marianne looked up at the knock on her door. Reagan entered, holding a manila folder. "Are your interns in here?"

"They're out watching the guys." She should be out there, as well. She told herself it was better to stay in and finish up the paperwork. She was lying.

"Perfect. I need you to sign this for me, then." She slid a piece of paper out from her folder and handed it to Marianne. "It's just a simple form explaining the relationship between yourself and Lieutenant Costa, as explained to your supervisor and the coach. It shows you were up-front about the situation and that you and he both agree it won't affect your working relationship."

Marianne snorted at that. When Reagan tilted her head in question, she shook hers. "Sorry. Allergies."

"Hmm." Reagan handed her a pen. "Just a signature, and then I'll get Lieutenant Costa's, and we should be all set. It's a formality, simply a CYA thing."

Too bad Marianne hadn't thought to cover her own ass. Otherwise she might not have been in this position to begin with. How the hell did she sign this piece of paper now, knowing that very soon, her relationship would likely be done? "Can I just give this a look through later and give it to you tomorrow? I've got a lot of paperwork to finish up."

"Oh." Blinking in surprise—because really, who needed an entire day to read through three paragraphs—Reagan lifted one shoulder in a shrug. "All right. No problem. No rush, I'd just like to have it on file before we start traveling." She started out, heels clicking over the linoleum, then turned back. "Have you had any more problems with the training room?"

"Problems . . . oh." Marianne sat back in her chair, surprised. "No, not that I can think of. Why? Was there more vandalism upstairs?"

"No . . ." Her voice trailed off, and Reagan glanced toward the door.

"They're not coming back in here. I told them to stand guard," Marianne assured her.

"We received some threatening mail at the main office." Reagan sat down in the chair Levi normally occupied and crossed her legs daintily. "Nothing too serious—nothing to call the bomb squad over. But it was enough to spook me. Nobody else seems to think it's a big deal."

Marianne knew there was something to a woman's gut feeling. But Reagan was younger, in her first job out of college. It could have been as simple as being unsure of herself and not wanting to disregard any potential problem, even when there wasn't one. "Did whoever sent them take responsibility for the vandalism here?"

"No, not in so many words." Chewing on her lip a little, Reagan switched her legs and drummed her fingers on top of the desk for a moment. The perfect manicure wouldn't hold up to that kind of beating for long. "I just don't want any problems."

Sorry, sweetheart. I'm about to dump a breakup in your lap by morning. "Understandable. I'm sure if the higher-ups aren't worried, it's probably nothing."

"Maybe." Sounding unconvinced, Reagan stood. "Enjoy the rest of your day."

Marianne hummed something noncommittal and looked at the sheet in her hand. With a sigh, she let it fall to the bottom of her stack of paperwork. She'd end up handing it back, blank, in the morning.

Kara popped her head in to wave good-bye, but otherwise Marianne's afternoon sailed on relatively uninterrupted. She managed to get nearly caught up on paperwork to the point where she wouldn't feel guilty about leaving it to a new trainer. When the Marines started filing in for ice bags, heating pads and help cutting tape off wrists, she put her problems aside and dealt with them, as well as her interns.

She'd end up dealing with Brad soon enough.

BRAD hung around the gym as long as he could stand, hoping to be the last guy in the training room. He needed to talk to her in her own space. For some reason, the conversation didn't feel right for her apartment. As if the temporary domestic bliss they'd experienced in her home wouldn't be able to stand the news he was about to drop on her.

Keeping it confined to her professional domain might be enough to get through this unscathed.

Yeah, right.

He walked in as Chalfant walked out. The guy looked raw, as if he'd taken too many beatings. "You okay, man?"

Chalfant tried a smile, but then just raised his hands and let them fall. "Last cuts are coming soon."

And Brad got it. The nerves were chewing on him from

the inside out. He clapped his hand over the younger man's shoulder and squeezed. "Get a good night's sleep. We'll talk about it in the morning. You can't let it get to you, or you're just creating a self-fulfilling prophecy."

"Easier said than done," Chalfant said with a grimace.

"Try some yoga before bed," he suggested. When Chalfant huffed out a laugh, Brad sent him on his way and stepped into the training room.

There were a few Marines finishing up their icing session. The guy intern was dumping out a bucket into the huge sink, while the girl sat chatting one of the guys up. And Marianne—his calm in the storm—moved from one table to the next, assessing and encouraging, educating and . . .

He grinned.

Handing out another pamphlet.

He walked in, and she turned immediately. The smile on her face faded, and he wondered what that was all about. He waved, then went to get a bag of ice and ask Levi to start his time on the sheet. The younger man glanced up with what looked like annoyance, but wrote his name and time down with a nod.

With no free table, he settled his back against a wall on the floor, stretched his knee out and closed his eyes. The best part about icing was the fact that it gave him an excuse to sit still for twenty full minutes.

As his body relaxed and his heart rate slowed, he heard Marines leave one by one. But it was as if he were hearing them from underwater, or from a great distance. For the first time in a long time, his mind felt uncluttered from the knowledge that he was keeping a secret from his coach. The simple act of unburdening himself to Coach had lifted a metric ton of weight off his shoulders.

He prayed the same thing would happen when he talked to Marianne.

He heard Nikki say her good-byes to Marianne and

Levi. Then Levi came over and nudged his left foot. "You're done. Dump the ice and you're free to go."

"Thanks." He stood stiffly—even when he was relaxed, sitting on the floor wasn't ideal—and tore the bag open, letting the last of the ice and water run into the sink. He watched over his shoulder as Levi grabbed his bag, took one last look at Brad, asked Marianne if she was sure she was okay, then took off. Maybe the crush wasn't on Nikki, but on his boss. Brad smiled at that. He couldn't blame the kid.

When he tossed the wet bag in the trash, he found Marianne sitting at her desk, back to him, making notes. He walked over and ran a hand over the nape of her neck. She jerked, then hunched away from his touch.

What the hell?

"Hey. Sorry, didn't mean to startle you."

She shuffled papers, stuck them in a folder, then turned. Her face was grim, and a sudden chill slid through his gut.

"What's wrong?"

She lifted her hands; let them fall back into her lap. "You tell me."

He raised a brow at her tone. She wasn't typically so snippy. He propped one hip against a file cabinet and crossed his arms over his chest. "I'd rather not play the guess-why-I'm-mad game. My sister plays that shit all the time and I suck at it."

Marianne's brows furrowed together. "This is a game? I asked you to tell me what was wrong. As your athletic trainer, that's not a game. It's a serious question."

Okay, so they weren't in lover-mode. Fine. "I wanted to talk to you about my knee."

Her face lightened slightly, and she leaned forward. "Sit."

He grabbed the other rolling chair and dragged it over. "I have some paperwork I need to hand you. It's in my duffel out in the gym. Basically, it's a torn meniscus. Not the worst injury, but something to deal with. And so we're going in tomorrow morning with Coach thirty minutes before warm up to talk to him about it."

She nodded slowly, watching as his hand unconsciously went to rub at the area just above his kneecap. "How long have you known that?"

He tensed. "It's been painful for a while, but not unbearable."

"That wasn't what I asked."

"About ten days."

Her eyes slowly slid closed, and her lips moved as if she were saying a prayer to herself. Brad waited patiently. Whatever condemnation she threw at him, he'd earned.

"But it's hurt all along, hasn't it?"

"Since the second day, I guess." He shrugged. "I've worked through it. It's not paralyzing pain or anything like that."

"I know what it is." She took a deep breath, then let it out and ran a hand through her hair. Some of the blonde hairs pulled loose from her short ponytail and drifted down to rest against her cheek. Her now-flushed cheek. Flushed from relief? Heat? Or anger?

"You've known for almost two weeks what was wrong, and you didn't tell me."

Okay, anger. "I wasn't ready to—"

"And because I didn't know, I wasn't able to do my job." The flush crept down her neck now, and her ice-blue eyes were like white-hot flames, searing straight through him. "And now, I get to go to the coach tomorrow and discuss this with him, and he's going to ask me why I didn't know this sort of important information two weeks ago, when you did."

"He already knows."

She blinked at that. "He . . . Since when?"

"Since the beginning of practice. I skipped yoga and talked to him about it."

She sat back in her seat with a chair-squeaking thump. "You went and talked to him without me?"

"Uh . . ." Brad knew a trap when he was walking right into one.

"You obviously did," she went on, without giving him time to pick an answer. She closed her eyes, then ran a hand down her face. "Great. Not only could you not talk to me about it, you went to the coach first." She laughed, but the sound was scratchy. "When you throw someone under the bus, you do it right."

"That's not what I did. That's not what I meant," he corrected when she shot him a glare so cold he wondered if he'd ever need to ice his knee again. He was losing his grip on the situation. Losing her.

"Look, I wanted him to understand first that—"

"That I can't do my job. That's what you basically said, by going there first. And you're right." She glanced down at the desktop, with its neatly stacked papers and files. "You're probably right," she said again in a low voice. "I should have pushed harder from the start. Played hardball. I would have, if you'd been anyone else. I take responsibility for that much. I just . . . from that first night we had dinner . . ." Her voice trailed off, and her eyes shifted from contemplative to accusatory. "Is that why you asked me out that first time? The night we went to dinner?"

"That was just dinner," he said weakly.

"I was bugging you about your knee." She held up a finger, then another. "You shot me down. I started again, and you asked me to dinner. To distract me? Was that . . ." Her eyes grew round, and his stomach roiled. If he'd have eaten lunch, he'd have lost it. "Is that what this whole thing was? Oh my God."

"No. Jesus H., no, Marianne. You're spinning." He stood, went to pull her into his arms. If he could hold her for a minute, just a minute, they'd both calm the hell down and they could talk it out more rationally. "I—"

"Tell me the truth." Her voice cut through him like tiny blades, but it was nothing compared to the hurt he felt when she scooted her chair out of his reach. "Right now, because I'm watching your eyes and I'll know this time. Did you ask me to dinner . . . did you start this with me to keep me from hassling you about your knee?"

He hesitated, and that cost him. He could see it in the way she shut down. "I asked you to dinner to stop the inquisition, but—"

The blood drained from her face, and if she hadn't been sitting down he would have had to lunge to keep her from falling to the floor face-first. As it was, he wondered if she'd just slide straight out of the chair into a puddle on the ground.

"I'm such an idiot," she whispered.

"No." He kept his voice firm, praying it would cut through whatever emotional bullshit she was letting block him out. "No, you're not. This is my shit. I should have—"

"I should have seen past my emotions. I sat there, and let myself love you, and let this go on longer than . . ." She squeezed her eyes closed for a moment. "I'm an idiot, and a fool. And most likely jobless. So." She clapped her hands together once, the sharp sound echoing in the empty training room. Then she stood on stiff legs and grabbed her bag from under the desk. "Just . . . whatever paperwork you have, slide it under the door before you leave. I'll grab it and put it in your file in the morning before the meeting. Thirty minutes before warm-up, like you said."

"You're leaving? Just like that." God, why couldn't she slow down and let him *talk* for a minute?

"Just like that," she agreed, looping the strap over her shoulder. She watched him for a moment, face still white, eyes a little hollow. When he didn't move, she waved an arm expectantly toward the door. "You have to go first. I need to lock the door."

"I can't . . ." He cleared his throat, struggling to talk around the lump. "I can't just leave with us like this."

"You can, and you will. Unless you want to be arrested for trespassing."

His legs felt like lead, and it had nothing to do with the afternoon's conditioning exercises. But he managed to walk out through the wide double doors of the training room and wait for her to close them. "Just . . . can you call me later? Please. Let me know you got home okay, or something?"

"I've been driving myself around Jacksonville longer than you've been in the Marine Corps. I'll get home just fine." She locked the door, then turned and headed for the parking lot. He started to follow, then remembered his duffel and ran to grab it, cursing a little when his knee caught and hitched his stride. When he got to the parking lot himself, her car was pulling out.

She was gone, and there was no way in hell she wanted him chasing after her.

Jesus H.

MARIANNE made it home—barely—before the tears started. How could she have been so damn stupid? She'd sat there and fallen in love with one of her athletes. Had given herself permission to. That was bad enough, though not the end of the world. But she'd let it blind her to his problems . . . or at least to the severity of them. She'd let it damage her credibility as a trainer.

Damn him for doing this to her. For not only breaking her heart, but her confidence.

She beat on the steering wheel, jolting when her fist hit the horn instead.

Fantastic idea, Marianne. Destroy your property. That'll show him.

She forced herself to take a deep breath, but that only ended in a hiccup, and she started all over again.

She was losing the guy she'd fallen in love with. Losing that sappy dream, the one that had caused her to doodle hearts and swirls on a notebook page. Just remembering that embarrassing moment made her cringe.

And now she was losing the dream of working in the big leagues. Colleges, minor leagues, farm teams . . . good-bye. Maybe taping up entitled high school jocks and icing down cheerleading injuries was just where she belonged.

Five seconds of that train of thought and Marianne knew it was absolute, utter bullshit. She was good at her job. She'd made a mistake, damn it, but who the hell *didn't* make one every so often? She'd learned, that was for sure. No way was she even getting remotely involved with an athlete after this. Burned once . . .

She would go into the coach's office tomorrow, lay down the error, tell him it wouldn't happen again, and accept the lecture she deserved. And she would treat it as a foregone conclusion that she would keep her job, because she was good at it. As far as working with Brad . . . she would be a professional, because that's what she was. A damn professional.

Her phone beeped, and she checked it. Kara.

How'd it go?

She knew her friend wasn't asking about practice. She was asking about Brad.

Not so good.

Wanna come over for pancakes? Son's cooking.

She nearly said no, because really, pancakes now? Heartbreak could not be solved by carb-alicious pancakes and syrup.

But then again, it couldn't hurt.

An hour later, she pushed away from the coffee table where she and Kara were sitting cross-legged on the floor, watching a *Project Runway* marathon thanks to DVR. "Those were amazing. Seriously. That kid needs to be a chef."

"He is sort of amazing, isn't he?" Kara smiled the warm smile of maternal pride, and maybe a little smugness. Marianne didn't blame her. Anyone who raised a halfway decent kid had a reason to be smug.

Marianne's bag rang, and Kara reached for it without asking.

"Go right ahead." Marianne waved and let her head hit the seat of the couch behind them. She patted her belly, too full to do anything else. "Tell whoever it is I'm currently in a breakfast-for-dinner food coma and I'll get back to them tomorrow."

"It's Brad."

She didn't move, but her entire body tensed. "Then tell him to fuck off."

"Kid in the room," Zach said wryly as he came in to grab their plates.

"Sorry, Zach." Marianne cracked an eye open and shot Kara an apologetic smile. "My bad."

"He's heard worse at school, I'm sure. Though he knows not to repeat it," Kara added with a warning tone.

Her son saluted her and headed back to the kitchen with their empty plates. A moment later, they heard the sink running.

"He cooks pancakes *and* does dishes? I'll take two."

Kara chuckled. "He's sucking up. I took away the Xbox for sassing off, and he's attempting to get back into my good graces so he can return to *Minecraft* a day or two early."

"Not gonna happen, is it?"

"Hell, no. But I'm not telling him that. I might get a load or two of laundry out of the deal before I drop the truth bomb." Kara held up the phone, which beeped with a voice mail. "Want to check it?"

"No. There's really nothing left to talk about." She held out a hand for the phone, but it started ringing again before Kara could pass it over. "Now who?"

"Brad again." Kara rejected the call, then turned Marianne's phone off before tossing it back in the tote bag. "There. You can check it tomorrow when you get to work."

"I love you."

"I know you do." Kara pressed her cheek to Marianne's head for a moment. "Do you need to stay here, or are you okay to drive back home?"

"I had eighteen pancakes, not beers. Ugh," she finished with a groan, rubbing her stomach harder. "You'd think I'd learn. Carbs never solve anything."

"But they taste delicious while you avoid your problems." Kara snickered as Marianne flipped her off. "Come on, Carb Queen. Let's get you back to your car."

CHAPTER

23

After voice mail number three—the third of which never even rang, just went straight to her inbox—Brad realized he was probably doing more harm than good at this point. His finger hovered over Marianne's contact, then he forced himself to scroll up and call his mother instead.

"Bradley!" Hearing his mom's warm greeting—rather than a cold voice mail recording—instantly kicked his mood up a few notches. "Still hanging in there?"

"Still hanging in. Some days, by my fingernails."

"Staying healthy?"

He debated a moment, then decided she could take it. "I hurt my knee, but it's not too bad. I can still box, so that's what's important."

"That's hardly what's important." Worry bled through the phone line, and he hated giving her even a second of concern. "Your health is the important thing. Making sure after this is all over that you're healthy enough to walk. Is it bad?"

"If it was bad, I wouldn't still be here. They'd have sent me home. It's really not that bad. I've got a doctor, a physical therapist and a trainer watching over me. Plus the coach."

"Well, okay. If you're sure."

"I'm sure. This is important to me." He flopped down on the bed and stared at the ceiling.

"It was important to your father, too. But it wasn't the only thing he had going on, you know. He had you and your brother. And me, naturally. We were his world, and running was just a small, satisfying corner piece of the total puzzle. We were the big picture."

He closed his eyes for a moment, and it was almost as if Brad could see a family portrait of them, as they had been right before his father had died. Smiling out from a puzzle that had the edges covered in their hobbies. His brother's baseball, his boxing . . . The image made him smile.

"That was deep, Mom."

"Uh-huh." Her sarcasm came through loud and clear. "Ready for something else deep? I need you to think about what you want your big picture to look like. Your love of boxing is great, and I get it. And your desire to do this for your father is beautiful. But it's not what defines you. What's your big picture, Bradley?"

"I love you, Mom." He wanted to tell her then, right then, that he'd already ruined his big picture. Marianne was finished with him—three unanswered, unreturned calls said that much loud and clear. So now what? His puzzle was just a bunch of edge pieces, with no middle?

"I love you too, Brad. Now, tell me more about boxing. Have you kicked anyone's ass lately?"

"Mom." He couldn't help but laugh, even as his eyes burned from resisting tears.

Ten minutes later, as he hung up the phone, he heard Higgs come in through the shared common door. After a minute, Brad went over and knocked on his door. Higgs answered with a clipped, "Come in."

"Hey." As Brad leaned his shoulder against the doorjamb, he realized this was the first time he'd come to Higgs' room, rather than the other way around. Had he been so closed off he hadn't even approached his own roomie once? "What's up?"

"I was just meeting my group for dinner. So." Tossing his backpack on the desk, Higgs watched him. "You missed yoga. Hot date?"

"I think my days of hot dates are over." He hesitated, then walked in and sat at the desk chair, much as Higgs had done in Brad's room numerous times before. Made himself at home. That's what friends did. "Cook's done with me."

"Women," Higgs scoffed. "They just can't get over it when a guy lies to them. How weird."

"Okay, asshole, if you're gonna be cute, I'll just head to my own room." Brad started to stand, but sat back down when his friend laughed. "Not funny," he grumbled.

"It's hilarious. Grandpa, Mr. I Work Alone, gets dumped by the hottie trainer the minute he realizes he doesn't actually *want* to work alone. Yeah . . . that's irony." Stretching out on the bed, Higgs grinned. "So what's the plan?"

"Plan . . ." Not following, Brad rested his good leg on the corner of the bed. "Uh, don't get cut?"

"Oh, boy. You suck at this." Roommate sighed and rolled his eyes. "I mean the plan to get hottie Cook back. You're not telling me you're just going to let her walk, are you? Because I didn't *think* you were an idiot, but maybe I was wrong."

"I didn't *think* you were deaf, but maybe I was wrong. She dumped me. There is no plan."

"I'm sorry, are you actually taking 'no' for an answer?

What the hell kind of Marine are you?" Higgs actually looked offended at the possibility that Brad was accepting the situation as-is. "When the woman you love walks away, you run after her."

"That sounds like an awful plan. Chasing after a woman?"

"You're not chasing after her." Higgs closed his eyes for a moment, as if in a bid for patience. "Have you never seen a chick flick before? The guy always fucks up, and then he does something spectacular to win the girl back."

"Big fan of the chick flick, are you?" Brad smirked.

"I'm a big fan of keeping the girl I'm with—whoever she happens to be that week—satisfied."

Brad rolled his eyes at the implied gigolo status.

"That has meant, on occasion, downing a tub of movie popcorn while seeing the selection of her choice. Side note . . . women who just got done watching a good romance are usually ready for some loving of their own."

"Stop. Just stop."

Higgs grinned and laced his hands behind his head. "Fine, be a prude. That's not the point. The point is, you're not running after her. Think of the drills we run. We're all in a line, jogging at a pretty moderate pace, then guy in the back sprints up front to . . ."

"Get in front of the line," Brad answered slowly, entirely unsure where this metaphor was heading.

"To get *ahead* of everyone. He's not running to chase after them, he's running to get ahead. So if he stopped dead in his tracks, the rest of the team would run smack into him. He's in their way now."

"Right. So, what you're saying is . . . I want her to run into me."

"There you go." Looking like a satisfied teacher whose student had finally caught on to the material, Higgs gave him a thumbs up. "So get in her way."

"Get in her way," he repeated slowly. The metaphor was making more sense than he wanted to admit. Either Brad was desperate, or Higgs wasn't half-bad in the romance department. "And I do that . . . how exactly?"

"Sweet Jesus, I have to do everything." Sitting up with a grunt, Higgs spread his hands out. "What matters to her? Besides you, and maybe family—because involving parents in the wooing of their daughter is just a line that I don't jump over—what is there?"

"Work. Her career." That much, at least, was obvious.

"So how can you incorporate that into getting her back? You use her career, some humor, a dash of humility, and you've got yourself a surefire way of making sure she can't miss you." He settled back against the headboard and grabbed the remote for his small TV from the nightstand. "Get in her way."

"Get in her way," Brad mumbled as he walked back to his own room. What the hell was he supposed to do for that? Write "I LOVE YOU" in athletic tape on her training room walls?

He froze with his hand on his bedroom door handle, considering.

Nah. She'd call that a waste of good tape.

There was nothing he could buy . . . she had all the equipment she needed provided to her. He couldn't help her keep her job . . . Coach Ace had already said he wasn't going to let her go. So what could he . . .

The lightbulb hit him in the back of the skull like a bolt of lightning. He scrambled over his bed and grabbed his phone and called Tressler.

"Hey. Grab the group and meet me at that craft store off of Western. Yeah, the craft store. No, I'm not bullshitting you, just do it. I'll be there in twenty. Tressler . . . I need you guys."

He hung up, feeling hope once more springing through him.

He'd been knocked down, but it was time to get back up and get in Marianne Cook's way.

MARIANNE walked across the gym toward the coach's office early the next morning, prepared to have her ass handed to her, and then fight like hell to keep her job. As asked, Brad had slipped his report from his doctor and PT under her door the night before. She'd come to the gym early to pick them up and read them through.

Thank God, the damage was minor, and not a real threat to permanent damage. She'd prefer he took the season off to rest and get back to full strength again, but it wasn't going to cause permanent damage to keep an eye on it, wear the brace and practice with caution.

Three things that could have been happening all along had he just been honest with her.

Since they weren't due to meet with the coach for another thirty minutes, she wasn't shocked to see Coach Ace's door closed. Either he wasn't in yet, or he was and didn't want to be disturbed by any early comers.

Prepare to be disturbed.

She knocked, then poked her head in. Coach Ace sat at the computer, staring at the keyboard with disdain. One hand ran over his snowy white hair with agitation. "Coach?"

He glanced up, frustration radiating from his body. "Get in here and type for me."

"Because I'm a woman?" she asked, deciding to start as she meant to go on: boldly.

"Because you're half my size and my damn fingers never hit the right keys at the right time." He stood and held out his chair for her. She sat, because she was at a loss of how else to say no. "Finish typing up this report here in the space. The cursor's already in place. Last one." He took a seat in the visitor's chair and waved at the paper. "Go ahead."

"Uh, I actually had something important to talk to you about." She put her fingers on the keys, finding the home buttons, then pulled them back. "We need to talk—"

"About Costa, I know. Type," he said again, softly. "I'm talking, you're typing."

She swallowed, then accepted that not only was she going to get her ass chewed out, she was going to be mildly demeaned in the process. Given some of the hazing she'd seen happen in gyms, typing a single report sheet wasn't much to complain about. She started at it, typing with the ease born of having a laptop since she was twelve years old.

"Now see? My fingers are too clumsy to go that fast. Or that accurately," he added, with a small smile. "I spend more time going backward than forward on that thing."

Marianne couldn't help but grin at that.

"Now, about Costa." He settled down in his chair—or rather, the guest chair. His huge frame wasn't made for a such a flimsy seat. She wondered if she'd be soon dragging him into her training room to ice down a chair-related injury.

"Costa is a leader. He might not be a leader on the scoreboard, but the boy's got the Pied Piper syndrome."

Marianne hadn't ever heard it put quite that way, but could easily follow the coach's meaning . . . and she agreed with him. She nodded once while glancing between the paper and the computer screen.

"I'd hate to lose him."

"That's what I wanted to—"

"And I'd hate to lose you."

There was the opening shot. "I'd hate to lose the team."

He nodded slowly, glancing around the room. She stopped typing to watch him. His dark face was devoid of any hint to his emotions. Pissed? Upset? Couldn't care less? She wouldn't have made a bet on any of them. "You see, that right there is why I'm about to say what I'm about to say. You'd hate to lose what?"

"Lose . . . the team?" Was that what he meant?

"There." He pointed one thick finger at her. "Right there. You could have said job, or this opportunity, or even your paycheck. But the first thing out of your mouth was 'team.'" He settled back again, a pleased smile on his face. "I think that says something, don't you?"

"I . . ." She looked down at the paper again, but her eyes were blurring. "I don't want to lose my job either, if that matters. Or the opportunity. And since I like being able to pay my rent . . . I don't want to lose my paycheck."

"Who does? But it wasn't first on the list. That's what matters to me. When it came down to it, you put the team above your own wants. There's the kicker."

She was quiet, blinking furiously to clear her line of vision so she could keep typing. If her fingers were busy, she could think better.

"I find it amusing," Coach went on in a calm voice, "that I sat in here yesterday and had someone else willing to put other people ahead of his own wants. Know someone like that?"

She didn't look up now, because if she did, he'd see the tear that rolled down her cheek and dropped into her lap. Maybe he saw it already. But he was kind enough—or embarrassed enough—to say nothing about it.

"I had a good Marine, a good boxer and a damn great leader sit in that chair yesterday and tell me he was walking because he thought I'd fire you otherwise. He was prepared to take the hit so you could keep your job."

She looked up sharply, tear—and embarrassment—forgotten. "He quit? He just . . . quit?"

Coach watched her silently.

"That stupid son of a bitch," she murmured, shaking

her head. When she got her hands on him, his knee was going to be the *last* thing he worried about. "That stupid, pigheaded, stubborn—"

"Much as I love to hear a woman wax poetic," Coach Ace said dryly, "I'll just say he didn't quit. He tried, but I shot him down. He can't leave. I need him. The team needs him."

She let her eyes drift closed. Her mind, having been so sharp with anger and frustration only moments ago, now felt fuzzy with relief. As if she were drifting on fluffy clouds of thought, with nothing concrete to anchor her anymore. The whole thing was just fucked up.

"So I'm keeping my trainer, and I'm keeping my boxer. I guess we're all done."

She cracked one eye open and held up the sheet of paper. "I'm not finished. Are you going to make me sit here and finish typing?"

He flashed a rare grin at her. "Nah. I just know that when people are nervous, doing something with their hands makes them easier to talk to. You happened to come in when I was struggling with the keyboard. Luck of the draw."

"Next time, I'll bring my knitting needles and we can gossip over the scarf I'm making my Nana for Christmas," she said, and he laughed.

Sobering, he stood. She did as well, and held out a hand.

"I promise our, uh, *situation* won't affect our work, on either side, from now on. Business only."

The coach raised a brow at that. "You mean to tell me I just confessed that man was ready to walk out of my gym to save your job, and you're not going to give him a second chance?" He whistled low. "That's cold."

"He . . . but he . . ." She blinked in surprise. "I'm sorry, I'm confused. Were you telling me all that to get us back together?"

He rolled his eyes and walked to his office door. "I'm

here to coach boxing, not play Cupid. This isn't Marine Matchmaking Headquarters. Date-A-Boxer," he grumbled. "If you can't take the information I just gave you and put two with two together, then the both of you aren't ready to date a turnip."

She wasn't sure if she was supposed to be insulted or amused. He opened the door ahead of her and she waited for him to walk through, but rammed straight into his back with her nose instead. "Ow!"

"Oh, uh . . . sorry." He took one step back, in which he stepped on her toes and nearly tossed her to the ground. "Sorry, sorry. My bad."

"Coach . . ." She danced out of the way as he quickly shut the door again. "What the—"

"You know . . ." He glanced around the office wildly, his hands shoved deep in his sweatpants pockets. "Could you, uh, finish that report really fast?"

She stared at him, dumbfounded. "Right now? You've got practice to get ready for. I've got a training room to supervise."

"No, see, because you were early and practice doesn't start for another"—he checked his stopwatch—"forty minutes."

She waited for a better explanation than that. He stared at her, a mountain of a man she'd be crazy to try to dodge around to get to the door. "You seriously want me to sit in here and type. Like a secretary."

"My fingers." He held up ham-sized hands, which really did have quite thick, blunt digits attached. With a soulful look, he glanced toward the computer and back again. "You'd really help me out."

Since crawling between his legs to get to the door wasn't an option, she sighed. "Just finish the form?"

"Just that one last form." He sat back down, grabbed

his clipboard from the corner of his desk and a pen and settled back in the chair. "Maybe one more. Or two. Three, maximum."

"One," she said firmly and settled down, resolving she would cave and do two as penance. It felt as if she'd gotten off easy on the ass-chewing she'd deserved. "Coach?"

"Hmm?" He was scribbling now, and she could easily imagine he was writing down boxing combinations, or conditioning drills, or group work.

"Would you have still boxed with a torn meniscus?"

"I did, for almost a year. I told him the same thing, and that the surgery isn't difficult, and recovery is more annoying than painful." When she chewed on her lip, he set the pen down and sighed. "He's a big boy, Cook. Don't make me play couples counselor, too. I'm not cut out for that shit."

When she took in his imposing scowl and irritated body language, her lips twitched. "I don't know, I think you might make a good one. You'd be one of those no-bullshit, straight-shooting kind of counselors that won't let guys lie and girls weep to get out of being open."

"Pass." He went back to his clipboard. But she noticed he brought his phone out of his pocket and spent more time texting than writing.

"Done." She pushed the first form toward him. "I hit save. Is that all?"

"One more." He handed her another from the manila folder. "Please?"

She sighed, as if completely put-upon, and went back to typing.

Brad would be by any minute to start their originally scheduled meeting. Would she stay? Or let him talk to the coach on his own? Maybe there wouldn't be a need to worry the coach about it, and they could just clear the air fully and move on.

Yeah, that would be good. Get out her feelings on the subject of their relationship—*I hate you for making me love you but I still love you and I hate that, too*—and he could say his piece and they could part ways as colleagues. Mature, rational and succinct.

Yeah. Right.

CHAPTER

24

Brad paced the gym floor, not sure whether he was ready to knock down the coach's door or run to the locker room to throw up. All he knew was he needed this to work more than he needed anything else.

"She's been in there forever," Higgs complained, walking over to Brad. He set his poster board down and propped an elbow on Brad's shoulder. "What the hell could they be doing in there?"

"Coach started to open the door, like three minutes ago," Chalfant said helpfully. "I think he caught sight of us and slammed it again really fast, 'cause we weren't ready for her yet."

"Because she got here early," Brad grumbled. He could only imagine what she was in there talking about. "If she'd gotten here at the time we set up, I'd be in there with her and I'd know what the hell she was thinking."

"Breathe," Higgs muttered. "Breathe, damn it. You're going to hyperventilate and swoon."

"Guys don't swoon," Chalfant said helpfully.

"Yeah, they pass out," added one of Higgs' group members.

"Everything's a joke." Brad rubbed at his forehead. He needed this to work. It *had* to work. He had to show her he could set aside his pride and be all in, the way she had been from the moment she agreed to jump headfirst into their relationship.

She deserved him to be all in, too. Hell, *he* deserved for him to be all in.

"You're more nervous than a virgin getting grilled by your date's daddy on prom night," Higgs joked, poking him in the ribs.

"At least Coach Ace isn't her daddy," Tressler put in helpfully. The rest of the guys cracked up laughing. Brad scowled.

"I think you're sweating more now than you do after two hours of cardio training." Higgs lowered his voice so only Brad could hear. "You doing okay, buddy?"

"No," Brad said tightly.

"Can I get out of this damn chair?" Tibbs asked.

"No," Brad said again. "Now sit down, shut up and be a good prop."

Tibbs grumbled, but stayed seated. It was the only way Brad would let him participate past helping to create his visual aid.

"Tired," Higgs breathed after a minute. "So tired. We got, what, ninety minutes of sleep thanks to making these posters? When is she coming out of there?"

"Pamphlets," Brad corrected automatically. "They're pamphlets."

"Right. Pamphlets." Higgs grinned at that. "Cook does love her pamphlets."

Here's hoping she loves this.

He started to ask Higgs to check the time again, then froze. Were those . . .

Were those footsteps?

"There's almost an hour before morning conditioning." He looked toward the hallway. "Who the hell would be here?"

"Uh . . ."

Brad swung around to stare at his roommate. "What did you do?"

"So, funny story . . ."

"What. Did. You. Do."

"Okay, okay, calm down. You're starting to scare me."

"I know where you sleep. You *should* be scared."

The door to the gym opened, and Graham Sweeney walked in, followed by his group. They each carried in their hands a poster, folded in thirds like the ones his and Higgs' groups were holding, to resemble a pamphlet.

"Are those . . ." Brad squinted. "Are those pamphlets?"

"They are. What?" Higgs said when Brad glared. "I thought we needed reinforcements."

"I don't even know what those say!" Brad wanted to wrap his hands around his roommate's neck and squeeze. So very slowly. Ounce by precious ounce of pressure, until his roommate's eyes bugged out like a cartoon character.

Higgs shrugged unapologetically. "What? If five is good, ten is better. If ten is better, fifteen is best. They like Cook, and they respect you. They want to help."

"Great, but . . . what the hell do those things say?"

"All the leftover ideas we scrapped because we didn't have time to make enough pos—pamphlets," Higgs corrected himself. "It's all stuff you agreed to, just didn't have time for. Seriously, nothing too off the cuff. Don't worry, they stay in the spirit of the thing."

"The spirit of the thing," Brad repeated through his

teeth. He was a man on the edge. He didn't want this ruined by anyone's attempt at humor.

Sweeney walked over and slapped Brad on the shoulder. "Big morning, huh? Early practice."

"Why are you here?" he heard himself ask before he could think better of it. Then he winced at how ungrateful it sounded.

"Because you're a teammate. Even if teams haven't been finalized, I think of you as a team member. We all do. And these infants respect the hell out of you, Grandpa."

At that, Brad felt his lips twitch. "I respect the hell out of you, too. Thanks." He shook Sweeney's hand, then grunted when the other man brought him in for a chest-thumping hug.

"Here she comes," Chalfant hissed. The sound echoed through the gym, and then the silent room was full of the shuffling of running shoes on hardwood as Marines scrambled to take their places.

The first face Brad saw was Coach's. He looked smug, and maybe a little satisfied.

And then he saw Marianne.

And prayed he was looking at his future.

WHEN the coach cleared his throat, Marianne nearly jumped out of her seat. "I think that's enough for now."

She looked down at the form she was typing out, then at the screen. She was only half done. "But I—"

"Cook, that's enough." His tone had edged into his hard-ass coaching voice. "Go get set up for your day. I'll work on it later."

She glanced at him skeptically, but shrugged. Fine then. "Okay, well, if you need me, you know where to find me."

He stood and waited for her to walk around the desk, then opened up the door. She hesitated this time, wondering if he'd pull the same trick and close her in again. When he raised a brow, she pointed to him, then the door. "I was just making sure you weren't going to repeat the last performance at the door."

"Smart-ass," he said fondly.

"It's genetic." With a smile she hoped he took sincerely, she stepped out of the office.

And straight into Pamphlet Heaven.

Everywhere she looked, there were Marines standing around, holding poster boards tri-folded like pamphlets. And they were all watching her expectantly. Concerned, confused and maybe a little scared, she looked back at Coach. He nodded and nudged her out into the gym fully.

She walked by the first Marine—Tibbs, who was sitting down like a good boy—and read the outside of his poster.

"Why Marianne Cook Is an Amazing Trainer," she read out loud. Tibbs opened the fold, and she read through several bullet points about her accomplishments as an athletic trainer . . . most of which weren't so much academic or career-related, but emotional. Things like, "She has gentle hands" or "She's efficient" made her smile. She swallowed hard when she read, "We trust her, all the way."

"Thank you," she whispered to Tibbs, then walked to Chalfant. He grinned at her, his freckled face looking so young and sweet, and presented his own pamphlet.

"Why . . ." She let out a short chuckle before she could finish the title. "Why Brad Costa Is a Kick-ass Boxer." She looked around for Brad, but either her eyes were too watery to find him, or he was actually not in the gym. "Tell me, Chalfant, why is he a kick-ass boxer?"

Without a word, the young Marine opened the pamphlet and let Marianne read Brad's finer points . . . which were listed in several different handwritings. Clearly, his group had gone in on this one together to write out why each of them adored him. He really was a wonderful leader. The idiot.

She walked to Tressler, who winked. She tried to keep a stern face, but failed miserably. "What do you have for me here?"

"This one's a good one." He held it up. "Why Cook and Costa Make a Good Team."

"Oh," she breathed out, her breath catching in her throat. Oh, God. There was no way she could read this one out loud. She read silently instead. It was done in Brad's handwriting, making it that much more special. He talked about their dedication, their willingness to push past obstacles to make the boxing team better.

It was sweet, but it wasn't a relationship-maker.

The next one made her double over in laughter. One of Higgs' men held up a pamphlet titled, "Why Marianne Loves Brad." That arrogant moron. She couldn't help but smile as she read the inside in the spirit he meant it . . . humorously.

Several more pamphlets pointed out what he respected about her, what he admired about her. Why he was sorry he'd evaded the truth. They were wonderful, affirming things to hear.

But they weren't enough.

Until she came to the last one. Higgs was holding it, and he smiled softly. "This one is the best one yet. It took me forever, so you better like it."

"I'm sure I will," she said, biting her lip to keep from grinning at the absolute insanity of this project. He flipped it around, and she nearly gasped. Only the reminder that there were nearly twenty Marines staring at her from behind kept her from making a sound. But she let her hand drift up to cover her trembling mouth as she read the title.

"Why Brad Costa Fell in Love with Marianne Cook."

She stepped forward and whispered, "Where is he?" as she read through the reasons. Because she made him laugh. She made him relax. She gave him perspective, kept him from taking himself too seriously, kept him grounded.

Because she was willing to make tough choices, and he loved her for caring more about his health than hurting his feelings or making him angry. Because she was it for him. Because he *recognized* her.

Marianne blinked rapidly to clear her eyes. A few tears escaped anyway and trickled down her cheeks. She wiped at them impatiently with the back of her hand. "Higgs. Where *is* he?"

"He's over here."

She whipped her head around to find Brad standing in the doorway of her training room. His posture said he was relaxed, with his arms crossed over his chest and one shoulder propped against the door. But she could see in his eyes the intensity and focus, and knew if she laid a palm over his heart, she would feel vibrations of energy.

She started toward him, then turned back around for a moment, cupped her hand and called, "Thank you!"

The Marines all waved and started for the hallway toward the parking lot—presumably to store the posters in their cars. But she couldn't let them go without hitting home that she appreciated their efforts.

"Oo-rah!"

The group paused and turned to look. A few held their fists in the air and as one, let out a booming "Oo-rah!" that echoed through the rafters of the gym. Her heart swelled at that moment, loving each and every one of them.

They left in a noisy, lovable huddle, and she waited until they were gone. But she couldn't ignore Brad forever. And when he reached for her, she didn't hesitate to walk right into his arms and wrap hers around his waist. Burying her face against his chest, she whispered, "I missed you."

He pressed a kiss to the crown of her head, then rested his cheek there. "I missed you, too. I'm sorry."

"Clearly," she said, laughing. "What the hell made you think to do this?"

"My lady likes her pamphlets."

She laughed. And then kept laughing, despite the fact that it wasn't funny so much as true. But her nerves were running a mile a minute and she couldn't catch up, and if she didn't laugh, she was afraid she'd cry. Laughing was safer, overall.

"I love you," he murmured when she finally took a breath.

Pressing her tear-streaked face into his shoulder—tears from laughing, she swore to herself—she nodded.

"I'm sorry, I didn't catch that."

She bit him.

"Ouch! Vicious. Now I'm gonna have to have the trainer fix me up."

"She's currently unavailable. I heard she was making out with her boyfriend." Marianne tilted her head back enough to smile at Brad's amused face. "Don't make a liar out of me."

He kissed her lightly, just a teasing brush of lips. She wanted more. So, so much more.

"I didn't hear you say anything back." He pulled away, and though his tone was light, she could see lingering worry heavy in his eyes.

"Maybe I should string you along."

"Maybe you should—"

"Children."

They jumped apart as if they'd been tossed by a catapult. Marianne's face heated, and she watched the flush creep up the back of Brad's neck as they both turned to see Coach Ace standing in the doorway, thick arms crossed over his chest.

His tone was serious, but his eyes hinted at humor . . . she hoped.

"Cook? You're not going to make the same mistake, am I right?"

"No, Coach."

"And Costa, well, we've already spoken, haven't we?"
He nodded. "Yes, sir."

With a sigh, he shook his head, chuckling a little. At
least, she was pretty sure that's what that chest rumble was.
"Don't screw it up this time, the both of you. I can't have
my athletes running out to the craft store every time you
two have a fight." He started to walk away, then turned back
to add, "Warm-ups in twenty-five, Costa. Don't make me
come back here and drag you out."

Brad nodded, unable to speak.

They turned to watch each other silently, eyes wide,
mouths trembling with the effort to hold back the laughter,
both mouthing to *stop it, shut up, no you shut up* until he
was out of hearing distance. Then they both lost the war
of the laughs and doubled over, falling against each other.
Brad leaned into the nearest exam table and pulled her
back to his front, cupping her from behind as the hilarity
subsided.

"Would you really have quit the team?" she asked a few
minutes later, after they'd simply stood with each other,
pressed together, absorbing each other's presence. "It's
what you've wanted since your dad died. How could you
give that up?"

He squeezed her tighter to him. "I would have lost this.
How the hell could I give this up for some boxing award?"
He nuzzled against her neck. Her eyes fluttered closed at
the sweet feel of it. She wanted to imprint the memory of
his lips right there, at the base of her hairline, forever.

"My mom talked me in circles a little. But really, it
came down to the reason making the team was important
in the first place. Because of my dad, yeah. I want it for
me, too. But my dad was the catalyst. The reason I even
considered trying out. And I think he'd be more disappointed in me if I'd let the team drag me away from you,

than if I'd been cut for whatever reason. So what was I doing, if not making him proud, and not making me happy? Nothing. It was nothing without you."

She sighed and turned in his arms, locking her fingers around his neck. "I'm not going to let you off the hook, you know. I read your paperwork, and I know exactly what you can and can't do, per doctor's orders."

His eyes narrowed. "Okay, but maybe just some modifications on the—"

"Nope." She pressed a quick, hard kiss to his mouth. "I'm not going to let you being my guy blind me anymore. In fact, I might be tougher on you than anyone from here on out."

"Great," he muttered, but she kissed him again.

"I'll be all over your ass for icing, and wearing your brace, and doing your exercises at home. Oh, yeah," she added when he winced. "I know exactly how much they suck. You're still doing them. Because if not, I'm kicking your ass. Then I'll step aside and let Coach kick it."

"Point made."

"We're doing this right this time. We jumped in so fast before, we weren't ready." She took a deep breath and gave him the most serious look she could muster when he was pressing against her with an impressive erection. "I'm ready now."

"Ready for what?"

"All of it. We're doing this right." She paused. "Maybe you should just move your stuff over to my place."

He shrugged. "Works for me. Though I'll have to keep a few things in the BOQ, for curfew nights when Coach asks us to stay here."

"Understandable." She grimaced. "And you'll have to have dinner with my parents."

He heaved a sigh. "It's inevitable."

"My mom will probably flirt with you."

"Two for one, score."

She pinched what little skin she could grab hold of on his stomach. He arched away. "Damn, woman." Capturing her wrists in one hand, he locked them between their bodies. "I love you."

"I love you, too." She rose on her toes to kiss him once more before they started their day.

"Hey, Marianne, I—oh." Levi stood frozen in the doorway of the training room. "Wow, uh . . . awkward."

Maybe a little. But not nearly as much as it would have been a week ago. "Sorry, Levi. We'll be out of here in a second."

"Okay." He started to back away, then glanced over his shoulder. "Do you know why there's a pile of Marines sleeping in the lobby like a litter of puppies?"

Marianne and Brad looked at each other, then both shrugged. Levi shook his head and walked toward the locker room.

"This . . . I've got to see." Marianne started for the door, jolting back when Brad pulled at her arm. "What? C'mon, how do you pass up that opportunity?"

"I don't. Bring your phone. We're gonna want photographic evidence." He waited for her to grab it from her desk, then kissed her hard and slapped her ass. "First one there gets to upload the photo to Facebook."

"You're so on." She sprinted after him, knowing he'd win.

But they'd both won, in the end.

TURN THE PAGE FOR A
PREVIEW OF JEANETTE MURRAY'S

AGAINST THE ROPES

COMING OCTOBER 2015 FROM
BERKLEY SENSATION!

Greg's nerves were on high alert, and had been since the second he'd ever-so-smoothly thumped Reagan's back. That delightful move had earned him the Dumbass of the Night award. And the hits just kept on coming. But Fate had thrown him a bone and given him a very good reason to get the luscious Reagan Robilard alone in her car.

"Just keep driving straight now," he said as they pulled through the main gate and past the sentry.

"There's nowhere to go but straight," she pointed out.

"You could turn right here for the hospital."

"I don't want that," she said, her voice tight.

"So keep driving straight."

She growled a little, the sound so cute and feminine he wanted to lean over and kiss the tip of her nose. But he resisted. One stupid move per night was his limit . . . hopefully.

"You ladies have a good night out?"

She smiled, which he couldn't see so much as hear in

her voice. "We were, until a few weirdos came and crashed the party."

"Weirdos?" Ready to defend her honor, despite being too late, he sat up straighter. "Who? What'd they look like? Did they bother you?"

"That would have been you three boys," she answered with a smug grin.

Oh. Right. He let his head thump back against the headrest. Damn. She had a wicked sense of humor on her. "How's the job working out?"

"It's far more action-oriented than I imagined, that's for sure. I never thought I'd be driving out in the dark to inspect slashed tires, or figuring out who keeps vandalizing the gym. I feel like I stepped into a Nancy Drew book instead of my first real job."

"First real job, huh?" She flushed slightly, the tint barely perceptible thanks to the street lamps. "Just graduated, I take it?"

"I did, yes." Her voice deepened when she wanted to sound important, he noted. "Took me a little longer because I had to work full time while I went, but I'm a proud graduate and ready to use my degree."

"Good to know." He settled back in his seat. "You'll turn here, then make another and the barracks will be dead ahead."

"Gotcha." She finished the drive and pulled into a space at the back of the lot next to Sweeney's SUV. "I should have brought a digital camera or something," she said, looking around her car. Her voice was tight, a little high-pitched now, telling him she was nervous. "I don't know if I'll need photos , but . . ." She bit her lip, and he put a hand over hers on the gear shift between them.

"Don't sweat it. We've all got cell phones with cameras. Between all of us we'll have plenty of photos."

"Oh. Right." She closed her eyes for a moment and took

a deep breath. A breath that pushed her more-than-a-handful breasts against the tight confines of her shirt. "Sorry, I'm nervous. This isn't the sort of thing they cover in marketing class."

"You're fine. You've got it." He stepped out, then debated going to open her door. She was, for all intents and purposes, on the job now. Would she see that as stepping over a boundary? Be angry he'd done something she could do for herself?

While he internally debated, she opened her own door and stepped into the warm night air, smoothing her dark pencil skirt down over her hips as she did so. And thank God for skirts that hugged those curve. Her body was a damn work of art; a true hourglass. He let her get a step in front of him as she walked toward the group congregated on the sidewalk in front of the building, just to give himself another minute of appreciation at the way her hips swung while she walked.

"Good evening, Marines." Her voice deepened into a husky, sexy tone that had him fighting an erection in the parking lot. "Problems with some tires, I hear?"

She listened as the guys explained having made it home from practice with no problem, parking, then finding the tires slashed when they'd come out to get dinner. She took notes on her phone, getting everyone's license plate, make and model, which tires were slashed and where they'd been parked in the lot.

"And nobody else's tires were slashed? The people who'd parked next to you, for example?"

"Only tires we see slashed are from the team's," Tressler said, looking supremely pissed and ready to brawl with anyone who gave him a wrong look. The hothead was in for a rude awakening on the mat if he couldn't keep himself together and shield those emotions better. "Except Chalfant. His got hit too, but he didn't make the team."

At Brad's growl, Tressler's eyes widened. "Which, I mean, he should have," he finished, then shot Chalfant a look. "Sorry, man. That's not what I meant."

"I know," the tall man said quietly. "It's okay."

"So what you're saying is the person who did this appears to have enough information about the team to know who to target, but not enough to know who was most recently cut," Reagan said quickly to diffuse any potential problems. "Someone who is paying attention, but doesn't have firsthand info."

"Yeah, that's what we've been thinking. You're good." Tressler nodded and grinned, which made Greg take a protective step toward Reagan's back. She glanced over her shoulder with a grouchy expression, but he didn't back up.

Tressler caught his eye, narrowed his brow slightly, then shrugged. At least the kid wasn't a total moron. He picked up on the subtle *back off* vibes fast enough.

After she'd gathered all the official documentation, she asked who had called the MPs. The younger Marines all looked at each other, each one shaking his head in turn.

"Nobody?" Reagan glanced between them, then fisted her hands on her hips. "Not one of you thought to report this? Your insurances alone will require that much."

"We thought we should wait to see what these guys said," another Marine—one of Sweeney's, Greg thought—said. "We figured it was their call, because things are so weird right now with the gym and the training room getting trashed."

"Can't fault them for thinking it through," Greg muttered by Reagan's ear. "Cut them some slack. They're babies."

She turned to cut him a frosty glance. "Half of them are just a year or two younger than me."

Whoops. He hadn't considered that. She'd mentioned being a recent graduate, but he'd simply assumed she'd gone back to school after working for a few years. So she was what, twenty-four? Twenty-five?

Not that he cared. He was only twenty-eight himself. But she gave the illusion of being older than she apparently was. Probably the same way she gave the illusion of being taller, more in control, more assured of herself. She projected it perfectly with wardrobe and attitude.

In full control now, Reagan started to pace in front of the group. Her heels made the sexiest clicking sound on the pavement of the parking lot. "Let's talk to the MPs and get that on the record. While we're waiting for them, we need to make some calls for rides to get you guys to practice tomorrow. Once that's done, we'll make appointments for you to get your tires replaced at whatever place your insurances will approve. We'll stagger the repairs so we can get them fixed without jeopardizing your training schedules."

She started tapping at her phone, and Greg nearly had to pick his jaw up off the floor at the change. He had the distinct feeling she'd left Reagan in the car and brought Ms. Robilard with her to work. Night and day difference between the unsure co-ed and the professional businesswoman.

And the other men noticed it, too. They scrambled to follow her directions, making calls or looking information up on their phones, taking photos and texting people about rides.

The woman knew how to light a fire under a group of Marines.

With a satisfied, if not a little grim, smile, Reagan nodded and clapped her hands once to get everyone's attention. They stopped talking immediately, and Greg nearly laughed at the image of a Kindergarten teacher getting the attention of a bunch of five-year-olds. "Right, I'm going to take some photos before I go, and then I will see everyone tomorrow." With a steely stare, she added, "This does not excuse anyone from practice in the morning. You've got plenty of time to arrange for a ride, so do it."

Most mumbled a quiet, "Yes, ma'am," before she walked

off to start taking photos of each car's slashed tires. Greg followed behind, hands tucked behind his back to keep from thrusting her against one of those vehicles and kissing her senseless. That was, without a doubt, one of the hottest things he'd seen in years. Her ability to take charge in the blink of an eye, command a group of hardass Marines, and do it in a sexy pair of heels and a body-hugging skirt . . .

She did a dainty little squat, keeping her knees primly together as she angled her phone towards the rear tire of a pickup truck. Her skirt stretched tight over her curvy ass.

Come to think of it, maybe that's exactly how she commanded their attention so well. Hmm.

"Did you need something else?"

His concentration broken, Greg blinked and uttered the ever-intelligent, "What?"

"You were staring." Reagan took another photo, the flash momentarily blinding him, then looked over her shoulder. "Did you still need something?"

"A ride back to the BOQ would be nice."

"Your friends are still here. I assume that's why. You could go with them." *Snap snap.*

"But then how would you get home?"

"GPS," she answered easily. "It's easy enough to key in 'Home' as my destination from an unknown place. Not so easy to key in the address of 'Barracks, Camp Lejeune.'"

Okay, she had a point there. "It wouldn't be very gentlemanly for me to ditch you now."

"You're not ditching, you're going home to get some rest. I'd actually prefer that, to be honest. The more rested you are, the better you train." She stood, teetering for just a second before he grabbed her arm to steady her. The short sleeve blouse she wore gave him the chance to feel the soft skin of her forearm under his thumb. He brushed once over the pulse on the inside of her elbow, felt it hammering, and knew she wasn't nearly as cool as she played.

"You want me to go home and get some beauty rest?" He lowered his voice, stepping in, wondering if she was ever without those damn heels—which yes, did great things for her ass—so he could actually look down at her instead of up half an inch. "I don't think you do."

"And that's why I'm the brains of this operation," she said lightly, stepping back. "Someone has to think about the greater good. Besides," she added, picking her purse up from the side mirror she'd hung it on to take photos, "you'll need your strength for battle tomorrow."

"It's training, not battle."

"I wasn't talking about practice. I was talking about dealing with me." And with that sassy parting shot, she slid between two cars and disappeared to continue her photo documentary.

"Higgs, let's go man. This day's a big cluster and I'm ready to hit the rack." Brad appeared by his elbow and tugged lightly on his neck. "Sweeney's dropping us back by home on his way."

"Oh, joy." He followed along, not at all willingly.

Discover Romance

berkleyjoveauthors.com

See what's coming up next from your favorite romance authors and explore all the latest Berkley, Jove, and Sensation selections.

See what's new

~

Find author appearances

~

Win fantastic prizes

~

Get reading recommendations

~

Chat with authors and other fans

~

Read interviews with authors you love

berkleyjoveauthors.com

LOVE
ROMANCE
NOVELS?

For news on all your favorite romance authors,
sneak peeks into the newest releases, book
giveaways, and much more—

"Like" Love Always on Facebook!
 LoveAlwaysBooks